Everything I Want © 2015 Natalie Barnes

Cover Design/Photography © 2015 Picture This Photography and Design

This is a work of fiction. Names, characters, places, and incidents are products of the author's imagination or are used fictitiously and are not to be construed as real. Any resemblance to actual events, locales, organizations, or persons, living or dead, is entirely coincidental. All rights reserved. The unauthorized reproduction or distribution of this copyrighted work is illegal. No part of this book may be used or reproduced electronically or in print without written permission by the author, except by a reviewer who may quote passages for review purposes only.

This eBook is licensed for your personal enjoyment only. This eBook may not be re-sold or given away to other people. If you would like to share this book with another person, please purchase an additional copy for each reader. If you are reading this book and did not purchase it, or it was not purchased for your use only, then please return to the eBook vendor of your choice and purchase your own copy. Thank you for respecting the hard work of this author.

Everything I Want

by

Natalie Barnes

Chapter One

I take one last glimpse in the mirror before I turn the light off. I walk out of the bathroom and into the bedroom of some Hilton hotel just outside of LAX. This could possibly be the day that my band gets signed.

Full of nerves, I take another glance in the mirror above the dresser to check myself out once more. My dark brown hair hangs long and thick to the middle of my back in the long layers I recently had cut into it. It's laying straight for now, but I know once I'm out in the heat and smog of LA, it will soon frizz.

I take a little bottle of serum out of the makeup bag that's on top of the dresser and I squeeze a small amount onto my palm. I rub my hands together and gently stroke my fingers through my hair, trying not to get too close to my roots right away so it doesn't appear greasy.

The smell is heavenly; not too fragrant, but leaving a fresh, clean scent behind. Once I put the hair serum away, I put on a little lip gloss, smacking my lips together. My tanned skin is glowing . . . thanks for the good genes, Mom and Dad. My dad is Italian and my mother is Native American. I've never had to set foot into a tanning bed or had to get airbrushed. All I have to do is put on my usual dark eye liner and mascara.

Fuck, I'm so nervous. All of a sudden, my cell rings. I drop the lip gloss and rush around the room searching for my phone. Where is the damn thing? I notice it on the chair in the corner of the room. By the fourth ring I answer it all out of breath; partly from searching so quickly for it and partly from nerves.

"What the fuck are you doing, Sophia? Taking a shit?"

Everything I Want

The guys in the band are all characters. Roger, my drummer, is always a jokester.

"Nope, not shitting," I say with a small smile crossing my face at his usual bluntness.

"Well, what the fuck are you waiting for, then?" he asks with a laugh, but I can tell he's serious.

"Be down in four minutes. I'm leaving my room now."

I hit end and leave the room, heading down the hall to the bank of elevators. Talking to Roger has calmed my nerves down a bit. Just a bit, though.

We arrive outside the studio with only a few minutes to spare. This LA traffic is fucking insane! It has taken us almost an hour to get here. As we all exit the taxi van, I notice my jeans have ripped even more below my right ass cheek.

Fuck! I love these jeans. They're my lucky ones. I wore them the first night I practiced with the boys when we decided to start this band back in college, the first time we performed in a little dive bar in downtown Ann Arbor, and the first time we hit the stage outside of Chicago for the metal festival last summer, which, by the way, is where we got noticed and received the offer to come out here and possibly be signed.

"Well, darling, you knew this day would eventually come," chuckles my lead guitarist, Cory, behind me as we walk in. "But, hey- the look fucking rocks, so don't sweat it!"

A Cheshire cat grin creeps across his face. I turn around and playfully smack him in the shoulder as we enter the building, giving him a scowl. He raises his hands in the air in defense.

I approach a large marble desk, seeing a very beautiful receptionist sitting behind it, talking on the phone. The image of a playboy bunny comes to mind, especially given her chest size.

Wow! I'm surprised she doesn't fall over. For someone with such a tiny frame, she sure is packing. Oh, great! The boys are gonna be drooling and getting hard-ons once they lay eyes on this one. I glance behind me before turning to speak with her. Sure as shit, they are all in awe of her. I give them a cheesy grin and roll my eyes at them before speaking with Miss Playmate of the Year.

"Um, yes, hello. I'm Sophia Ariel and this is my band, Dollar Settlement." I gesture toward the guys. "We have an appointment with Lux Lufer."

I give her a small smile with my hands behind my back, trying to seem reserved or some shit. She gets a glimpse of the guys and a big smile spreads across her face, showing off perfect Barbie teeth. She then glances back at me.

"Why, yes! Mr. Lufer has been expecting you. Just take a right down the hall to the elevators. Go to the sixteenth floor. You will see another receptionist there. I will buzz her and let her know you're on your way up. Then just wait for Mr. Lufer to buzz you in."

She gives us one last smile before picking up the phone to call, I'm assuming, the upstairs receptionist.

"Thank you," I reply, and wave to the guys to follow me down the hall.

"Holy shit!"

"Damn!"

"Fuck me running!"

These guys and their perverted mouths. They're like my brothers, but sometimes I feel like a mother hen. I push the button

Everything I Want

to call the elevator, and all of a sudden, the door opens. What, no wait? I need a little more time before going up there. This is such a huge opportunity, and it's only a matter of seconds away. When the doors close, I turn to the boys.

"So, are we ready?" I ask nervously, but still trying to seem upbeat.

"Hell, yeah we are, sweetheart!" Jared says excitedly.

Roger's looking me over; he can tell I'm nervous as hell.

"What's the worst he's gonna say, Sophie? He doesn't like our fucking music or doesn't see making sales with us?" He quirks his eyebrow up at me. "He obviously knows we're fucking good. He's seen us in Chicago, and he called just a couple weeks later offering to bring us out here. He must like our shit."

Roger leans against the wall and looks up, smiling. He must already be thinking we've got this. But one thing I've learned in all my years on this earth is not to get your hopes up.

"Thanks," I say, smiling at him. "If I start babbling like a girl in there, I give you permission to shut me up ASAP."

They all laugh.

"Oh, sure."

"We fucking know better."

The elevator doors open, and we're there. Not even a stop on the way up to let anyone else on? Hmm. Maybe it is a sign of something good, but like always, I'm not getting my hopes up.

It's absolutely beautiful up here. The lighting is dim. The floors are marble and the walls are covered in nothing but gold and platinum records. Just inside the reception area sits a large, dark leather sectional with a marble coffee table in front of it. Behind the sofa is a huge built-in wall aquarium, filled with exotic fish that I never have ever seen before. If you look closely, you can see through to the other side to what I'm guessing is a conference room.

I turn left and smile at the lady sitting at the desk. She looks a little older than Miss Playmate from downstairs, but she is just as beautiful. She stands to greet us.

"Good morning! I'm Rachel. Would any of you care for a beverage while you wait for Mr. Lufer?"

I see the boys getting ready to throw a bunch of drink orders at this poor woman, so I turn to them and give them my stern mother hen *not now* look. I turn back to Rachel and smile.

"No, thanks," I tell her. She nods and takes a seat back down at her desk.

I make myself comfortable on the sofa, regretting turning down the drink. Shit! Maybe a little scotch would've helped ease my nerves right now. Rachel's phone buzzes. She stands again, gesturing to her right toward the metal double doors.

"Mr. Lufer is ready to see you now."

I hurry up and say a silent prayer in my head for the strength to get through this. Shit! Here we go!

The office is amazing. The blood-red walls are also covered in albums. The office has dark hardwood floors and the windows on the far wall are tinted. The lighting in the office is also dim. Sitting right in front of the windows is a massive steel desk with two black leather chairs in front of it. Mr. Lufer stands, wearing a charcoal colored suit. His black hair is slicked back with a little salt and pepper coloring the sides. He is a short man, so when he approaches us, the guys are like trees towering over him.

Everything I Want

"Hey, how's it going?" He smiles as he shakes all of our hands. "Please take a seat."

He gestures toward the black leather sofa and the two chairs in front of his desk. We all take our seats with Roger and I taking our places right in front of his desk.

"So . . . let's get to the rat killing, shall we?" he laughs. Lux seems like a really cool guy.

"I want to sign you guys. A five album deal. And you must tour before the release of any new albums."

He leans back in his chair and rests his feet on his desk. He has some pretty nice shoes. They are so shiny I can literally see myself in them. Wait! Did he just say he was signing us already? I didn't realize I was staring at him with my mouth wide open. I'm left speechless.

Roger leans over to me and starts patting my back, and all I can hear is the echoes of excitement from the other guys in the background.

"I will go over the terms of the contract with you guys now, if you're ready?"

He looks right at me with a puzzled look on his face, no doubt because of what my face must look like right now.

"Okay," I squeak. "Good."

He proceeds with the details of the contract. After everything is said and done, we all stand and take turns shaking Lux's hand.

"All right, guys and gal."

He turns and gives me a half smile before continuing out of his office. "I know these next five weeks are going to be pretty damn tight. I'm going to be putting Dollar Settlement on tour in a little over a month, so we have lots of work to do. I'm about to show all of you the studio. Get comfortable. You will be seeing a lot of it from now on."

We go down a few floors in the elevator when Lux speaks up again.

"Now, one of the reasons why I'm pushing so close to this tour date is because I need an opening act for one of my main bands. The other group I dropped because they wouldn't stop dicking around."

The doors to the elevator open, and we all follow his lead down another dimly lit hallway.

"So anyway, I know you guys can do it. And your material is great, so I'm not worried about that. But don't start fucking around, because I do like to run a tight ship here."

We approach the metal double doors at the end of the hall. They are just like the ones to his office. He turns around to face us and gives us an all-out smile. I wonder what band it is? Lux stays quiet for a few more moments, building up the tension before he speaks again.

"The band you guys will open for is Undead Society."

"Fuck, yeah!" Jared, my bassist, exclaims.

Undead Society is one of his favorite bands of all time. We all look at each other with excitement and a couple high fives go on. They are truly one of the best metal/rock bands out there. Think of Corey Taylor from Slipknot or Stone Sour, with maybe a little "Lamb of God" style thrown into the mix.

Lux turns away and pushes the metal doors open. All of a sudden, we hear loud jamming going on. Wow! Talk about excellent soundproof walls. One more dark little hallway to go down, and then we're in the booth.

Everything I Want

Staring into the glass, I notice the sexiest man I have ever seen in my life yelling into the mic that's standing in front of him. I instantly know who he is. Tristan Scott! Lead singer and one of the guitarists for Undead Society. Wow, he's so fucking hot! Butterflies take flight in my stomach.

Chapter Two

I can't seem to take my eyes off of Tristan as Undead Society wraps up. He stands really tall, about 6'5", and he's put together like a bodybuilder. Only, his muscles aren't obscene and gross looking like some of those guys on TV. The way he wears his black sleeveless shirt makes my mouth water. It's plastered to his chest from how ripped and toned he is. The little bit of sweat he has on him helps, too.

His thick, wavy, dark hair is kind of grown out, but trimmed short on the sides and back. Oh, how I would love to stroke my fingers through it! I can't see his eyes because he's wearing dark aviator sunglasses, but short facial hair covers his face, and he has the most full, kissable lips I have ever seen on any man. His pants are loose fitting, but not gangster loose. The distressed jeans hang off his broad hips with a black belt keeping them in place.

He's so sexy. Damn, I could stare at him all day. His left arm has a tattooed sleeve, and his upper right arm has what looks like a tattoo that goes down his side or back. Not really sure what it is, but, wow!

Now I'm glad I'm wearing my lucky jeans. Besides the new rip I have in the back, they are very form-fitting with a hole from years of wear and tear on my left knee. I'm also wearing a simple, tight white V-neck shirt that shows some cleavage. I'm not like playboy lady at the reception desk, but a full C cup is good enough, I think. With the shirt being white, you can easily see my black bra underneath. The dark eyeliner and mascara make my blue eyes pop even more. I mentally give myself props for not looking jet-lagged today.

I glance around at the guys, who are all taking their places in the booth and getting ready to meet Undead Society, since, after all, we will be with them for seven weeks. The door to the booth opens and Caleb, their lead guitarist, enters the room first. He is kind of surprised when he notices all of us there just hanging out. The rest of the guys come in, with Tristan bringing up the rear. I notice instantly that he is staring at me. My stomach starts flipping all over as if I've just been on some big drop ride. But then I notice his clenched jaw. What the fuck?

"Hey, guys!" Lux says. "Just wanted you to meet the new band I signed today. They will be joining you on tour. They're Dollar Settlement, and they can jam. I went out and saw them in Chicago last month."

Lux looks over at me and points.

"This is Sophia. She's lead vocals. Don't let that pretty face of hers fool ya. This chick has a set of lungs on her."

I blush and look around the room. The rest of the guys smile and give me a quick nod, except Tristan. He just glances at me, then turns his attention back to Lux. Well, I *think* he glanced at me. It's too hard to tell with those damn sunglasses on. Why the fuck is he wearing them in such a dark room? Maybe he's high or something. Or maybe he's trying to come across as a badass or some shit. Whatever! He can kiss my ass.

Lux turns toward Roger, who is standing a couple feet away from me.

"This here is Roger. He's the drummer."

Roger reaches out and shakes all of their hands. What a nice gesture. You can so tell he is a small town Michigan boy. When he reaches for Tristan's hand, he looks so small. Normally, Roger is our giant at 6'2". But standing right next to Tristan, Roger seems average.

"This is Cory. He's the lead guitarist, and Matt, who is rhythm."

Lux looks behind him to see a still shocked-looking Jared, and gives him a reassuring wave closer.

"And last, but not least, is Jared. He's bass. And I think he's a big fan."

Lux and a few of the other guys laugh while Jared shakes it off. Everyone except cranky Tristan, that is. Damn it! I can already tell this is going to be a long fucking seven weeks.

"Okay, so before I leave you guys to all get to know each other, I have just a few more things to say to the newcomers."

He looks at me and my boys.

"This is your studio now. You guys have to get pumping now that you guys are in a time frame. You can start right away, tonight, whenever. Just get fucking cracking, all right?"

He gives another toothy smile.

"Outside is Beth. She will have the keys to the studio for you guys. I will let security know as well. Day or night, I mean it. Oh, and one more thing . . ." He points to the quiet man sitting at the board with his hat bent forward. "This is Gage. He will be here almost all of the time to set up for you guys. And if he's not here, then call him. Time is money, so I don't want any of it wasted. Understood?"

The last part kind of sounded like something a father would say. Or maybe even a sheriff.

"You got it, Lux," I say with a smile.

I'm so ready to get in there and start rehearsing. The rest of the guys all nod and exchange handshakes before going in and check out the room. As I turn to follow them, Tristan looks down at me coldly.

Everything I Want

"This isn't no bar gig. You fuck up on tour, it makes this label look like shit. I have shares here, so I don't want myself looking like shit. You got it?"

Um . . . What in fuck's sake did this piece of shit asshole just say to me?

Keep calm, Sophia. Be professional.

I repeat this in my head three or four times to calm myself down. If the other guys were in here, Tristan would be lying flat on the floor right now. Well, maybe not, because he's so huge, but he would've definitely gotten smacked at least once. The boys can be very protective of me. I look up at him, trying to stare at what I think are his eyes. Between the darkness in the room and his sunglasses, it's hard to tell.

I cross my arms allow a little smirk to play across my lips.

"I think my little band can manage. Are you done? Because I have some work to do."

I smile as sweetly as I can. Shit! Being fake nice like this really hurts my face. I want nothing more than to claw this motherfucker's eyes out. I know my band is damn good. We've worked hard for the last eight years straight. We have been a band since our freshman year of college, and play all of our own material, too. No covers. Sometimes we throw some covers in our gig for fun, but mainly, it's all our shit.

Did I mention *Tristan* is a piece of shit?

I don't even give him a chance to respond as I walk past him. This booth is kind of small, and when you have someone as big as Tristan in it, well . . . I accidentally brush my arm against his as I try to get into the other room.

That brief touch sends instant shockwaves through my veins, cooling and heating my blood all at the same time. Damn. I don't want him to see me rubbing the goose bumps off. When I finally get inside, I can hear the main door outside the booth slam shut.

"What the fuck was that?" asks Matt.

I just shrug my shoulders.

"Well, since we're all here now, do you think we should start?" I glance over at Gage, who is in the booth looking out at us and nodding.

Good! I'm all of a sudden in the mood to scream.

The guys start unloading their equipment, plugging things in and warming up. I bend down to take a water out of the mini fridge because I have a feeling my throat is going to be sore by the end of the day. I grab the headphones that are resting on the mic in front of me and place them on my head. Gage gives us directions, and I start my vocal warm-ups.

"Ready?" he asks after about fifteen minutes.

I look behind me, seeing the boys all ready to go with smiles cracking their faces in two. I turn around and nod at him through the glass.

"Good to go."

Cory starts playing 'Boss.' Oh, yeah! Now I'm ready!

****

I'm lying on the couch in the booth, staring at my phone. It's already midnight. Wow! We've been here for almost twelve hours.

Everything I Want

My throat is sore and my vocals are turning a little raspy now. Roger is asking Gage questions about the controls.

I never noticed it earlier, but this is way more advanced than any other studio I have ever been in before. Knobs and buttons are everywhere on the deck. Flat screens are placed on all the other walls. It truly is a sight. I can't believe I looked past it before. It was probably because Tristan was in here, switching my gears from hot to cold so damn fast.

I stretch out one last time before getting up. I'm so exhausted from traveling to LA, the interview this morning, and then jamming all day. I say it's time to grab a shower and drift off to sleep.

Just then, Jared and Matt come barging in all loud and kind of buzzed. They decided a while ago to have a few beers and a joint. Whatever, though. If they don't go over the edge on wasted-ness, they can jam out pretty good, if not better, I think.

"Where's Cory?" I ask.

Jared points to a door on the opposite end of the recording room.

"Ah . . . I think he's just loading our shit in the back there."

"Oh, okay." I start walking toward the door. "I will meet you guys down by the cab."

"All right," Roger says before letting Gage know what time we will be showing up again tomorrow.

I peek my head into the door and notice Cory leaning against the wall with his back to me.

"Hey, we're leaving now," I say, taking a few steps closer to him. Something seems a little off. "Are . . . are you all right, man?" I ask.

"Fuck! Yeah, I'm all right." He turns to face me, his nose bloody. "Just overdid it in there, you know?"

"Oh, my God!" I shout as I clasp my hands over my mouth. "Shit, Cory! Let's get you to the bathroom. Are you feeling okay? Shit!"

"No, I'm fine. Just this annoying nose thing. It started bleeding when we wrapped. But I didn't want to make a mess or scene out there, so I just came in here to wait it out."

Cory chuckles to himself. Yep, still must be a little buzzed. After he gets done with cleaning himself up, we head toward the elevators.

Once inside, I turn to him.

"I know it's none of my business, but maybe you shouldn't do so much next time. Really, you shouldn't be doing it at all right now, since we have so much shit riding on our backs, you know?"

He looks down at me and shakes his head slightly.

"Sophia, I'm fine. It's not like I'm hardcore into it. If I was, I would probably be lying on the floor right now or wanting to keep jamming. I hit just a little to keep it flowing for tonight since I'm only running on a few hours here."

He smiles and rubs my shoulders for a minute; then the elevator doors open, and we're now at ground level. I turn to Cory and give him a hug.

"This is only the beginning for us. We have to take care of each other, okay?"

I kiss him quickly on the cheek.

"I know, Sophie. Thanks."

He grabs my hand, and we leave the building and jump into the cab.

Everything I Want

A while later, I'm lying in bed with my extra-large Pantera "Cowboys from Hell" t-shirt that was once my dad's. It's already 2:00 a.m. Today has been a day with so many emotions. I brush my hair after my gloriously refreshing shower, then cover up with the quilt my grandmother made for me when I was little. I know I'm a nerd, but I always bring it with me whenever I travel.

Lying here in the darkened hotel room, I start thinking about the deal, recording, poor Cory, and—of course—Tristan. Ah, Tristan, Tristan, Tristan. How can someone so ridiculously talented and devastatingly handsome be a major prick for no reason? I wrap my brain around it numerous times, trying to think about what I did to piss him off.

Hmm, nothing.

Maybe it's because of what Lux said? The band before us screwing around? And Tristan did say he had some shares in the company, so maybe that's why he was on a little edge. I don't know, but it kind of makes sense, right? Well, I just have to prove to him and Lux that Dollar Settlement is the real deal, and we're not going anywhere. All of a sudden, I feel my eyelids getting heavier. The last image that crosses my mind is of Tristan's full, soft lips.

Chapter Three

It has already been four weeks in the studio. We're busting ass trying to get this album done before we start touring next Wednesday. Putting in twelve to fifteen-hour days every day is brutal, but I know it's going to be more work when we start touring.

The boys are holding up pretty well, too. And I'm happy to say that there haven't been any more incidents with Cory like our first night here. But I'm a little bummed that I haven't seen any of the Undead Society guys around. Well, Tristan, I mean.

The first time I met him, I thought he was an ass, but maybe it's because of the stress of the other band not being able to pull their weight. So I understand that and want to let him know not to worry. I have great respect for his band. Shit, they've been in the game for almost ten years now, but I haven't been able to tell him that because I haven't seen him yet. Well, I can always do it when we start the tour, I suppose.

As I'm doing touch-ups and backtracks to our song, "Forgive Me," I notice movement in Gage's booth. I overlook it and finish the song. Gage's voice pops through the speakers.

"All good. Do you wanna come in and listen?"

"Sure."

I remove my headphones and place them back on the mic.

Damn LA and its heat! Shit. I know this place is equipped with the most modern central air system, but I'm practically dripping with sweat from singing and screaming my ass off these last eight hours. Ew! My Deftones t-shirt is practically hugging me now, which sucks because all I want to do is rip the damn thing off. And jean shorts, forget about them. They just make it all the more uncomfortable.

Everything I Want

I pulled my hair off my neck a while ago because my overheating body made it frizz, so now it's just up in a ponytail. I didn't even bother putting makeup on today. Why? Because I'd only sweat it off in two hours. Besides, I'm just around the boys, anyway. No need to impress anyone.

I push the door to the booth open and see Jared sitting on the couch with a huge-ass smile spreading across his face. I turn to my left and lo and behold! Who do I see? Tristan!

Damn! Now I wish I would've put on a little makeup, or at least some eyeliner or mascara. I give him a quick nod then turn back to Jared.

"Where's the rest of the guys?" I ask.

"They went out for some beers and smokes. They should be back in twenty, though."

He is so excited to be here right now. Undead Society is one of Jared's favorite bands, so he's in his element right now.

"Are you ready to listen to the full song now?" Gage asks as he turns his chair back to the deck, messing with a few more switches. "I think I have it all put together."

I glance up at Tristan. He's just standing there with his arms crossed in another sexy, sleeveless shirt that stretches his tattoos out a bit on his muscular arms. Shit!

Get this sexual idea of him out of your head, Sophia! I yell at myself. This is business now.

I take a seat by Jared, cross my legs, and open the cap to my water for a quick swig. Gage pushes one more button, then my song starts to play through the amazing system in the booth. I can't help the grin that forms on my lips.

Cool, Sophia. Remain cool. Don't show too much emotion around Mr. Scott over there. Damn it! I hate it when my conscience is right. I bit my lower lip to keep the grin at bay.

A few minutes later, the song finally finishes. Gage turns to Jared and me.

"Sweet. I think we can call it a wrap on this one. Nice, Soph—"

Tristan interrupts Gage, shaking his head.

"She needs to go over the chorus again. A little lower next time."

He turns to me with a cold stare, his eyes seeming darker. Excuse fucking me. Really? I thought I did a damn good job. I've been working on it . . . let's see . . .

All fucking day!

"Yeah, right . . . I'm going to have to disagree with you," I say in the way that Bill Lumbergh says it in Office Space.

Looking up at him through my lashes, I give him a glare. Sitting down while he's standing is even more intimidating. Jared has this look of shock on his face, like he can't even believe that I'm speaking to Tristan Scott this way.

Tristan is staring at me like I'm some bug he is getting ready to stomp on with his unlaced Timberlands. He rubs his hands together then tucks them into his back pockets and gives Gage a beastly cackle. He turns his head and glares down at me.

"Well, since I do have a say for Lux, I say do it over. You sound like Mickey Mouse." He then looks down at Gage. "You should know better."

His voice is so deep that it intimidates and excites me all at the same time.

Everything I Want

Wait one fucking minute! Did he just say I sound like Mickey Mouse?

I should tell this motherfucker he sounds like Justin Bieber just to piss him off! In a second, I'm on my feet before I even realize it. I wish I was wearing heels right now to have better eye contact. My 5'6 frame just isn't cutting it to go rounds with Skyscraper over here, but I have nothing. I look back over to Jared; he is on the couch, immobilized. Well, there goes my backup. I turn back around to face Tristan again.

"Fine! I will redo it!"

My voice comes out in a low growl. I never heard myself sound that way before. I push through the door leading back into the recording room and grab the headphones, pulling them back on my head.

"Let me know when we're ready," I say sarcastically, because I know Mr. Know-it-all is still in there.

"Ready," Gage says over the speakers. I close my eyes to tune everyone out and begin.

It's 3:00 a.m. and I'm exhausted, but we're finally done for the night. I must have gone over the same fucking lyrics thirty more times before Mr. Know-it-all Douchebag gave me a nod from the booth that told me it was good enough before he walked out.

All the guys, except Roger, have already left for the night to get some sleep. Aw, my. I told Roger he didn't have to stay, but he insisted. So pretty much most of the work is done now; all that's left is some fine-tuning. Eleven tracks in five weeks. That's fan-fucking-tastic, considering it takes some bands months to do!

Natalie Barnes

The morning is slowly making its appearance in my hotel room. I'm lying in bed trying very hard to fall asleep, but I just can't stop thinking about Tristan. Why do I let him bother me so much? I've only been around the guy a couple times. And why the fuck does he think he is our manager? I may have to have a little talk with Lux about this.

On the other hand, maybe not. We are just getting started, and I don't want Lux thinking I'm trying to be a diva or something. But, damn . . . would it hurt Tristan to be a little kinder to me? I mean, I'm new to this; so cut me some fucking slack. I noticed last night—or earlier this morning, whichever way you look at it—Tristan was treating the rest of my band with some respect, but not me. Fuck it. I will just bite my tongue. For now.

****

It's all darkness, and I hear 'Beautiful Tragedy' playing. My eyes pop open. It's my phone. Still a little groggy, I rub my eyes and sit up, looking from my left to my right.

"Where is the damn thing?" I mumble, then lift up my pillow and grab it.

"Yeah?" I choke out.

My voice is a little raspy from sleep and from putting in all the hours yesterday.

"Good afternoon, Sophia," Lux says cheerfully. "Be ready in thirty minutes, okay? I'm sending a driver over to pick you and the other guys up to take you to the studio. We have to start getting ready for the tour."

Wait! Good afternoon? What time is it? I glance at the clock on my bedside table. Shit! Three in the afternoon!

"Yeah, okay. Cool. I will let them know. Thanks."

I press end and slowly climb out of bed and take a good stretch. I then dial Roger's number. It only rings once before he picks up.

"Hey, sleepyhead. We were wondering when you were getting up."

"Yeah, I know. Sorry about that."

I'm trying to talk, but I can't stop yawning.

"Listen, Lux is sending a car over in thirty minutes. You guys be ready. We have to start going over things for the tour."

"Yeah, we know already, Sophia. Tristan called me a couple hours ago."

What the . . . ?

"Oh, he did?" I try not to sound annoyed. "Okay, then. Well, I'm just gonna grab a quick shower. Be down in a few."

"Cool. See you then," Roger says to me.

"Um . . . Why did he call you?" I ask quickly before ending the call. Shit! Maybe I shouldn't have asked.

"Because he's meeting us there to help us out and prepare. After all, he does know a few things about this kind of shit and has done this a few times before."

I hear Roger laugh slightly. And I swear I can almost hear his eyes rolling, too.

"Okay. I just thought Lux was going to be doing it. That's all. I have to go. Bye."

"Bye bye."

Roger then clicks off. I wanted to end the call immediately so Roger wouldn't keep talking or asking annoying questions.

I'm drying off from the quickest shower I have ever taken. I decide on wearing light blue jeans and a black three-quarter sleeved, button-down shirt. I quickly brush my thick hair and throw it up into a loose bun. I brush my teeth and apply a little—not too much—eyeliner and mascara. I do one spray of perfume, then I go and grab my shoes. I feel my phone go off in the back pocket of my jeans as I'm getting my shoes on. It's a text from Cory.

Car here u ready?

I stand quickly and slide on a couple knitted bracelets and one of my silver, metal ones on my wrists. I then shoot back a text.

Walking down the hall now. Couple minutes.

I knew I wouldn't have any time to make my hair totally presentable, so that's why I opted for the bun. When my hair finally dries, it will have loose waves. Okay, I'm ready to get this ball rolling. The tour is now six days away, and there is so much to be done.

Walking out of the hotel room, I grab a twenty dollar bill off the dresser and stuff it into my other back pocket. Going down the hall, I notice an older woman checking me out. Not in a sexual way, but more of a curious way. I've been living here for the past month, so maybe she wonders what in the hell I am doing here. I don't know, but the look on her face kind of creeps me out. I give her a closed-mouth smile as I approach the elevators. She rolls her eyes at me and walks away. There, that takes care of that. I laugh as I wait for the elevators to take me down.

Chapter Four

We pull up outside the studio. The day, of course, is hot and humid, so I hurry my way into the cool building. Lux is standing in front of the doors, greeting us as we walk in. Beside him stand Tristan and Caleb. Oh, boy! Will I ever get over this feeling of titillation I get whenever Tristan's around? I want to taste him and slap him all in the same moment. Fuck, it's so annoying. I shake off the image of Tristan in my mind and look over at Caleb, giving him a small smile and wave.

Caleb's head is shaved, and has tattoos and piercings all over. At first glance, he may seem kind of scary, but when you start talking to him, he is a very sweet and intelligent man. Meaning, don't judge a book by its cover.

"Hey, everyone!" Lux calls out. He's now standing in the center of our group, turning slowly in a circle looking at each one of us.

"We have to get some photos done of you guys today. Tristan and Caleb will take you guys downtown to meet up with the team."

Tristan and Caleb are standing back a little ways. Caleb is grinning ear to ear. Tristan, on the other hand, is standing there with this stone-cold look on his face, showing no emotion. Figures!

"I'm thinking that some industrials would look good. Does this sound okay?"

Lux glances at me then the guys. I'm thinking that industrials would look pretty sweet. We all nod at each other, then I turn back to Lux.

"Yeah. That sounds cool, actually."

I can't help the super-excited grin dancing on my face. Matt raises his hand slightly like we're back in class or something.

Everything I Want

"I have one question."

Lux nods at him to go on.

"Shoot."

"What's industrial?"

I turn back to him with what must be the dumbest look on my face.

"Really Matt?" I quirk my eyebrow up at him.

"I know what 'industrial' is, Sophie," he says, making air quotes. "All I was wondering is . . . Are we gonna be using metal and shit?"

Aw, my. I really can't give him a hard time about this because the look on his face says that he's really trying to understand.

"Yes, Matt. That's exactly what you guys will be using," Lux says to him, speaking very slowly. He then shakes his head and looks around at all of us one last time. "You guys are going downtown by some warehouses. That's where the shoot will take place. Now, any more questions?"

Everyone turns back to Matt. He looks at all of us.

"Hey, back off. Shit! Next time I won't fucking speak."

You can tell by the tone of his voice that he's trying to be serious, but the expression on his face is that of a wiseass. We all laugh and throw a couple jokes at him. I walk over to him and give him a quick squeeze. When I turn back around to face Lux, I notice Tristan glaring at me.

"We got shit to do. Let's go."

He walks past us, heading out of the lobby doors. Lux shakes his head then waves us on.

"Good luck!" he says before heading toward the elevators. How come Tristan came to mind when Lux said "Good luck?"

Caleb holds the door for me as we leave. It's nice to know that his guitarist has some fucking manners. Two vehicles are out front parked in the street. Both of them are SUVs with tinted windows. I so don't want to be in Tristan's vehicle. I notice Caleb entering the first one. I see Matt and Cory opening the doors to get in. Shit! I have to hurry so I can get a spot. When I approach, I notice the back of it has trunks and cases filling it.

"Hey, girl! Over here!" I hear Roger yelling, holding the front door of the second SUV open for me.

Damn! I mumble some profanities to myself and roll my eyes.

Stop acting like a brat! I scold myself.

"No, no, that's okay. You can take the front. You're bigger than me. I can squeeze in the back with Jared."

"Don't be silly. Ladies first, remember? Now get in."

Roger's pulling the tender gentleman card, but right now, all I feel is annoyed.

Tristan leans forward onto his folded arms that are resting on the steering wheel.

"*Someone* get in!"

I take one last look at Roger and give him a little scowl. All that's given back to me is a cheesy grin. I take my seat in the SUV, reaching up to grab the seatbelt.

"Sophia, do you mind moving your seat up a little?" Roger asks me.

"You know, you should have just sat in the front like I said. You're much bigger than me."

Everything I Want

I buckle myself in and reach for the button on the side to move my seat forward. I'm so close to the dashboard now. Roger isn't the slimmest one in the bunch, if you know what I mean, and he's very tall, too.

We turn onto the freeway and head north. I have no idea where we're going. The only parts of LA I've seen in the past month are the studio and the hotel. Yes, I know. I'm lame. The guys tried getting me out a couple times, but all I could focus on was doing my best job on the album. Roger and Jared start talking about some club they went to the other night.

Reaching forward in my seat, I push the button for the radio. I really don't want to hear about their sexcapades. Tristan glances down at my hand. I find a station that's playing Alice in Chains' 'Hole.'

Great song. I've always loved nineties rock music, especially from ninety-four on down. I turn it up a little louder when Roger starts talking about some easy whore he slept with. Ugh! Guys are such pigs! That's why I made sure never to be one of those girls. I've only been with a few guys and I'm proud of it. Like, literally, three. But I can say that sometimes it has definitely been tough.

There's something about Layne Stanley's voice during this song that makes my nerves shiver. I look over to Tristan and I notice how he rubs his right palm up and down his upper thigh. Just that small action brings up the image of his rough hands on my body. Thoughts of what could be are teasing my skin. Oh, my God! Change thinking process now!

I stare out at the freeway when, all of a sudden, I hear Tristan's voice.

"So . . . you like Alice in Chains, huh?"

"Yeah," I say. It's the only thing I can get out of mouth right now.

What is this? Is he actually being nice? It's probably because Roger and Jared are in here so close. I look up at him and notice his right hand combing through his hair. He looks so damn hot right now.

Damn, my stomach. He makes me so nervous. He glances down at me and uses his index finger to slide his sunglasses back into place on the bridge of his nose. I can't keep staring at him, so I turn and gaze back out the window.

"What other bands do you like?"

Wait, is Tristan actually making conversation?

"Well, I like pretty much alternative and rock. A few of my favorites are Deftones, Pantera, Avenged Sevenfold, In This Moment, and you guys . . ." I trail off.

"Well . . . thanks," is his only response.

Okay? I guess? Why, oh, why did I just admit that? Shit. Shit! Now his head is going to be even bigger. I take a quick glance up at him. He has this little half smile playing on his lips. Wow! He is so hot wearing those aviator sunglasses, his wavy hair falling around his broad face, his tight gray t-shirt complimenting his muscular chest so perfectly . . .

Mmm . . . Damn it! I have to stop letting my thoughts run away with me. I press my thighs together to stop the dull ache that's been growing between my legs since I got into this damn car. That's it! Roger has shotgun on the way back.

We take a right toward our exit. We're at a stoplight now, and this gorgeous car pulls up next to us. I think it's a Ferrari. Yeah, it has that dancing-looking horse emblem on the hood. Shit. When I

Everything I Want

actually notice it, there are a lot of nice cars around. I see one of these kinds of cars every once in a while back home, but it's rare. Sports cars in Michigan are not so good. One word: winter. As I'm thinking of all of this, Tristan pulls me out of my train of thought.

"We're about five minutes away now. There will be some costumes at the site. I think a stylist will be available if anyone needs help or anything."

"Wait. Like what kind of costumes? Halloween and shit?" Jared stupidly asks.

"No. Unless you want to wear that shit. Basic shit, you know?" Tristan uses his thumb and gestures toward me. "I think the only one with really any choices here is her."

Roger speaks up from the back.

"I tell you guys what. I'm not changing my fucking clothes. I couldn't care less."

"That's probably because they won't have anything in your size," Jared says, then busts out laughing.

"I'm not fat, you fucktard! I'm big-boned. Fuck! My dick alone wouldn't be able to fit into the bitch pants you wear."

"Sure, Roger," Jared says to him, still laughing.

"All right, children, knock it off."

I have to talk to them like this sometimes. I glance back over at Tristan, and he's smiling a little. He's so unbelievably attractive when he's like this.

We arrive at the location. These are warehouses? Detroit always comes to mind when I think of warehouses. Like the Packard plant. Actually, that's not a bad idea. I'm going to have a little talk with Lux about setting up some video shoots in Motown.

"So what's going to happen now, exactly?" I ask Tristan. "I mean . . . I— We've never done anything like this before."

Tristan pulls off his shades and his eyes are a little softer now.

"There will be a stylist and photographers. That kind of shit. All you guys have to do is get ready, and they will direct the rest. If you have any ideas, make sure to let them know. Lux won't be stopping by, so that's why I'm here to make sure it goes okay."

"Sounds easy," Jared says.

I climb out of the SUV and go over to meet up with Cory and Matt. They're laughing at something Caleb just said.

"Yous ready?" I ask them both.

"Yeppers," Matt says, then looks down at me, still trying to control his laughter. What the fuck did Caleb say that's so funny? All of a sudden, I hear a very flamboyant voice in the background.

"Hello, hello, hello!"

This really tall, thin man with long, blonde hair comes out. He's wearing black leather pants with a matching leather vest and a red bandana tied around his neck. His eyes are rimmed with heavy black eyeliner and his fingernails are painted dark red. Oh, boy! I hope the guys behave themselves, or I'm going to freak. I hurry up and turn around to face them.

"Better fucking behave yourselves!" I say quietly to them before I turn back on my heel.

Tristan chuckles at my comment to the guys. He must know when we go out in public, sometimes it is like a fucking zoo.

"Ooh, la la! You're so fabulous! I'm Frankie. Frankie Heart."

He winks at me then embraces me in a big hug. Wow, okay.

Everything I Want

"And you must be my Sophia. And these are the boys, hmm?"

They all look uncomfortable while Frankie checks them out. Roger and Jared are trying so hard not to laugh. Cory just has this confused look on his face, and poor Matt . . . Well, I don't really think he knows what to think. Actually, I think Matt might be a little high when I get a better look at his face, what with his bloodshot eyes and all. Frankie gestures his delicate hand at them.

"Give me names of da boys."

"Well, this handsome man right here is my drummer, Roger."

I smile and grab Roger's hand to pull him closer. He seems to be dragging his feet a little. Frankie stretches out his hand for Roger to grab. Roger takes it and shakes once, firmly.

"Roger."

"Ooh . . . Love the grip! Gotta hold onto them sticks tight, huh?" Frankie says teasingly.

Everyone but Roger bursts out laughing, even Tristan. Roger doesn't know what to do or say but nod. He's trying not to be rude, and I can tell Frankie is just pulling his chain a little.

"Yeah, I guess."

I nod over my shoulder to Jared.

"This is my bass player, Jared."

"Nice to meet you, Jared. OMG! I love your pants!"

Now Roger starts wailing in laughter. Jared glares at him. I have to hurry up and change the subject fast before these two start ripping into each other.

"This is Matt. He's one of my guitarists."

Frankie winks at Matt.

"Charmed, I'm sure."

Matt's more of the pretty boy of the group, so he gives Frankie this all-American smile. I think Frankie is going to have a heart attack. Matt loves fucking around with people. Stupid ass. But he is kind, though.

"And, finally, this is Cory."

Cory walks up to Frankie with his right hand extended.

"He is lead guitar," I state before taking another quick glimpse at Tristan.

He and Caleb are now standing behind me. Tristan has this sexy smirk playing on his lips with his arms crossed in front of him. Caleb whispers something in his ear and Tristan nods. I wonder what he said?

Frankie yells something towards the warehouse, but I don't make it out because my mind was wrapped around Tristan and Caleb's muted conversation.

"Okay! So everyone, this is my assistant, Chloe. She's fabulous. Now let's play, shall we?"

He claps a couple times. You can definitely tell he's excited about this.

Chloe is short and a little stubby. She has short, purple hair and her cute little dimples have piercings in them. She dresses like someone who lived in Seattle back in the early nineties with her baggy olive-colored pants and red flannel shirt unbuttoned at the top. She's wearing what look like skate shoes. She gives us a shy smile and a low wave.

We head toward the warehouse where everything is set up and displayed. I instantly spy a table and a rack, which I know is for me, and beeline right for it.

"Chloe, darling, take these fine men to their tables. I wanna have some fun with Miss Ariel over here." Frankie circles his index finger at me. "She's gonna be so much fun!"

Chloe leads the guys away, talking with Roger. Tristan and Caleb then enter our designated area. My stomach flips again at seeing Tristan come through the door, staring back at me.

Chapter Five

Frankie starts pulling out all these great-looking corsets. Some are made up of dark leather and others of red satin and silk, with an overlay of lace. Stunning! All of these pieces are absolutely stunning, and I want them all. I'm dazed until Tristan's deep voice snaps me out of it.

"You sure you should be making her look like a whore?"

He gives Frankie a stern look, then cuts his dark eyes over to me.

Frankie giggles to himself then looks at me, rolling his eyes.

"Don't be silly, Tristy. I'm the professional here, boy. If I needed advice about heavy metal or whatever, I would ask you, but this is fashion and it's what I do. Mmkay? Now go run along with the other boys."

Tristan looks pissed. Yep, there's the guy I remember! I was wondering where he was hiding. Not!

Frankie has his hands now on his slender hips, giving a little shake. He is clearly not intimidated by Tristan's wrath. I admire Frankie even more.

"I just don't think you should be having her shit hang out all over the place. She's a fucking musician," Tristan growls, ignoring me completely now.

Oh, now Tristan has gone and done it. Frankie takes a couple steps over to him and starts waving his hand in his face. All the guys at the other table look up for a second before returning to what they were doing.

"Excuse me. Lux called *me*, okay? Why? Because I'm fucking awesome, okay? And last week, Lux showed me the video from their

Everything I Want

Chicago show, and this girl was pretty much wearing the same garments on stage. It's called a show! So you don't need to be here."

My mouth has now literally hit the floor. Fuck Tristan for trying to judge my costumes. I have to remind myself later to give Frankie a much appreciative hug. Tristan turns and gives me the shit eye before walking over to the guys' section. I have no fucking clue what possessed him to even be this way over wardrobe. I look over at Frankie.

"Thank you," I whisper to him.

"Baby doll, it's no problem. I've worked with him a few times. He's never gotten this involved before, but he always has little remarks to make. Now, let's go to hair and makeup and get you ready to rock, because girl, when I'm done with you, you're gonna fucking own the shit."

We both laugh, and I follow him through the next area to get ready.

I'm sitting in the dressing area that they have designated off from the other side of the warehouse. Black curtains hanging from standing iron rods are the only things shielding me. Stand up lights and a makeshift vanity are the only other things back here. The stool I'm sitting on is hard, cold, and very uncomfortable.

This girl named Kelsie is doing my hair. She's dressed in an oversized white see-through blouse tucked into tight, black, high-waisted slacks. Her pants kind of remind me of the movie *Cry Baby* when the grandmother called the girls from the Drapes' pants, "hysterectomy pants."

Kelsie has on these seven-inch, red Mary Jane pumps that make her legs look so long. The way she has her hair and makeup done reminds me of Dita Von Teese. She brusher, blow dries, and curls my hair. Good thing I have thick hair, because if not, I would be kind of worried about going bald with the way she's pulling on it.

Frankie leans in with his little black makeup palate and brush.

"Pucker up them Jolie lips, hun."

He starts painting on this red, red lipstick. He won't even let me look into the mirror until he's finished with me. And it's already been over an hour.

I hear the guys behind the curtain getting kind of restless from waiting. I asked twenty minutes ago if Caleb wouldn't mind going on a beer run since I didn't really know how long it was going to take me.

"All done. Wow! My best masterpiece yet. Girl, you're gonna break lots of hearts and give a whole lotta hard-ons."

Frankie's grinning and clapping to himself. What did he just say? I laugh because he's so blunt and full of fun. I love people who are themselves and don't give a rat's ass about what anyone else thinks.

"Hey, Frankie, do you mind grabbing me a beer? I'm getting kind of uncomfortable and would like to have one, just while I'm waiting to get done."

Frankie shakes his head with a little smile on his plump lips.

"Do you wanna ruin my beautiful lip work? Hmm . . . What about I track you down a straw? But. Be. Very. Careful."

He turns on his heel and pushes the curtain to the side. All of a sudden, I hear Frankie scream.

"Eek!"

All of the guys start laughing, and off in the distance, I hear Roger's low mumbling.

Everything I Want

"I'm not changing my shit! It's pretty much the same shit on that table."

Frankie's boot heels go clicking off in Roger's direction.

"It's a shoot! Change into wardrobe!"

Some more mumbling goes on, and then I hear Frankie again.

"Fine. Fucking whatever! But I don't want my fucking name on his name when it comes to stylist."

Frankie bursts back into my little area. I thought there for a minute that he was going to take the whole rod down when he threw open the curtains the way he did. He blows out a puff of air, sending the pieces of hair hanging in his face flying. He hands me a beer with a straw in it. I grab it from him and smile. I've never had a Coors with a straw in it. I laugh to myself a little.

"Thank you," I look at him and say.

"You're sweet. But that barbarian, Roger . . . with his oil stained pants! I mean, I picked out some damn good pieces."

He's shaking his head now and heads toward the curtains again. He stops right before he reaches them and turns slightly. He peers over his shoulder with this up-to-no-good look.

"I think you look like the rock goddess that you are. Everyone will think so. Well, everyone but maybe . . . Tristan."

He gives me a quick wink of his eye before disappearing back through the black curtains again. What in the hell is that supposed to mean?

Kelsie is done with my hair and just finishing up with some spray. Frankie is all excited to turn me in my chair.

"Open your eyes, sweetheart," he whispers in my ear.

I slowly open my eyes and gaze at myself in the mirror. Wow!

"Oh, my God!"

I shake a little, trying not to cry and ruin my makeup. Frankie stands beside me, crossing his arms.

"You like it, huh?"

"Of course! I fucking love it!"

I'm staring at myself in the mirror. My eyes are the very first things that get my attention. My sapphire blue eyes are all dolled up in this very intense, smoky look. I have these individual eyelash pieces on, making my eyes even more prominent.

My full lips are painted this burlesque red color that makes my teeth even more stunning. My thick, walnut brown hair is blown out and full of soft waves. Kind of looks like a mix of "just fucked" and "supermodel." I absolutely love it!

I stand up and turn slowly, checking myself out in the full-length mirror.

"Not too shabby."

I turn around quickly and see Matt. He smiles and then takes a drink of his beer.

"I just wanted to see how you were doing, but if you look like that every time we perform, me and the other guys are gonna have to work double time keeping you safe."

I smile at his sentiment. He's sweet.

"Don't worry, Matt. We don't have Frankie with us on tour. And I sure as hell don't know how to do all of this detail."

Frankie is now sitting on a stool off to the right of me, smiling.

Everything I Want

"Maybe Cinderella's 'fairy' godmother may join you."

I go back to checking myself out once more in the mirror. I'm wearing this black leather strapless corset that hooks in the front and matching black leather mini shorts; it's very edgy and normally something that I would never wear. Blood red stilettos with metal spikes for heels add some color and even more edge to the outfit. It's kind of funny that Frankie said I look like a rock goddess because now that's how I feel, wearing this outfit. It's like I've changed my identity or something.

I pull on elbow-length leather gloves that have the fingers cut out, and turn to Matt.

"Give me one more minute to finish my beer."

Matt winks and then nods at Frankie.

"Sure thing."

Frankie takes a couple steps closer to me.

"I'm gonna let Jay, the photographer, know we're almost ready. Oh, and one more thing . . . You look absolutely beautiful. Don't let anyone make you feel different."

He then walks out of the curtain. Why does Tristan come to mind at Frankie's words? It's probably because when I walk out of here, he's going to shit!

Actually, I kind of like that idea. Take that, motherfu—

Stop it! I say to myself. I definitely have liquid courage going on. Breathe. It's just some pictures. Okay, here I go!

I pull open the heavy curtains, making sure not to make eye contact with Tristan. I take a few steps closer to the guys when I notice Lux is here. He's right in the middle of a conversation with

Jared and Cory when he stops mid-sentence. He's staring at me with wide eyes.

Suddenly I hear Roger say, "Damn, girl!"

I glance over to my left and notice him standing there, wearing exactly the same thing he came in with; bike oil-stained jeans with an old, dark-colored Metallica shirt that he ripped the sleeves off of himself. His shoulder-length, curly, light brown hair is pulled back into a low, tight pony tail with a dark blue bandana on his head.

Matt looks handsome, wearing a black suit with a dark shirt unbuttoned at the top and pulled out from his pants. His dark hair is messed-up looking. Cory is wearing ripped, dark blue jeans and a white t-shirt. The tattoos on his arms and hands are all showing. His blonde hair is shaved close to his head. He's got an Eminem thing going on.

I peek over him and notice Jared. He's wearing form-fitting black jeans with a leather jacket and a black and red shirt underneath. His dark hair is styled as if he were going out on the town or something.

I'm starting to feel just a bit silly hearing all the compliments and whistles from the guys until Tristan's low, dark voice speaks up.

"You look like Taylor Momsen."

I glance over at him. He is leaning against the wall with his arms crossed. What an asshole! Right when I open my mouth to say something, I get cut off by Caleb.

"What the fuck ever, man!" Caleb turns to me. "You're smoking!" he says.

The tendons in Tristan's arms and neck flex as he stands tall. Grabbing a beer from the table, he rolls his eyes.

Everything I Want

"She dresses the same as the kind of chicks you hook up with, so what's the fucking difference?" Caleb points out.

I know Tristan is a rock star, and it's pretty obvious that he has hooked up with many women, but I can't help but feel a tinge of jealousy when Caleb says that. Why should I even care about the asshole? Damn beer for making me feel this way. Yes, I had a six-pack of beer and this is how I get? Girly and shit?

"All set?"

We all look over at Jay, the photographer, and his assistant. He walks up to us explaining what ideas he has and is asking us our points of view on things.

I'm leaning against this jacked-up sheet of metal with one leg propped up on it. My other leg is standing on some broken concrete that looks like someone took a jackhammer to it. Trying to keep my balance in these damn shoes while trying to look sexy is tough shit.

Jay is kind of annoyed with me because I guess I'm not doing the poses right. I'm not some damn model; I'm a singer. He is even shorter than Lux, and he looks Sean Connery-ish. I see his assistant bouncing all over the place, from picking up cables to changing the lighting and moving some of these metal props around. He does a lot. I don't know his name, but he's a big guy like Roger and Tristan.

"Okay. I want Sophia in the middle. Roger and Cory take to her right side. Yes, good. And Jared and Matt, go to her left. Okay, good. Now, Sophia, put your arms up on Roger's and Jared's shoulders but just your elbows. I want your forearms coming out and your wrists loose. Good. Okay. Now tilt your head back and up to the side a little. Bend your legs slightly."

I do as he tells me, having my chin up and my head slightly cocked to the side. I squint my eyes a little, trying to appear more badass or maybe sensual. Whatever way it comes out, I don't really care.

As Jay starts snapping, I take a quick glance with my eyes to Tristan. He's now sitting in a chair leaned back with his arms still folded in front of him, but this time, I notice him watching me. Well, glaring coldly, to be exact. But I have to admit it; I like the attention he's giving me, even though he is an asshole. I like that he notices me. Just then, I have the urge to push my chest out a little more and move my head slowly to the other side.

Getting my pictures taken like this, and feeling the Coors Light in my system, really makes me feel powerful. Less than a week away, I will be performing onstage. And I can't wait.

Chapter Six

I'm leaning against a cool cement wall. My left leg is propped up behind me. The fluorescents are very dim and flicker every so often. I hear the guys down the hall in the dressing room partying. I really should be in there with them, but I'm so fucking nervous right now. So, I decided to wait out here in the hall and have some time to think to myself.

I look down at what I'm wearing. I'm in my "stage clothes," which consist of something that someone might wear in the bedroom privately or at a strip club, to be honest. I'm wearing a black and lilac strapless corset made of satin and lace with cheeky black and lilac hipsters on. I have on a black garter belt that's attaching these sheer black thigh-high stockings; I'm also wearing five-inch, black, open-toed pumps. My black silk robe is lying on the concrete floor next to me, so I bend down carefully to retrieve it. I put on the silk garment and tie it around myself. I have plans to take it off during our opening number, 'Scars.'

Just when I tie it, I hear Tristan.

"Nervous?"

I peek up at him through my long eyelashes. He's looking down at me, and I see his chest moving up and down with his breaths. Tristan reminds me of a statue in Greece or somewhere over in that part of the world. His body is well-built, and he is wearing jeans that are a little loose and held up by a plain black belt. His black t-shirt contours well to his arms and chest. I can see almost every muscle of his upper body straining through the thin cotton material.

His dark hair is messy, and his face appears as if it hasn't been shaved for a week or two. I like facial hair. I want to take my tongue and graze it up his strong jaw to feel the stubble. My mouth goes dry.

Everything I Want

"You fucking all right?" he asks me with a raised eyebrow.

I didn't realize that I've been staring. Since he is waiting for me to answer, I shake my head softly and clear my thoughts of him.

"Yeah," I respond quickly. "Just . . . ah . . . a little taken aback by all of this, you know?"

I gesture to where the crowd is waiting on the other side of the cement wall. Tristan looks up for a moment, then looks back at me. All I can see are these dark, carnal eyes searching mine. And right when I think he is going to say something thoughtful, he ruins it.

"Try not to fuck up tonight."

That's it! I'm pissed off now. I'm not biting my tongue; no more.

"What's your fucking problem, dude?"

I cross my arms and push my leg off the wall, looking straight up at him. It's my turn to raise my eyebrow at him. He cackles hatefully at me, the sound rolling out of the back of his throat, almost sounding like a growl.

He takes a step closer, hovering over me. Damn, he smells so good! He smells of man, body wash, and a little whiskey.

"Nothing's my problem, but you are opening for us. And you wearing a robe and hooker shoes indicates to me that you might fuck up."

An evil smile dances across his face now, showing off his teeth and crinkling the corners of his eyes.

"It's not what you wear, Sophia, but if you have talent."

I want to slap him. I want to slap him hard or bite him. Hmm . . . Wait, don't think of biting, 'cause that route leads my brain elsewhere. Motherfucker! The whole time I was in LA, I wore t-shirts and jeans, except during the photo shoot, of course. And as far as talent goes . . . Lux noticed my band at a festival, heard my real voice—not one done up or played in studio. Before I can stop myself, words spill out of my mouth.

"Why do you hate me so much?"

Damn . . .

He shakes his head and starts laughing harder; then he quickly turns all serious again. His eyes are so sharp and his words so bitter that they pierce me.

"I don't hate you," he says before I can rephrase. "I just think you're annoying as fuck."

He studies me, trying to see my reaction. I give him my shit glare. Just as I'm about to open my mouth to tell him to kiss my ass, the door opens and my guys pour out, laughing. Tristan takes a step back, still with that half-smile lingering on his broad face. He looks so cocky right now. I smile sweetly at him, batting my eyelashes, hating every second of this fake 'being nice' crap.

"Ready, Sophia?"

Cory's walking over to me. He seems really ecstatic right now. Roger comes in, stepping in front of Tristan. Tristan is now in the background with his group coming over to him. Lux walks down the hallway to my left.

"On in three minutes!" he shouts. "Get your asses on stage."

Lux is beaming right now. As we approach him, he gives us a little pep talk. I can't help but feel the cold stare of Tristan's eyes burning a hole in the back of my neck.

We follow Lux's lead up the stairs, and all of a sudden, we're on the stage. I can really hear the crowd now. Shit! I'm so fucking nervous! Maybe I should have smoked that joint with the boys, or at least had a beer. I feel like I'm going to cry, puke, laugh, scream, or pass out all at the same time.

I rub my sweaty palms on the silk robe; I feel my palms starting to stick to the fabric. I know the guys are saying something to me, but I can't process it. It's all fuzzed out right now. It's like I'm underwater or like I have cotton shoved into my ears.

Shit! Why did Tristan have to say "Don't fuck up"? I was so sure of myself that I wouldn't, but now I feel like I might. I've sung in front of lots of people before, but nothing comes close to this. I mean, we're in Las Vegas and there's sixteen thousand people waiting for us out there. Granted, they're really waiting for Undead Society, but this will definitely put a good word out for Dollar Settlement.

As long as you don't fuck up.

Shaking my head, I tell my little inner bitch voice to shut the hell up.

Lux starts clapping.

"All right, it's show time!"

Shit! I don't think I'm ready yet. I feel Roger's hands on my shoulders, trying to loosen them up a bit. Jared walks up beside me and winks; then, he heads for the stage. Cory and Matt follow him. Damn it! I can't pick my feet up. Shit! I'm so scared.

"Breathe, girl. Breathe. You got this," Roger whispers into my ear.

He nods, calling my attention to look up at him. He gestures with his head off to the side where Tristan and his band are making their way up the stairs.

"Let's show that fucker how Dollar Settlement does it."

His face looks like it's going to break with the huge grin splitting his face. I quickly glance over at Tristan, then back at Roger. How did he know that Tristan pissed me off? Maybe because every time I'm around the guy, I end up in a bad mood. Well, Roger's little talk seems to work. I'm not as nervous as I once was. Now I'm in the mood to kick a little ass.

I grab his hand and hurry us onto the stage. It's dark in the arena, and the rest of the guys are already in their places. I walk up to the mic and close my eyes tightly.

Breathe. Just breathe, I say quietly to myself a couple of times.

I reopen my eyes; all I see are thousands of hands, lights from phones, and lighters. Wow! I cannot describe this. I will never forget this moment as long as I live. I don't know why, but I look over my shoulder and see Lux in his suit, standing offstage and giving me the thumbs up; Tristan's behind him with his guys, just watching me intently. I look back to the front when I hear Roger start knocking his drumsticks together. Faded purple and dark blue lights turn on me. It's showtime!

I start singing the opening to 'Scars,' soft and pretty-sounding; then, as the song starts to progress, my voice goes a little deeper and I begin to wail. I feel this burst of adrenaline rush through my veins. I'm starting to move a little more, and the audience really seems to be enjoying us. I know the big reveal is coming up when I hear Cory change riffs. I put the mic back on the stand and hold onto it for dear life. I'm standing there, going back to my "pretty voice."

I sway my hips softly and slowly undo my robe. Tristan's words filter through my head again.

I just think you're annoying as fuck.

Well, fuck him. He wants to not like me for no reason. I'll give that son of a bitch a reason. Suddenly, I hear Roger wailing on the

Everything I Want

double bass and I know it's time when Cory starts up again. I let the silk drape over my shoulders, baring my front to the audience. As I begin to holler into the mic, the garment falls slowly to the stage.

"Woo!"

Thousands of screams pierce my ears, almost over my own voice, and I love it! This is truly the best thing I have ever felt in my entire life. I'm moving effortlessly around the stage. When I'm up here like this—performing and looking this way—it gives me such a rush.

Now the song is ending. I walk back over to the mic stand to place my mic on it. As I'm holding onto it, I lean in to announce my band.

"How's everyone tonight?"

There's more screaming, and my face feels like it's breaking because of the huge grin I'm wearing on it.

"I would like to say we're Dollar Settlement!"

I motion my arms behind me at my boys, who are waving and greeting the audience into their mics. Roger does this quick little double bass beat, showing off.

"Now, I want all of you . . ." I bring my hands, palms up, toward the crowd. "To let us know if we should keep playing by showing me some hands, and I want to hear some fucking screaming! And if all of you aren't satisfied, then we'll leave right now."

Thousands of hands raise, and more screams come from the crowd. I turn to look over my right shoulder, and I see the silhouette of Tristan's massive body in the dark. I can tell he's pissed. I give him a Cheshire cat smile and face the crowd again.

"This next one is, 'Boss.'"

Cory starts to shred on the guitar, and it's time to wail again.

We've now finished up our set, and I thank everyone for being out here tonight. They are going nuts, screaming and chanting, "Dollar Settlement." The feeling I got from performing tonight is the best high ever, and I don't want to come down.

I make my way offstage. Some metal music blasts through the speakers, and the roadies start clearing our equipment and setting up Undead Society's. I approach Lux, who is nodding his head at me.

"You guys fucking nailed it!"

He pats my sweaty back and then starts talking—well, I guess shouting—into Roger's ear because it's so loud in here. Tristan brushes past me kind of hard, making me fall into Lux. What the fuck? I can tell my comment at the beginning of the show got to him. Good.

Lux looks down at me and all I can say—well, yell—is, "Damn shoes!" Lifting my heel up to show him.

He smiles and goes back to talking with the boys. Just then, the lights turn back on with this faded orange and red coloring, illuminating the stage. Tristan is standing in front of the mic with a guitar on his back. He leans down into the mic and starts his introduction.

"How the fuck is everyone tonight?"

Tristan's deep voice rumbles through the speakers as if it was the sound of thunder coming. I thought the crowd went nuts for us, but this is absolutely insane!

"Before we get started, that was some killer band, hey?"

Everyone starts applauding again. Oh, he's complimenting us. Well, that's nice. Damn, he switches gears so fast!

Everything I Want

"Especially the chick. Am I right?"

Where is he going with this? All of my band and Lux watch on patiently to hear what Tristan has to say next. My body begins to tremble.

"Chicks like that remind me of one thing."

He turns to Caleb, who I notice, is shaking his head no. Oh, no! What's about to happen? Tristan's laugh comes through the mic so dangerous and raw, I start to panic.

"Our first song of the night . . . 'Harlot.'"

His band then takes off jamming, and the audience roars even louder than before.

"What an absolute douchebag!" Frankie's high pitched voice says behind me.

Cory looks over at me, confused, but I'm paralyzed.

Paralyzed at what Tristan just said to thousands of people. Paralyzed at him singing hard into the mic. And paralyzed at how pissed I am at him, but I can't seem to tear my gaze away from him, either.

I stand there watching his whole set play through. In some songs, Tristan just wails, and in others, he plays his guitar with the rest of the guys. Not once did he look my way to see my reaction. Cory and Roger went right back into the dressing room, I'm guessing to burn one. It's just Matt, Jared, and me standing on the sidelines, watching Tristan's band play.

Frankie steps in closer and whispers loudly in my ear.

"I'm gonna make sure tonight at the after party that you're gonna look like the 'Harlot' he says you are."

What? I turn to him with this disgusted look on my face. He must see my horrified expression because he leans back in.

"Don't worry, my sweetie. You will still and always be fabulous. I mean, when you're not performing, your look is simple and pure as apple fucking pie. But tonight, with what that motherfucker did, I'm gonna make you look like a siren. Besides, it's your first VIP event, and you have to rock it in character."

Frankie is smiling this devilish little smile down at me. I turn back for a moment to look over at Tristan, and he's still just giving in to the mic.

"Sure, I guess. Why not?"

I give up. Tristan is an absolute asshole, and I want nothing more than to kick his ass on the charts and on tour. On the charts will have to wait, but for now, I will have to upstage him. And I will. Frankie grabs a hold of my hand and leads me down the stairs.

Chapter Seven

Within thirty minutes, Frankie has touched up my makeup. I still have smoky eyes, just cleaned up some. He opted for nude lipstick instead of the bold red I was wearing earlier onstage. I've changed into this all black strapless corset. I love how the corset pushes my chest up, making my C cups look almost like they're Ds. I definitely have that hourglass look going on from wearing the corset so tightly, but I don't know how women back in the day could wear these all the time. It looks amazing but feels very uncomfortable.

I still throw a little of myself into the mix, and I change into light blue jeans that hug my waist perfectly. My jeans have some rips throughout my knee areas and the backs of my thighs, but I love the edgy look they throw off, and they're very comfortable, too. I don't really care what I wear on my feet, so I'll just keep the black peep-toe pumps that I wore onstage earlier. My feet are getting a little sore, but I figure if I'm drinking and sitting then it won't be so bad. Right?

I'm glad that I have my own dressing room. I'm getting ready for the after-party away from everyone else. I sure as hell don't want Tristan to see me pissed off about that little stunt he pulled at the beginning of his show. Now, he will come off and see that I'm not there. Maybe he will think that I didn't even witness it.

Matt knocks once on the door and peeks his head in.

"The car is here to take us. You ready to go, girl?"

"Yeah," I say back to him while I grin from ear to ear, checking myself out.

Everything I Want

I turn and thank Frankie for another wonderful job he's done.

"I don't really know how you plan on this look getting back at Tristan, but I do feel really good and can't wait to go out and attend my very first after-party."

Frankie leans on my chair, his large, delicate hands holding onto each of the arm rests. He's staring at me in the mirror, where our eyes meet up.

"Isn't it obvious?" he asks.

What? What's obvious? I don't get what Frankie is asking me. He must notice what I'm thinking now because the look on my face is a little confused.

"He wants you, but he cannot have you."

Frankie pushes himself off the chair and looks over to Matt.

"She's all set. I will see you guys there later," he says, then walks out, the clicking of his boots on the tile floor the only sound in the room.

What the fuck did he just say to me? His tone was almost cryptic. Tristan wants me? Yeah, okay. I really don't think that's it. He had this bug up his ass when I first met him. I think it's something deeper than that. Whatever it is, I have to figure it out and solve it, because we are going to be around each other for seven more weeks.

We arrive at some club downtown for the after-party. We are only staying in Vegas for one night, so I guess I won't be trying my luck at any tables tonight. Maybe make an appearance and then sneak out? No, I can't do that. It does sound tempting, though, especially having to be around moody Tristan all night.

This is actually my first time being around him and his band in a semi-casual setting. Usually we are in the studio or in meetings, preparing for the tour.

The guys and I walk up to the front of the club. There are bouncers at the entrance and a crowd of people roped off, waiting to get in. I feel safe right now because I have all my boys around me. The bouncers nod and quickly open the doors for us when we flash them the cards that Lux gave us at the beginning of the night. Once inside, I notice he is waiting for us. I check him out, not in a sexual way; it's just that he always wears such nice suits.

"Hey!" He waves to us. "The party is up there."

He points to the third-level balcony. This club is incredible! It has an open dance floor with blue lights underneath, illuminating the club all over with the glow. The booths are all white, and on each side of the dance floor are two bars made of what looks like blue glass. You can see every floor since each floor's balcony wraps around the entire perimeter of the club. I look up to check out the second-floor balcony. People are leaning against the glass railings. The third floor has more of those blue lights from the dance floor shining overhead.

We follow Lux to a private elevator. A sharply-dressed man holds the door open for us. The elevator is all white, inside and out, with even more blue lights inside of it, casting a dim shadow on the inside. We arrive on the third level, and I notice that it's still pretty loud up here from the club's open-floor plan, but it is a bit quieter than the bottom level.

"You want a drink?" Cory leans in and asks me.

"Yeah, um . . . I guess I'll have a gin and tonic."

Cory's smile grows.

"Good girl. It's about time you let your hair down. I'll be back."

I laugh at him because he finished the last part with a terminator-style accent. I can tell that the boys are all excited seeing me out because I haven't really partied with them in over a month. I've been

Everything I Want

so damn busy in LA, and I just wanted to focus on my vocals being the best that they can be.

Roger pulls my hand.

"Hey, over there is a sectional booth. Let's grab it."

He lets go of my hand and heads that way. I follow him up to the booth, and he and Jared scoot in. I take a quick glance to check everyone out. Lux is leaning over the railing, talking to a couple of people. I wonder where Tristan and his band are? Maybe if I'm lucky, he won't show up and I can enjoy my night out without having glares and cocky comments thrown my way. That would be nice.

I climb into the booth, sitting on the edge, when Cory walks up with our drinks. He places mine down in front of me and asks me to scoot. Roger looks down at my drink and Cory's.

"Where's my drink, fucker?"

"You're a big boy, Roger. Go over there and get your own damn drink, you lazy ass," Cory laughs.

"Hey, Matt!"

Roger yells over to the bar, where Matt's standing. He's already talking to some blonde in a really short, tight red dress. Matt looks up for a moment then goes back into conversation with the blonde.

"Motherfucker is ignoring me. Well, hell."

Jared is sitting there quietly, checking everything out. Roger pushes his way out of the booth. The booth shakes a little from Roger's weight pushing down on the table.

"Don't break the fucking booth, dude," says Cory, looking up at Roger with a shit grin on his face.

"Fuck off!"

Roger starts walking away.

"Hey, man!" Jared yells to him. Roger turns and looks back at us.

"Let me fucking guess. You want a fucking drink, too?"

Jared smiles and nods.

"Yes, please."

"Motherfucker," Roger says to himself, shaking his head as he walks up to the bar.

I pick up my drink from the table and bring the glass up to my lips. The cool, pine-tasting liquid runs smoothly down my throat. It's so refreshing and feels so good on my dry throat from all the singing and screaming I did earlier.

Yep, I'm with my boys and having a couple of drinks. This will be a good night.

"So what did you guys think of the show tonight?" I ask Cory and Jared.

Jared rubs his hands together then places them back on the table.

"It was fucking awesome!"

Cory takes a drink from his beer and sets it down while agreeing with Jared. He turns his body slightly toward me.

"What was that shit with Tristan about earlier tonight?" he asks with this amused look on his face. What the fuck do I say to this?

"I have no fucking clue." Shaking my head at the thought, I take another drink. "At first, I thought it was the previous band. You know? They fucked up somehow. But now I think he's just fucking jealous."

Everything I Want

"Who's fucking jealous?"

Oh no! Fucking Tristan is standing over us with Caleb.

Cory takes another casual drink of his beer, playing the cool card; Jared's face looks like he just shit his pants. Right then, Roger walks back up to the table with his and Jared's drinks.

"Here's your drink, you little shit."

He slides Jared his beer and takes a seat on the other edge of the booth. Roger takes a quick sip and nods his head, greeting Tristan and Caleb. He pulls a cigarette from his chest pocket and lights up.

"So what did I miss?"

"Nothing. We just got here," Caleb says to him.

I hope Tristan doesn't know that I was just talking about him. I've always seemed to have this kind of problem, you know? Opening my mouth before looking around me. I'm literally just staring at my drink in front of me when Caleb starts talking to me.

"Hey, Sophia, you smashed it tonight!"

He is grinning ear to ear, but all I notice is Tristan's heated gaze. I hurry up to look back at Caleb.

"Thanks. Um, you guys wanna sit?"

I scoot into the booth closer to Jared. I really don't want to be around Tristan, but my hospitable personality takes over.

"Cool." Caleb points to Cory, Roger, and Jared. "Rest of these guys met the band, but you haven't. I'm gonna go grab a drink and bring them over. You need anything, guy?"

He looks over to Tristan, who is just standing there with no emotion showing on his face. I can't tell now if he's still pissed or what. He looks around the bar for a minute, then shakes his head.

"Nah. I'll be up at the bar."

I see his eyes wandering over that way, where there's two blondes staring back at him, waving. Fuck me. I feel like rolling my eyes but stop myself. Better get used to it. After all, he is a rock star, and I'm sure he gets tons of ass every night. Fucking sick.

Tristan goes over to the bar, and Caleb looks back at us.

"Everyone good here?"

Caleb and Tristan are total night and day. I look over to my boys, who are all wearing shit grins and joking around with each other. I now realize that we just made it through our very first concert, and it's time to celebrate.

"Actually, Caleb, would you mind getting a round of tequila shots and maybe another gin and tonic for me?" I ask him sweetly, batting my eyelashes. I will make tonight a good one and not let Mr. Fuck ruin it.

"All right, Sophia! Let's get 'er done."

Roger pounds on the table and Jared and Cory burst out laughing.

"You got it," Caleb says before making his way up to the bar.

Cory leans in on the table signaling us to get closer to hear him.

"Who's babysitting tonight?" He gestures his thumb toward me.

Oh, boy. They always get like this when we go out, and it's annoying. I cross my arms and give him a scowl.

"What the hell, Cory?" I nudge him a little with my shoulder. "I'm a big girl. I can take plenty of care of myself."

"I guess I'll fucking do it. Jared's a little bitch, so he can't do it."

Everything I Want

Roger pushes on Jared's shoulder while Jared is trying to take a drink of his beer. He ends up spilling a little on himself. I'm pretending now not to listen to their "babysitting Sophia" conversation, and I take another drink.

Caleb and the rest of the guys, except Tristan, make their way over to our table. Cory scoots closer to me to let Caleb in, and Roger scoots toward Jared to let Dave, Ryan, and Gunner in.

This sectional booth is pretty huge, not like the kind you see at some typical dining establishment. But even this is full capacity, with Caleb's leg hanging over the side; and I'm practically on Jared's lap. I look around at all the guys. I know, from being a fan, who the Undead Society guys are, but I've never really been formally introduced.

Let's see. I know Dave is rhythm guitar. He has very long, light brown hair and is also covered in tattoos. Ryan is bass—kind of like my Jared—with almost black hair styled a bit and is very thin; but he has more of a rugged look going on than my baby-faced Jared. And Gunner is their drummer. He reminds me of a Californian surfer with his dirty blonde, medium length hair. He also has tattoos, and has really nice fucking teeth, like they could use his mouth as a model in some toothpaste commercial.

Caleb introduces them to me and I finish my first gin and tonic, getting ready for the shots we have sitting in front of us. I'm loosened up and not feeling so shy anymore. I lean over the table to grab my glass that has a lime wedge resting on top of it.

"Ready, fellas?" I lift my glass. "To a successful first show and many more."

We all clink our shot glasses together and take our shots.

Chapter Eight

Yuck! I hate tequila! And the lime really does no justice, but I instantly feel the warm tingle of the alcohol. This is great. We're all laughing and talking.

"So, Sophia, where are you guys from again?" Ryan asks while looking at all of us.

Well, most of us since Matt's not here; he's trying to get some ass that's sitting up at the bar, wearing the tight dress.

"Ann Arbor!" I yell through the noise of the music.

Is it me? Or is the club playing it louder?

"Cool. So Michigan, I take it?" He asks.

I lean toward him across the table.

"Yes, sir. All of us are from Michigan. Where you guys from?"

I smile at them, glancing at each one of their faces.

Ryan grabs his drink.

"Pretty much all of us are from California, except Tristan. He's from Wyoming."

Wyoming? Well that kind of makes sense. I mean, he's the size of a tree and has that backwoodsman look going on. Yes, I can definitely see Tristan being from Wyoming. After Ryan takes another drink he nods at Roger.

"So how did you guys get together?"

"College. Well, I didn't go, but my roommate went. One night there was this party, and this little thing went on this makeshift stage and started wailing. It blew my fucking mind how good she was. So I approached her afterwards and asked if she wanted to start a band."

Everything I Want

Roger's face lights up from reminiscing about our past. "I already knew Cory, and so we kind of just looked around on campus 'til we found these two fucks."

He nods towards Jared and the direction Matt is standing in, then begins laughing. Jared smiles, shaking his head at Roger.

"Cool," Caleb says.

We all start talking about our early band stories. Finally, a waitress in a white cocktail dress comes over to take our order. It's about time! I really should slow down a bit, but I'm having so much fun with the guys. Also, I'm still on this adrenaline high from the show earlier. Nope. I'm not slowing down. Well, not yet, anyways. I look up at our very pretty redheaded waitress and decide to take it upon myself to order for everyone.

"Can we get another round? Oh, and a round of tequila shots too, please. And keep them coming!"

I smile over at Jared; he has this half-smile on his face now. The waitress leans in toward me, with her ass in Caleb's face and her breasts in Cory's face.

"Sure thing, darling. What's in your drink, sweetheart?"

They love it. Perverts. She has this accent to her. I'm guessing Texan?

"I'll just take a Coors Light from now on. Thanks."

She gives a quick nod of her head and then she's off.

"Fuck yeah, girl!" Roger pounds on the table causing it to shake a little. "Let's party!"

Ten or twenty minutes pass, and we're all still laughing and joking around. My cheekbones hurt from all the smiling I've been doing. Ryan, Dave, and Gunner are pretty cool. Matt comes over with a chair and pulls up next to our table since there is no room left in the booth. He looks around at all of us.

"How's it going?"

"Where the fuck were you?" Cory asks.

He should already know the answer to that. I have a feeling I don't want to hear this part of the conversation, so I start checking out the club from up here. I scan the room we're in. I don't realize it, but my eyes end up sliding their way over to Tristan. He has one blonde on his lap, and the other one has her arms draped over his shoulder. Just then, he looks up at me and our eyes lock.

All of a sudden, I feel my face starting to feel warmer; and the dark look in his eyes does something to ignite my core. I quickly turn back to the guys. Shit! He caught me staring at him. Damn it! I feel so embarrassed. He probably thinks I want to jump him, too. Well, maybe I kind of do; but I will be regretting that thought tomorrow.

Thankfully, the waitress appears with another round. I hurry up, grab the shot from her tray, and slam it, not waiting for the rest of the guys to join.

"Damn!" Gunner whistles through his teeth at me. "You sure can hold your own, hey?"

I shrug my shoulders at him, pretending to seem innocent.

"Don't let them pretty blue eyes fool ya," Roger says to him. "Even though she didn't go out back in LA, she can hold her own."

"No way."

Caleb looks over at me like he has a hard time believing what Roger just told him. Yeah, I guess it is kind of hard to picture. After all, I'm not that bold-looking; but like I said before, don't judge a book by its cover.

"Oh hey, Tristan!" Roger gives Tristan a wave.

What? All of the guys greet him, but I'm not going to. I'm not even going to look up at him. Instead, I take a drink of my beer. Jared glances around.

"Hey, man! Wanna pull up a chair?"

Just then, Caleb scoots out.

"No bother. I need to stretch my legs anyways."

Cory looks down at me, then looks at Caleb leaving the booth.

"Actually, I have to hit up the bathroom," he says, and winks at me.

Son of a bitch! I'm just getting ready to make up some excuse to leave too when suddenly Tristan's massive body sits down beside me, trapping me in. Fuck me.

He's so close, even closer than when we were in the SUV together last week. I breathe in his scent; he smells so good it's intoxicating me even more. I'm definitely drunk. It isn't good to be this drunk around him. Out of the corner of my eye, I can see him staring down at me. He's probably getting a good cleavage shot right now. I can feel my cheeks warming up again.

I glance down at the table, and Tristan's leg rubs up against mine. Right now I must keep reminding myself that he's a dick, because the way our bodies just barely touch sends this jolt of electricity pulsating through my entire body. Tristan being this close to me makes me feel weak, and I crave his touch on every inch of my body. Okay, Tristan is an arrogant piece of shit. Why am I even letting this guy give me this kind of a reaction?

"So has your name changed at all?"

Ryan's voice snaps me out of my trance. I don't say anything, just sitting there quietly for a moment.

He continues on, asking, "I mean, Ariel. Is that your last name?"

I shake my head a little, trying to find the words to speak.

"No, it's my middle name, actually. My last name is Mancini."

Ryan nods then takes a drink.

"Cool."

I'm starting to squirm a little. I'm going to finish this beer and then I'm going to make up some excuse to leave. Yes, that sounds good.

Tristan stretches out his arms, laying them flat on the table when he's done and starts talking to his band about what he thinks could be used in the next show. Really? I mean, I'm all for being professional, but we just did our show. Time to unwind and fucking relax a little. I look over at Jared, rolling my eyes and sticking my lips out, mocking Tristan.

"Is something the matter?"

Tristan's deep voice causes me to jump. Jared starts laughing at me, and I just sit there for a moment. For some stupid reason, I thought that when I turned my back away from him, he wouldn't be able to see me.

"No. Nothing's the matter."

I turn back toward him a little, clearing my throat. I give him my little sassy, teasing grin. The alcohol is definitely making me cockier now.

Tristan narrows his eyes at me, but this smirk forms on his beautiful lips. While the other guys pick up the conversation again, Tristan leans into me and whispers in my ear.

"Then why the fuck were you mocking me?"

He slowly pulls back from me, placing his left arm behind me and resting it on the booth. Now I feel intimated, but I don't want him to see that. Straightening myself up and squaring my shoulders, I look him dead in the eyes.

"Well, maybe because you dedicated fucking 'Harlot' to me."

I quirk my eyebrow up at him and cross my arms. Doing so pushes my breasts up even more. I notice his eyes moving down to my chest, and he slowly licks his bottom lip before he pulls it into his mouth. His eyes slowly graze my chest for a moment longer before making their way back up to meet mine again.

Fuck me running. Okay, I think I should go and use the bathroom now. This is just getting too intense for me to even handle now.

"I need to use the restroom. Can you let me out please?" I manage to get out quietly.

Tristan just stares blankly at me. I can't tell what he's thinking right now.

"Go ahead. I'm not stopping you."

Um . . . I think this requires him to—I don't know—move the fuck out of my way?

"Well, actually, you are. You see, you need to move out of my fucking way."

Holy shit! I can't believe I was so bold just now, but it felt good. Tristan's eyes widen, and a humorous look crosses his face. He shakes his head softly.

"Climb over me if you have to go that bad."

What? I'm not climbing across his stuck-up ass. He just wants to put me in an embarrassing position by either crawling across him or asking the other guys to all get out. So I do the immature thing. I lower myself to my knees below the table, just like when I was a kid eating out with my parents. Tristan looks surprised, and Jared's looking at me like, "What the fuck are you doing?" No one else seems to notice. They are all getting smashed, and they're partying hard now.

I have all these knees in my back, and Tristan's knee in my face. I hear Jared laughing. Tristan peeks his head under the table and gives me this cocky smile.

"You should have told me that you wanted out. It would have been much easier for you than doing it that way."

Motherfucker! I did say I wanted out! He's just putting on a show 'cause of Jared being right there. As I get on all fours, I punch Tristan's shin. But all that does is hurt my hand. Ouch!

"What the fuck?"

Tristan starts bellowing with laughter, but I'm pissed. Hurrying up and trying hard not to bump into anybody, I crawl my way out from under the table. The floor feels so gross on my palms.

Once I'm out, I look up and see Matt staring at me while I'm on my hands and knees. I don't know what else to do but plaster a cheesy smile on my face. His eyes widen too, looking shocked to see me like this. Oh, great. I know this doesn't look entirely good. He bends his head down and whispers to me.

"What the fuck are you doing underneath the table, Sophia?"

I give him this look with my eyes that says, 'please don't ask any questions' as I bite my bottom lip. He shakes his head and takes a drink from his beer. After he sets his bottle down, he extends his hand for me to grab. I take hold of it and he steadies me to my feet.

Standing up, I dust myself off.

Everything I Want

"Yo! How the fuck did you get there, Sophie Mophie?" Roger stops mid-sentence and stares at me. "You're like fucking Houdini. I didn't notice you even leaving the table. Shit, I didn't realize I was that drunk yet!"

Roger starts laughing; then, he waves the waitress back over. Before walking away, I stop and turn to my right and very discreetly, I raise my middle finger at Tristan. He flashes this huge, toothy smile at me. I give him one more glare, then I head toward the restrooms.

I'm so annoyed right now, I'm seeing red. It's definitely killing my buzz. To top it all off, he didn't even explain to me why he pulled that little harlot stunt tonight.

After being on that gross floor, my hands feel sick. Once I use the restroom, I scrub the hell out of them, then dry them off and look at myself in the mirror. I'm a little flushed-looking now, but that could be because of the booze or Tristan working me up. I notice that my eyeliner has run a smidge, so I take my fingers and gently wipe away the black residue from under my eyes.

Thankfully, everything else still looks good. Okay, when I get back out there, I won't let that asshole ruin my night. This is my first night out in a while, and we've just finished our first show. I'm celebrating, damn it! I'll have just a couple more beers then back to the hotel I go.

I turn toward the door, and right before I push it open, I let out a breath that my lungs must have been holding in. Shit! I guess I'm pretty drunk already. As I walk back into the VIP room, I instantly notice Frankie standing at the bar. Thank God!

Squeezing my way through the now-crowded dance floor, I hear Roger's laugh all the way over here. I look over at him and see him having a good time, and that puts a smile on my face. I'm so proud of all my boys tonight.

Coming up to the bar, I poke Frankie in his right side.

"Where have you been?" I ask him.

He looks over his shoulder at me, and his face immediately lights up, showing off his teeth and his full lips. Frankie loves his lip injections.

"I had other . . . arrangements to tend to," he grins mischievously.

"Ohh . . . Did you get some, Frank-ie?" I slur a little bit, and that makes me start laughing.

Frankie gives me this curious look and leans in to me.

"Girl, are you fucked up right now?"

"Nope! Not yet, but getting there."

"Well, let's just see about that, shall we?"

He turns to the bar and waves his hand at one of the female bartenders. She looks up at him through long, dark bangs and wipes the counter down before making her way over.

"I'm gonna need a shot of Grey Goose and . . ." He looks back over at me. "What are you drinking, sweetheart?"

"Coors Light, please," I tell him.

Frankie rolls his eyes and continues our orders with the bartender.

"And one dirty Coors Light. Wait a second . . . make that two shots of Grey Goose."

He glances down at me with a dirty little smirk as if he has something up his sleeve. Oh, no. I don't know about this.

Everything I Want

"I don't think that's gonna work too well. You see, I'm already drunk and have been drinking tequila, gin, and beers all night."

"I think the idea was to get you wasted, girl."

Fuck me!

Chapter Nine

The bartender returns with the two shots of vodka and my beer. Frankie nods and pushes some cash at her. I reach out with both hands and grab my shot and beer from the counter. He reaches for his with one hand, and with the other, he picks up a Bloody Mary that he must have already ordered before I came out of the bathroom.

"Okay, here's to the start of a fan-fucking-tastic friendship."

He clinks his shot glass against mine, and we down our shots. If I was sober, I probably would have felt the burn of the vodka a little more, but with my buzz on, it's less noticeable. Frankie is now sipping on his drink with his dainty, well-manicured pinkie sticking out.

"So . . . Having a good time so far, sweetie?"

I roll my eyes at that question and Frankie narrows his. He fishes the pickle out of his drink and points it at me.

"Girl, let me tell you something, mmm-kay? If you rolled your eyes because of who I think, then you just need to step up. Don't let him ruin your night or this experience for you. All right?"

I can't help my laughter. Frankie is trying to be a little serious with me, but all I can focus on is his damn pickle flopping all over the place when he speaks. He must have noticed it too, because he looks down at it and bites the end off, giggling when he does.

I cast a glance over the booth; all the guys are still there, minus Cory and Caleb. But now, I notice one of the blondes that was with Tristan earlier tonight is back. She is squeezing into the booth with him, and for some fucking reason, I hate it.

"Hey, Frankie, do you wanna dance?" I ask, turning away.

Everything I Want

Frankie nods slowly and grabs my hand.

"I thought you'd never ask. Let's go downstairs, more people."

He points over the balcony. I agree and follow him to the elevator.

We approach the dance floor, and it's packed! The lights underneath it are made up of different shades of blue and they move in a rolling motion, making it almost look like you're dancing on water. It's pretty fucking sweet, but definitely not a good thing to keep staring into when you're drunk.

Frankie takes hold of my hand and pushes through the crowd. I follow behind him, trying not to fall flat on my face. Wait! I don't mind dancing at the edge of the dance floor, but he's taking us to the center. Figures. Frankie, from what I've gathered, loves attention.

He drops my hand and whips around. Placing one hand on my right hip, he pulls me close against his lean body and starts to move. I don't really listen to modern day dance stuff, but the song on isn't that bad. The bass is pumping through the speakers that are surrounding the entire dance floor—the whole club, for that matter.

My body is feeling warm and fuzzy from the drinks, but now I can feel the music take its effect on it, too. My hips move to the rhythm of the music. I raise my arms above my shoulders and close my eyes, feeling every beat run through me.

I start rolling my chest every so often, and Frankie does the same with his on me. By looking at it, you wouldn't be able to tell that Frankie is gay with how he's dancing with me. He's such a good dancer, which is a bonus for me, because it makes it easier for me to follow his lead.

We are now on our third song, and I can't get enough of dancing. Frankie is the best person to party with; he's carefree, funny, and dances extremely well. Having a flamboyantly gay friend is totally fucking awesome. I feel like I can pick him up and place him right on my bed at night, just like a little girl would do with her favorite doll. That's how Frankie is to me. Only, really, I'm his doll, because he's my stylist. He does such a damn good job at it, too.

I can feel my footing isn't at all the greatest right now with these heels and the buzz I have going. I've lost my balance a couple times already, but Frankie leans in and saves me every time. So I decide to turn my body around and push my back up to his front. I start swaying my body down his with my hips. He starts moving back with his body, going side to side. I would feel uncomfortable doing this kind of dancing with someone else, but . . . it's Frankie and he's gay, so it's okay.

Making my way back up his body, doing the same moves that I did going down, my arms reach up and rub his chest with my hands. I turn to face him again. His face is splitting with his grin, and he shakes his head. Just then, I feel arms circling around my waist, pulling me away. I abruptly turn around to see who's grabbing me.

What the fuck? Some random guy who looks like Rico fucking Suave is trying to rub up on me. I don't think so! I'm getting ready to push the motherfucker off and tell him to get lost when Frankie steps in. He pushes the guy away and yells, "Back off, bitch!"

Wow! Frankie being all dominant and shit. I never even knew he had that side to him before.

He grabs my hand and leads me off the dance floor. I would've taken care of it. I would've just peeled my heel off and slapped the fucker in the face with it, but I guess this is the more subtle way of handling it.

"Want a drink?" Frankie's fanning himself with his dark silk button-down shirt.

"Um . . . I guess?"

Everything I Want

I don't really need one anymore. I'm pretty drunk as it is, but thirsty as hell from dancing.

"Actually, can you get me some water? I'll grab a beer when we head back up."

Frankie smiles at me then leans in at the bar.

I turn back around, facing the dance floor again. I would have to guess that there's about two hundred people—maybe even more—on the first level alone. This place is definitely intense!

Frankie hands me my drink and downs two shots for himself.

"Ready?" he asks me, licking the vodka off his lips. Then we're back out dancing again.

After a couple more songs, I'm ready to sit down again and have a beer. Right as we're heading off the floor, a familiar tune pumps through the speakers. I stop suddenly, pulling Frankie to a halt. He notices it, too, and jumps a couple of times and starts clapping. It's Marky Mark's 'Good Vibrations."

I don't care what other people think of this song; this is dancing music, for sure! Excitedly, I pull Frankie back with me and we bounce, grind, and wave our arms in the air to the music.

When the song is over, Frankie and I head back to the VIP area.

"I need to tinkle," he whispers in my ear, and makes his way to the restrooms. He stops and turns around. "Get us a round!" he yells back at me. I nod okay at him and smile.

I order our drinks, and I'm just standing there waiting for them to be made. I can see that none of the guys are in the booth anymore. They're all mingling around. As I watch the bartender prepare Frankie's Bloody Mary, I feel this warm presence right behind me.

"Having fun?" Tristan's deep voice whispers into my ear, causing me to still.

His lips tickle my earlobe and send shivers down my spine. I spin around, brushing up against him. Fuck! He is right on me.

Looking up at him through my lashes, I nod silently at him. I go back to facing the bar, but Tristan is still standing behind me. Damn it! What is he doing right here? Especially behind me like this? It's less crowed at the other end of the bar. I feel him press his hard chest to my back. He speaks up to the bartender, who is all in favor of dropping her other duties to come over here and take Tristan's order.

"Can I get a scotch?" he requests, leaning down on me.

Looking back up at him, his eyes are dark and dangerous-looking. Must be from the booze he's drinking. I think? I don't know if I'm freaking out or not, but I swear I can see something more in them. I'm just not sure what it is.

His strong arms are tight against his gray, short-sleeved t-shirt. The way he crosses them in front of his chest is causing his tattoos to stretch against his muscles. The sight of that alone makes me want to do some very bad things to him.

His hair is tousled, falling around the sides of his broad face. I hate to admit it because he's such a dick, but damn, being drunk and not having gotten laid since my ex and I broke up almost a year ago is making me so horny right now. Not a good thing to be feeling around Tristan right now.

"So, you dance?"

I turn around to face him, our bodies inches apart. I give him a puzzled look.

"I noticed you dancing down there. You look pretty good."

Everything I Want

As of right now, I'm in a state of shock. Usually, only insults come out of his mouth, but Tristan's saying I looked good dancing. It makes me feel nervous and excited all at the same time. He was watching me dance? And for how long?

"Cat got your tongue?" he asks, leaning into me more.

His eyes are searching mine. Shit! I'm so out of it right now. Tristan threw me off track with his compliment; now I don't know how to act or speak.

Shaking my head slightly, I reach for my drink. After I take a sip, I glance back up at him. I feel incredibly vulnerable right now as he towers over me, and I don't really like it.

"Uh, yeah. Thanks. Honestly, if I wasn't drunk right now, my ass wouldn't even be out there."

I giggle to myself for being so honest and modest with him. As I mention the word "ass" to him, I notice Tristan taking a few steps back and checking out my body. What the fuck is going on right now? Did he really just check me out?

"Well, I think you should have your ass out there more often."

He's so calm right now that I can't tell if he's being serious or just fucking around.

Tristan reaches in and grabs his drink off the bar. While reaching in, I feel him brush up against me again. Is he doing this shit on purpose? I feel lightheaded from his proximity to me. I really can't handle this right now. I'm drunk and obviously turned on. And I have hot asshole Tristan standing right here in front of me. Now I'm starting to believe that maybe he's flirting with me. That reminds me. Where is fucking Frankie when I need him?

"Yeah, well I don't really go to clubs often, so . . . And besides, weren't you the one that called me a harlot? For dressing and dancing this way on stage earlier tonight? Isn't that kind of being hypocritical?"

I end up sounding a little bitchy when I didn't mean to come across that way. But after I throw that back in his face, an arrogant smile plays on his lips.

Rubbing his chin with his hand, he takes a moment to think about the words I just threw at him. I just stand there looking up at him and waiting for him to respond. But he doesn't. Instead, he cackles to himself.

Finally, Frankie shows up, interrupting our awkward conversation.

"Sorry, girl. There was a fucking long wait for the toilets. By the time I was done, I couldn't even powder my nose. I didn't want to leave my girl out here for so long."

He squeezes past Tristan, not even noticing the tension in the air.

I look up at Tristan in annoyance, wondering when he's going to leave, but he just stands there, looking at me with this smirk on his face. I can't help it; I still want to know why he dedicated 'Harlot' to me.

"Oh, girl, I will be right back. I have to say hi to someone I know real quick," says Frankie before rushing off.

So now it's back to just Tristan and me. Well, I might as well finish what I started with this harlot business. I'm drunk and I can't let it go. I take a step closer to him, bending my neck back as I look up at him. He follows my moves, his demeanor still cool. He leans in, his face now right in front of mine with just an inch separating us. I can smell the liquor coming off his hot breath, and I feel just that much more intoxicated.

"Tell me something, Sophia. Why do you think I did that?"

Everything I Want

"I don't know why. That's why I'm asking you, dumbass."

Holy shit! I can't believe I just said that. I guess all this pent up anger towards him is finally spilling out. It feels really good letting it out. His eyes dance at my insult, and then a glare takes over his eyes, hardening them. He leans in so close now that I actually take a step back, bumping into the counter behind me.

"Because, Sophia. That's exactly what you are," he growls.

He reaches his arms around on each side of me and places his hands on the bar top. I'm caged in, unable to move. The only thing I can do to escape him is look down, but I don't want him to know that he intimidates me. So I stand my ground and stare back at him into his eyes. Once he knows he has my full attention, he continues.

"And if not, then you're nothing but a fucking cocktease."

What? My eyebrows raise so high that I can feel the skin on my forehead stretch. What a dick!

"You son of a bitch!" I spit at him.

You can feel the air around us getting dense. Frankie pushes his way back through to me.

"Excuse me, Grizzly Adams!"

I'm stuck staring into Tristan's eyes. While I'm glaring at him, his eyes crinkle at the corners and his lips go up slightly in a smirk. He steps back and takes a drink of his scotch, never taking his eyes off me.

"Fuck you," I mouth at him when Frankie's back is turned. I spin around quickly so I don't have to see his reaction.

Another hour passes and I'm still up at the bar with Frankie. Roger comes barreling over to me and hangs off my shoulders.

"Rea-dy?" he asks.

He is so wasted right now. I grab hold of him, steadying his swaying.

"Yeah, let's go."

I look around and I see Jared. I give him a nod, letting him know that it's time to go.

"I'll catch the next one!" Jared yells to me over the noise of the other partiers when he sees me heading over to the elevator with Roger.

He's with Cory and Matt, and since there's only one elevator in the VIP lounge, he will have to wait. As Roger and I stumble onto the elevator, Tristan makes his way in, too. Great!

The elevator is filling up with random drunk bodies with everyone pushing and crowding each other. Tristan steps up right behind me. Trying to act unbothered by his proximity, I remain as still as I can with my eyes straight forward, trying to focus on the elevator doors.

Some drunk-tards stagger their way around the tiny space we're all standing in. I lose my footing when they crash into me, sending me reeling back against Tristan. Before I can fall to the ground, Tristan wraps his arms around me and steadies me on my feet. Rubbing my backside against his front, I feel him tense up. I can feel his hot breath on my scalp. My legs tremble and my core ignites. *Fucking alcohol!* I'm so not thinking clearly right now.

As we descend the few short floors, I feel Tristan's growing erection on my back. Holy shit! I feel dizzy and hot as if I have been in a sauna for too long. My heart starts racing, and my center begins a slow ache. As soon as I see the doors opening, I'm out of there like a bat out of hell, leaving Roger behind.

Without looking behind me, I climb into one of the SUVs parked outside that I know is one of ours. Fumbling with my seatbelt, my heart races like I just ran a marathon. I peek out the tinted window to see if any of the guys are coming yet. I notice Tristan strolling over to the second SUV, his eyes turned in my direction.

For a moment I duck down, thinking he can see me. I slowly rise in my seat and look back out the window. He's standing there, his eyes angry and cold, his mouth set into a tight line, causing his jaw to clench.

I lean back into the cool leather seat. My head feels incredibly heavy and very dizzy. Rubbing my hands on my face, I try to comprehend what the fuck just happened in the elevator with Tristan's . . . uh . . . thing. This is going to be one hard tour. I just know it!

Chapter Ten

I wake up with a pounding headache. Damn! How much did I drink last night? I roll over to my left side, and I grab my phone on the pillow beside me to check the time. 9:30 a.m.! That means all I had was five and a half hours of sleep. Shit! We have to be at the airport by noon. That doesn't really give me any time to just lounge around like my body wants me to. Our next show is tomorrow night in St. Louis.

I figure it's time to start moving around. I can always sleep on the plane, and I'm definitely not going out tonight no matter what the boys say. I know the guys will probably want to, but they have way more tolerance built up than I do.

Swinging my legs over the side of the bed, I stretch my limbs a little before getting on my feet. Damn it, my head is killing me right now! I stumble over to the table by the window that overlooks the Vegas strip.

Grabbing my bag, I dig around for some Tylenol. Taking two pills in my hand, I turn to the mini fridge that I know is stocked with water. When I bend down to grab one, I cringe at the sight of the mini shots that are in there as well. Hurrying up, I place the two pills on my tongue and gulp down most of the water.

Standing there and waiting for my stomach to relax, I reminisce about last night. I had so much fun with Frankie and the guys. I laugh quietly to myself at the thought of how excited Frankie and I got when 'Good Vibrations' came on. Yes, that was lots of fun.

Okay, I think I'm good to get up now. Walking slowly on wobbly legs, I head for the bathroom. I should've shut the curtains last night because the sun shining through is not a welcome sight right now.

I make my way through the bathroom door and close it softly behind me, resting my back against the cool wood. Then all of a sudden, it hits me. Tristan! Tristan in the elevator, to be exact. My head falls back and bangs against the door.

Closing my eyes tightly, I try to remember through the fog that clouds my memories. Tristan leaning against the wall of the elevator, looking so delicious with his piercing dark eyes, messy hair, and masculine arms crossed against his strong chest; feeling his heat against my back and how his arms wrapped tightly around me when I almost fell. And how his whole body went rigid, especially that *other* part of him.

I can still feel and smell his hot breath, and my skin tingles at the memory. I hate that he turns me on so much. I also remember the angry and cold expression that he had on his face when we got into the SUVs, like I pissed him off or something. For what? Turning him on? Um . . . I don't think getting shoved practically on top of him in a packed elevator is my fault. But, hey, Tristan's pissed at me. What's new? He's already been pissed off at me for doing absolutely nothing to him before, so let's add a new imaginary problem, shall we?

Shaking my head and trying to get rid of all thoughts of Tristan, I bend over to turn the water on. I don't need to keep thinking about how I may have turned him on. I just need to relax a little and get something in my stomach; then maybe I will be able to start fighting off this hangover.

The small bathroom instantly fills with thick steam. Peeling off my Pantera shirt and black lace boy shorts, I climb slowly into the shower and let the hot water pour down on me. It feels so good, massaging away the dull muscle aches from last night.

Turning my back, I just stand there for what seems like five minutes. Slowly, I face the water again and bend over to grab my body wash and loofah. The aroma of passion fruit, Shangri-La peony, and vanilla orchid take over. Letting my head fall back, I inhale the aroma. I scrub myself thoroughly before turning around to wash my hair.

After I'm done with my hair, I stand under the spray for a few more minutes before shutting the water off. Climbing out of the shower, I feel lightheaded. It must be from a mixture of the hangover, lack of sleep, and the intensity of the heat from the shower. My empty stomach doesn't help; I feel like I'm on some fucking carnival ride.

I grab one of the fluffy towels from the wall and dry myself off with it, carefully brushing the towel over my skin. Any rapid movements right now might cause me to throw up. Once I'm done, I wrap the towel around me and step in front of the mirror.

I wipe off the steam that has collected on the glass with my hand and stare at my reflection. My tan skin looks pale, and I have dark circles under my eyes. It's probably from the lack of sleep last night. My blue eyes seem glazed over and droopy. I look like total shit right now.

Grabbing my lotion, I squeeze a small amount onto my palm and rub my hands together, pressing softly on my face. Next, I reach for my toothbrush and begin brushing my teeth. It's amazing how much better you feel when your mouth is clean. The cool, minty foam takes away all of the leftover alcohol from last night, and awakens my senses.

I go back into the bedroom when I'm finished. The Undead Society guys get the top floor suites with all the perks, but since my band is just starting out, we get the average rooms. I don't mind at all, though; I've already gotten used to these kinds of rooms from living in LA this past month.

Getting my bag, I pull out my slightly flared black yoga pants. I don't fucking care at all today about looks, only comfort. Next, I find my gray sweatshirt that's ripped on the top, off the shoulders. I remember doing that on purpose because of *Flashdance*. I thought that chick in the movie was awesome.

I pull out a white strapless bra and cotton thong. I really want to wear panties, but it would show too much through the thin material of the pants. And besides, the thong is cotton so it's more comfortable than the lace one.

Dressing quickly, I reach for my phone on the bed. It's time to wake the guys up. It's already after ten, and they have to start moving. Maybe breakfast downstairs, I think? Knowing not to call Roger yet, I dial Matt. Roger needs to be kicked awake right now to get him up, not some little phone call. Matt's phone rings four times before he picks up.

"Good morning!"

Oh wow, he sounds peppy after a night of partying.

"Hey," I say back in a low voice so that my head doesn't explode. "Wanna grab something to eat downstairs before we head to the airport?"

Matt laughs a little into the phone, probably knowing that I feel like shit.

"Yeah, that sounds good. Jared's in the shower right now so . . . Do you want to wait for him or just head down now?"

Ugh. Jared is known for sitting in the shower 'til the water runs cold. Call me selfish, but I really don't want to wait any longer than I have to, to put something in my stomach.

"Let him know to meet us down there. And Cory and Roger, too," I add.

"Well, Cory left an hour ago, and Roger is still sleeping." He starts cackling. "I could punch him in the face, though. That would sure as hell wake him up."

He laughs harder. Where's Cory? I wonder. I will have to text him. I hope everything is okay.

"Fuck off!" I hear Roger curse in the background, pulling me away from my thoughts of Cory, as Matt laughs at whatever he just did to him.

"Meet you down there in ten, okay?" I ask.

"Sure."

I hang up and brush my hair at record speed, practically ripping through it. When I'm done, I put on some sunglasses, hoping they will shield me so others won't be drawn to my hungover appearance. Stepping into my flip-flops, I grab the room key off the dresser.

I don't see Matt as I wait for the elevator. I hope he's already down there. When the doors slide open, I look up and see Tristan and Caleb standing there, waiting for me to get in. Oh, no! Not him again!

Caleb has the hugest grin on his face; Tristan briefly glances down at me before looking straight forward again. You can't even tell that these guys were up most of the night partying. Caleb looks like he just stepped out of the shower. His shaved head is shining, and he is wearing fresh-looking jeans and a red t-shirt.

Tristan is wearing really faded jeans with a bunch of rips down the front. They remind me of this book I read a couple of years ago that's all the rage now. Red Room of Pain jeans! They look hot as hell on his muscular thighs. He also has on a navy colored hoodie that has been torn open at the neck. His hair is wavy and soft-looking. I'm very conscious of the fact that I look like shit. Shit! Now I wish I would've taken a little more time on my appearance.

Stepping into the elevator, I feel awkward at what happened last night. When the doors close, Caleb begins to talk.

"Did you have a good night last night?"

I nod, glancing over my left shoulder at him.

"Yeah. It was fun," I say calmly, giving him a shy smile before turning my gaze back in front of me.

Feeling the familiar heated gaze on the back of my neck, I squirm. I know it's Tristan staring down at me. Being this close to him again and smelling his cologne takes effect on me. I hate that he affects me this way.

"You were pretty wasted when I saw you stumble around last night, Sophia. It's cool to see you cut loose. I was starting to think that maybe you were a little uptight."

Tristan starts to cackle. Spinning around, I glare at both of them. Showing Tristan my 'fuck you' eyes. I don't know why, since I'm wearing sunglasses, but I still thought that they might be able to tell.

"What do you mean 'uptight'?" I ask Caleb, crossing my arms in front of me, but I make sure to put on a playful smile because I like him.

He raises his hands up defensively, shaking his head.

"Oh, it's nothing, Sophia," he says, laughing. "I meant that I never see you out. Even when you guys were in LA for a month. It's cool to see you let loose every once in a while. You deserve it."

As we land on the ground floor, I nod at Caleb before getting off, careful not to look over at Tristan.

I head straight for the restaurant, Caleb and Tristan only a few steps behind me as we all go down the hall. Thinking now that maybe yoga pants probably weren't the best thing to have put on, I feel self-conscious when I hear Tristan and Caleb mumble something. It's probably Tristan calling me a cocktease again or some shit like that. Finally, Caleb clears his throat.

"Are you eating alone today, Sophia?"

I look over my shoulder at him, shaking my head.

"No. Matt and Jared are meeting me."

Shit! I just remembered. I was supposed to text Cory this morning. I'll have to do that once I'm in the restaurant. I wonder where he is?

As we go inside, I see Matt sitting at a table in the center of the room, strumming his long fingers on it.

"Hey, you," I say to him as I pull out my chair.

"Hey," he smiles back.

Taking my seat, I pull out my phone to text Cory.

Where r u? Grabbing something to eat downstairs right now.

After I hit send, I look back up at Matt. He's grinning at me.

"What?"

He leans forward on the table with his arms crossed on it, his blue eyes gleaming with humor.

"I like the sunglasses."

"Well, I feel like shit," I say, rolling my eyes. "And I know I must look like it too, so . . ."

"You don't look like shit, Sophie."

Everything I Want

Matt smiles again. Leaning back, he nods for me to come closer. I lean in on the table now, waiting for what he has to say next.

"You still look good, even hungover. Those guys over there were checking you out hardcore when you came in here, if that's any indication."

He raises his eyebrows in amusement. My eyes widen.

"What guys?"

"Tristan and Caleb."

He nods in their direction. Glancing over my right shoulder, I notice Caleb is up at the buffet, but Tristan is sitting at the table, stirring his coffee. He looks up at me briefly with hooded eyes. Closing my stunned mouth, I hurry up and glance away. Matt starts laughing.

"You big jerk!" I swing up and playfully smack his arm.

After we place our orders, I get a text back from Cory. Thank God! I was beginning to worry.

I'll be down in 5.

Raising my head, I see Roger and Jared coming into the restaurant. Jared is looking all nice and cleaned up; styled hair, dark blue jeans, and white t-shirt. Roger, on the other hand, looks groggy and messy. His curly hair is pulled back into a half-assed pony tail. He's wearing a blue bandanna on his head with sunglasses on, like me. He has on this faded black sleeveless shirt that looks kind of wrinkly.

Roger stumbles up to the table first, and I notice that he must have taken a shower, too, because his messy hair still looks damp. Jared gracefully pulls up a chair to my right and takes a seat, lacing his fingers together on top of the table.

The waitress returns, placing my food and Matt's down, and grabs Roger's and Jared's drink orders. I'm having plain oatmeal with some fresh berries and maple syrup, and a tall glass of orange juice. I didn't want or need anything too heavy in my stomach just yet. Matt ordered a farmer's omelet and toast. He starts cutting his omelet up, and I'm mixing my berries into my oatmeal, when I see Roger taking a napkin and wiping the back of his neck with it.

"What are you doing?" I ask.

He stops and tosses the napkin down on the table. He leans back in his chair, gesturing with his thumb over to Jared.

"This little prissy bitch here decided to use all of the hot water up, which I think is fucking funny because we're in a goddamn hotel. But he still manages to find some way to." Roger shakes his head and continues. "I pretty much just washed my 'nads and pits, then I was outta there."

Jared smirks at him. Roger pulls out his chair.

"I'm hitting the fucking buffet."

Jared glances at the menu, then gets up to follow Roger.

I take a bite of my oatmeal and it's delicious. When the warm, gooey goodness hits my stomach, I instantly feel a little better. Looking over at Matt's plate, I can see that he's already halfway done.

"Geez, Matt," I laugh. "You seem like you're starving or something. How can you eat that fast, especially after drinking?"

I pick up my orange juice and take a sip.

"I don't know. I got up at nine, worked out for forty-five minutes, and then showered. I guess the exercise helped me work up an appetite."

He shrugs and continues with his meal.

"Damn. Maybe I should've tried that. But my head was killing me this morning."

"Yeah, when I feel like shit, usually working out a little kills my hangover. I'm ready for another night now."

He smiles at my cringing face. Yuck! Not me tonight, that's for sure.

Just then, Cory enters the restaurant, and his clothes look clean. He's wearing jeans and a vintage Nirvana t-shirt. But his eyes . . . His eyes are blood red and bugged out. Either he didn't sleep at all last night, or he is stoned out of his mind. He pulls up a chair on my left side between Matt and me.

"Good morning, guys," he says to us.

"Hey, how are you?"

I pull my sunglasses down the bridge of my nose a bit and quirk my left eyebrow up at him. He knows I'm onto something because he gives me this puzzled look as he pops an ice cube from his water into his mouth.

"Ahh . . . fine," he says slowly, clearly.

"Okay, then."

I know it wasn't just pot. His eyes wouldn't be bugged-out looking, and he wouldn't be fidgety, either. He would've been laid back and have more tired-looking eyes. Nope. My guess is that he did some coke again. I hope he doesn't keep going with this. Ever since that one night in the studio, I have been worried about him.

Roger comes back to the table and practically drops his plate on it. I laugh to myself a little because Frankie was kind of right. Roger is barbaric. His plate is smothered in sausage gravy. I can't even tell what's underneath it. Fucking eh.

Jared sits beside me, and I can at least tell what he is having; bacon, a cinnamon roll, and yogurt. Roger must have noticed it too, because his face blanches.

"What the fuck, Jared? Yogurt?"

"What, man? This shit is good. Not like that heart attack shit you're eating."

Jared peels the tab off of his yogurt and digs in.

"This is what grown men eat, Jared. Not bitch food like yours."

Roger digs into his plate.

"So, how you doing, Sophie?" he asks after a few bites. "You look like hell."

What?

"Well, Rog. I don't feel that great, so of course, I might not look like it."

I roll my eyes at him and start eating my oatmeal again, laughing a little. Gotta love him. And sometimes wanna slap him.

After we finish our food, we go back to our rooms and collect our things. We make our way down to the lobby, waiting for our cab. Undead Society gets to travel to the airport by limousine. Not us. But maybe someday. Hopefully, we will be as successful as they are.

Chapter Eleven

Once we reach the airport, we drive through gates that lead us to a runway where a private jet is waiting for us. Undead Society flew via private jet from LA to Vegas, but we came on a commercial flight, so this is fucking insane.

Stepping out into the hot Vegas sun, I pull my hair up into a sloppy bun. I was just starting to feel decent, and I don't want my hair on my neck, making me feel too hot again. It might trigger something in my hangover.

Lux walks up to us and smiles. He's wearing another suit, but this time, it's all beige with a white shirt underneath. He has a white silk handkerchief in the breast pocket.

"How's it going, everyone?" he asks, looking at each of us.

"Good," we all reply, and nod at him.

"Let me just say again that last night's performance was great. You guys, and lady," he adds, smiling at me, "killed it! So we are just beginning, and there will be way more shit to come. But if you guys keep this up like last night, in time . . . Well, let's just say the world will know every single one of you guys by next year."

He gestures toward the plane.

"Get on. Undead is already on board. You will be sharing with them. Your equipment left two hours ago on a separate plane. The rest of the crew is flying commercial. They will be in St. Louis this evening. Enjoy your flight."

He's walking toward his limo when he stops suddenly.

"Oh, by the way. I have some other clients I'm meeting up with for dinner tonight. I will see you guys tomorrow at the show."

And with that, Lux ducks into the limousine and takes off.

I'm the last one to step onto the jet. It's small, with tan leather sofas lining the walls and a mini bar set up in the far left corner. There is a table in the far right corner, and beyond that, there's a door that leads to a private bedroom. The décor is light and airy with shades of cream everywhere. I see Gunner sprawled out on the right hand couch, grinning up at me with his arms crossed behind his head.

"How's it going?"

He nods, but I can't see his eyes with his shades on.

"Fucking sweet! Booze!" Roger exclaims as he heads straight over to the bar.

Can't take him anywhere, I swear. I glance around for a spot to take a seat. I'm still really tired and would like to do nothing more than pass out; but with nine guys on this small jet, it's kind of impossible to really find a comfy spot.

"Hey. Is anyone claiming the back room?" I ask loudly so that they can all hear me.

Roger doesn't even notice. He's too busy making himself a drink. Fucking alcoholic! Jared and Matt take a seat at the table with Caleb and Dave. Ryan is on the other couch across from Gunner, but Roger is making his way to sit next to him. I really don't want to make Gunner sit up. I would feel kind of bad and bitchy to ask.

"I think the back room is still free," Gunner says suddenly. "Tristan is still in the pisser, so you better claim it while you can."

I smile at him and thank him for the heads up and make my way to the back room. I need to fucking sleep a little, or I will turn into a zombie. I need to get my body trained for this shit. Performing and partying.

As I turn the door handle, I notice it's unlocked. Phew! That's a good sign. A bed all to myself sounds amazing. I turn the handle and gently push my way through when I notice Tristan standing there, removing his shirt. I see each one of his muscles flex and tighten. Damn.

Tristan's upper body is now completely bare. I must look like a damn fool right now for staring, but I can't pull my gaze away. He is a total Adonis. He has smooth, olive skin, and every muscle is ripped and defined at its best. I mean, the guy has a freaking eight-pack, with a deep V that leads down . . . There's just a dusting of dark chest hair on his defined pecs. His ripped jeans hang snug and low off of his narrow hips with an inch of black boxers showing. He might be a jerk, but right now, he's one absolutely fine ass jerk.

I snap out of my trance, pulling myself from my wandering mind and eyes. Damn. I'm so embarrassed. He's just staring back at me with no expression on his face, but the look in his eyes seems to be surprised a little. It's probably at me barging in here, and I can only imagine that I must look like a damn goldfish right now with my mouth hanging open and my eyes wide.

"Oh, shit. Sorry," I mumble as I swiftly turn around to head back out.

"What are you sorry for, Sophia?"

Oh, God. I love how he says my name. Stopping, I turn back to face him and gesture with my hands to the room.

"I didn't know that this room was taken. I just came in without knocking so . . ."

Tristan's mouth raises on the one side, revealing a cocky half-smile. His eyes glisten and darken at the same time. My body begins to react at the look he's giving me.

"Well, you don't need to be sorry for opening a door. If I wanted privacy, then I would've fucking locked it."

His voice has some edge to it.

I catch myself furtively checking him out and I see his smile fade. Giving him a slight nod, I spin back around, trying to leave the room. Again his words stop me in my tracks.

"Were you looking for a spot to crash?"

"Ah, yeah, but it's cool. I can go rest out on one of the couches."

Hurry! Get the hell out now! I scream at myself. Grabbing the handle, I push up on the lever.

"Well, babe, you can always crash in here with me if you want."

I glance back at him with a, *what the fuck are you talking about?* look.

Tristan gives me a teasing smile, showing off his perfect white teeth. His head tilts back a bit, his arms folded over his broad chest. The sight of him doing this sends moisture to my center. I close my legs tighter, trying to relieve the pressure.

I cross my arms and copy him, quirking my eyebrows up and sucking my cheeks in a little. I have to hide this sudden attraction to him, so I decide to look like I'm annoyed. Which, by the way, right now, I am. But I'm more annoyed at my traitorous body for feeling this way than I am at the invitation he's just given me.

"Ahh . . . No thanks, Tristan. I'll be fine out there," I say to him in a smart ass tone. I turn around and start walking out the door; then I wave my left hand up at him in the air. "Thanks, anyway."

The door shuts behind me, and I let out a breath of air that I must have been holding in. I seem to do that every time I'm really nervous. I was beginning to feel hypnotized by him in there. Shit.

I take a seat next to Roger and curl myself up. I place my earbuds in to tune everyone around me out so I can rest for a little while. I don't mind being out here, though; it's just a little noisy for me to be able to really sleep well, is all. I will just have to jam softly to keep the rest of the guys' noises at bay.

I scroll though my playlist and end up picking "Perfect Circle" by Three Libras. It's mellow enough for me to fade away to. The music begins to play softly, and my mind floats away with the gentle lyrics of this song. I drape my left arm over the couch and rest my head on it. Soon, I drift off.

I feel weight pushing down beside me and the warmth of someone's skin close by. I flutter my eyes open to see what's going on. Tristan is sitting beside me with his arms resting on the top of the couch. His left hand is barely grazing my neck. I jerk suddenly, taken aback at his proximity. Roger is still on my other side, talking to him. Tristan notices my movement, softly looking down at me. Sitting up quickly, I scoot myself away. How long has he been sitting there?

"How long have I been out?" I ask, looking over at Roger.

He puckers his lips and looks up while rubbing his chin, thinking.

"Probably a couple of hours. We're about to land soon, which reminds me . . . better make one more drink."

Roger gets up and goes over to the bar.

"Sleep well?" Tristan's deep voice pulls my attention back to him. Before I can answer, he says, "Don't get used to this. We're catching a bus after tomorrow night's gig."

Everything I Want

He's cocky again. What does he think I am, a diva or something?

"I know," I respond, my tone flat.

But really I don't. I should've, though. I mean, it is my first tour. Even though we are with Undead, I just thought being with that band gave us a few more perks than if we were with some other band.

Tristan is just staring at me. At least now he has his fucking hoodie back on. I would've been too distracted if he didn't. Tristan stands and walks over to the other couch now to sit beside Gunner. He's so tall that he has to crouch when standing up. Why couldn't he have just sat over there in the first place?

Matt calls out to me.

"Hey, Sophia. Remember that one time on New Year's when you drank all those Jaeger bombs? Fucking eh. Talk about blowing chunks."

He starts laughing with Caleb at the table at his little story. My eyes go huge again. Why did Matt have to bring that up? I barely remember that night as it is, let alone having everyone on the plane laughing now. Well, almost everyone. Tristan is just sitting there, but I did catch a quick, tight-lipped smile crossing his face.

"Come on, guys," Cory chimes in while dealing the cards. "What did you expect? I mean, she's fucking tiny and doing them bombs all night was going to catch up with her. We all knew it. Remember?"

He looks around, gesturing toward me.

"We had that bet on how long she would go. Jared won that one, by the way."

Cory starts laughing at me.

"Yeah, the only thing he's ever won," Roger says.

I look over at Jared and scowl at him. I can't believe they had bets on me! Especially my sweet, dear, quiet Jared. Motherfuckers. I look over at them, crossing my arms.

"Fuck off! That was over four years ago. I can take any of yous on now. Well, maybe not Roger," I add.

They all burst out into fresh laughter.

"Yeah, okay, Sophia. Well, maybe Jared, 'cause he's a little yogurt-eating bitch," Roger says.

"Fuck you, man!" Jared retorts, shaking his head.

"I'll throw down five hundred saying you can't."

Tristan speaks up.

"You have to outdrink Jared and one other."

He raises his eyebrow at me with a mischievous grin on his face. Is this guy really throwing money down on me?

"Fuck, yeah!" Roger wails excitedly. "Let's do it tonight!"

Oh, no. Not tonight, please. I'm way too hung over.

"No. No, Roger," I say, shaking my head. "I'm too hung over from last night to be doing anything like that tonight."

Tristan's grin widens at me.

"What, Sophia? I knew you wouldn't be able to handle it. It will be the easiest money I have ever won."

Oh, so now I'm being challenged, huh? What the hell. I know I'm being peer pressured right now, but I don't care. I want Tristan's cocky mouth shut and proven wrong. Before I have any time to think about it anymore, I jump in to it.

"All right. I'll take the fucking bet. But if I win— *when* I win, I want the penthouse suite for the rest of the tour."

Oh, yeah! That's a good one. I shouldn't be getting spoiled like that, but some of the places we go to are really fucking nice; and we just have begun touring, so it makes it worth my while.

Tristan eyes me carefully then nods in agreement.

"Fine. If you win, then you can have my room for rest of the tour."

"Fuck yeah! It's gonna be fun tonight!" Roger goes on again, excited. "Jared and Matt versus Sophia."

Matt gets up and walks over to the bar to set down his drink.

"Better stop this now since I'm sure I will be having plenty more tonight."

He smiles at me with his deep blue eyes full of light. Oh, dear lord. What did I just get myself into?

When we land, I grab my belongings. All of the guys are still laughing at me. Why did I agree to this? I'm caught in the middle of their game. I prepare a mental checklist of what I have to do to get ready for tonight. No backing down now. Squaring my shoulders, I make my way off of the jet.

Chapter Twelve

We're all hanging out in Tristan's suite tonight. Even Frankie is here tonight to support me. When we landed, I texted him and told him what was going on. When I got to the hotel, I worked out, ordered room service, and took another shower to prep myself for tonight.

Tristan's suite is beautiful. It's this large, open room with a bar and a kitchen on the back wall. It has a marble island with four steel stools in the center of the kitchen area. On the other side of the suite are tall glass windows with a beautiful view of the Gateway Arch. Couches are set up in a giant U at the center of the living area, with an oak dining table off to the left. On the eastern wall is a door, which I'm assuming leads to the master suite, and a giant flat screen TV.

I take a seat next to Cory on one of the stools. Tristan comes out of his bedroom, looking mighty fine as usual. He's wearing light blue jeans and a black thermal shirt with the long sleeves pushed up to his elbows, showing off the ink covering his left arm. He must have just taken a shower because his hair is pushed back and hanging behind his ears, exposing his broad face.

Roger gets up from the couch.

"All right, let's get tonight happening!" he shouts, making his way over to the bar. "You guys have to have all of the same drinks. No bitchy wine coolers, Jared."

"Whatever, man. Your mom likes them when I bring them over," Jared retorts, rising to his feet and following Roger.

"Fuck off!" Roger says to him and approaches me. "What would the lady like to start with?"

Hmm . . . I know starting with liquor is probably best. You know how the saying goes- "Liquor before beer, you're in the clear. Beer before liquor, never been sicker."

"How about seven and seven?" I suggest, looking at Matt, who nods in approval.

As Roger starts making our drinks over by the sink, Tristan stands directly in front of me on the other side of the island and makes himself a drink while talking to Cory. I perch myself on the stool. I feel much better about my appearance now than I did on the flight earlier. I'm wearing a tight black vintage Guns and Roses t-shirt that shows a little of my belly, and faded jeans that hug my hips. My hair is pulled up into a ponytail, and for makeup, I just settled on eyeliner, mascara, and lip gloss. Not too much, but just enough to give me a sexy edge.

Roger slides my drink down to me.

"For the lady."

"Thanks."

I grab it from him and take a sip. Not bad, but he did make it a little too strong for my liking. Note to self: have Cory make the next round.

As I'm sitting at the bar, I notice Tristan glancing over at me as he's talking to Cory with his arms crossed. I decide that I need to move. I spin around on the stool and scan the room for Frankie. He's over at the table, sitting and talking to Jared and Gunner and playing with his phone. I get up from the stool and make my way over. I can't help but feel Tristan's eyes on the back of my neck as I walk away.

"Hey!" Gunner says to me as I approach the table. His eyes are red, and a lazy smile sweeps across his face.

"So, what you guys doing?" I ask.

Jared holds up cards then begins shuffling them.

"Wanna play euchre?"

"Sure! I'm in," I smile to him.

"What's euchre?" Gunner asks as he scratches his head.

"The best freaking game ever! But we need one more player."

"Oh, not I," Frankie says, shaking his head while looking back down at his phone. Jared looks around the room.

"Hey, Matt!" he yells, signaling with his hands for Matt to come over.

Matt joins us, and we teach Gunner the basics of the game. I start off because Jared's instructions are confusing as hell. I explain a trump, a bower, and a set. Frankie's mouth is wide open in confusion. Yeah, it can be a little difficult at first, but it is a great fucking card game. Gunner is looking at us with the same expression as Frankie.

"So you're saying a trump is the suits, and bowers are both black and red? Fuck, man."

"We'll just start playing, and you'll get the hang of it. You can be on my team," I say to him.

He agrees and we start playing.

Good time must have passed because we're now on our third drink and our second game. Of course Gunner and I lost the first one, but this game is close by points and he seems to be enjoying himself. After we're done playing that hand, Frankie gets up.

"I need a fucking cigarette! Wanna come out to the balcony with me, Sophia?"

"Sure."

I grab my drink and stand. I hear giggling all of sudden and glance over my shoulder to find three chicks sitting on the sofas. One is sitting on Tristan's lap. What the fuck? I must have been really into the game to not hear them come in.

I follow Frankie out to the balcony. The October air has slightly cooled, but it's nothing like Michigan would be right now. I'm pretty buzzed already; I hope I can get through this night without failing.

"How's it going, girl?" Frankie asks me, leaning over the balcony.

I look through the glass doors and see Tristan. He has a chick on his lap with his arm around her, but he's staring at me. Fuck it! Time to get wasted.

I turn quickly back to Frankie.

"Well, I could go for another drink. And maybe some weed."

"Lucky for you, sweetheart, I can help you out with both."

He winks at me and heads inside. Moments later, he comes back out with another drink in one hand and a joint in the other.

I light up the joint and inhale, holding it in my lungs as I feel my head swim a little. Shit. This might be the beginning of the end for me tonight, but I don't care.

Frankie and I carry on our conversation while drinking and smoking. We're jamming out to music from my iPhone, transistor radio style. Pantera's "Cemetery Gates" comes on and I swear, closing my eyes, I can literally feel the music on my skin.

"Want another round, sweetheart?" Frankie asks me.

"Mm-hmm," I say to him, keeping my eyes closed while leaning over the edge of the balcony. The breeze feels wonderful.

"Okay, doll. Be right back."

Standing out on the balcony, Pantera is done playing and the next song that comes on is Metallica's 'Bleeding Me.'

I love this! Drinks and good music are all I need. I feel the coolness of glass press on my arm. I jump a little from the shock and get ready to slap Frankie for his little joke when I realize it's Tristan, standing there beside me looking down with his dark eyes and holding my drink. I take it from him slowly, just staring at him as I take a sip.

"How you doing?" he asks with his deep voice.

"I'm doing," is all I can manage to say.

Shit! Why do I always get like this when I'm around him? I'm turning into some kind of fucking pussy when I'm drunk.

We stand there in silence for moments 'til he breaks the ice again.

"Matt's going strong still, but I don't know about Jared. We might be able to get this bet."

He takes a step closer to me, causing me to back up to the railing. I'm kind of trapped now. I stare up at him as he looks down at me. He places his arms on each side of the railing beside me, caging me in. A slow, cocky smile plays across his lips as he dips his head closer to mine. I can feel the heat of his body on my very own now, and I can smell the cologne and whiskey on him. It's a very intoxicating mixture. My head starts to instantly feel heavier.

"You know, Sophia. If all you wanted was to sleep in penthouse suites, then you don't need to do this. My bed is always open to you if you just ask."

What the—?

I raise my left eyebrow at him.

"Excuse me?" I say to him, trying to back up even more, but I can't due to the railing that's already digging into my back.

He leans in even further, his face only an inch away.

"You fucking heard me," he whispers.

Instantly I'm wet. Fuck my stupid, traitorous body. How can his arrogance turn me on? I quickly shake it off on the inside.

"What the fuck is wrong with you, dude?"

He backs up a little with a cold look on his face, but I keep going.

"Seriously? One minute you're talking shit and then the next, you're coming on to me? Please!"

"Fuck you, bitch!" he says, fully removing himself from me.

Good! I've pissed him off. I gesture toward the suite and the chick still sitting on the sofa.

"I'm not one of your fucking groupies that you can toy with, so you might as well go back in there and continue what you were doing."

He doesn't like what I just said because now he's back on me.

"Sophia—"

Right then, Frankie comes barging out.

"Fucking shit! So much snow going around in there you'd think it's a fucking blizzard!"

Thank God! Tristan abruptly turns on his heel and leaves.

"Um . . . What the fuck just happened?" Frankie asks, pointing his finger over his shoulder at Tristan.

"Motherfucker thinks I'll drop my panties for him."

"Ooh! Don't you hate it? The sexy as hell ones are so damn conceited. Shit!"

I give him a "whatever" look and he stops me.

"Don't go there, girl. I know it's only a matter of time before you two fuck. Whenever you guys are in the same room, you can cut the sexual tension with a knife. That's how tender you two are."

I look at him, but then I burst out laughing. What did he just say to me?

"No, Frankie. Never going to happen."

Shaking my head, I finish my drink.

"Come on. I need to kick Matt's ass now."

I grab his hand and lead him back into the suite.

Once inside, I'm sick. Tristan has that girl straddling his lap while he sits on the bar stool, but really, that's not what's bothering me so much. It's Cory doing a line on the coffee table. I stomp my way over to him.

"Hey!" I say, but the music is so fucking loud that I can't even hear myself say it. "Hey!" I yell again in his ear and push him. "What the fuck, man?"

Cory wipes his nose and sniffs.

"Calm down. It's only one hit. I don't say shit to you."

"That's because I smoke pot! Not shove shit up my nose!"

Cory glares at me and stands.

Everything I Want

"I need another beer. You want one?"

He's changing the subject on me now. I shake my head no at him, glaring as I do. He just leaves me standing there while he walks away.

What the fuck?

"You okay, girl?" Frankie asks.

"Yeah, I guess. I'm ready for shots now."

"Okay."

Frankie and I go over to the sink, which is right by Tristan and his whore. I call Matt and Jared over.

"Ready, fellas?"

They smile and nod while Frankie starts pouring our tequila shots. I just can't care right now. I will just have to have a talk with Cory tomorrow. I down three right away with Jared and Matt. Roger is clapping from behind us.

After another few shots, my vision is blurred. My head is dizzy and my balance is off. I'm leaning against the counter laughing at whatever Frankie has just said. Jared looks sick. His skin is pale, and he's just leaning against the wall.

I glance over, and Tristan is still sitting on the bar stool with his whore. Hmm . . . That's nice. Just then, Warrant's "Cherry Pie" begins to play through the surround sound; and I'm up on the island in a flash. I don't know what's gotten into me, but it feels good. I start swaying my hips with my palms pressed down on the sides of my thighs.

"Fucking eh!" Roger exclaims from the back of the room.

Cory's and Caleb's jaws are on the floor.

I sway my body even more, keeping my legs together but swaying down and back up. When it hits the chorus, I pull my shirt off, revealing my black bra. I grab my hair tie and pull it out, shaking my head as I do. Now everyone is watching and cheering me on. I throw my shirt at Frankie and continue on.

Halfway through the song, I'm kneeling, leaning back, doing this rolling motion with my upper body, and gracefully pulling myself back up to my feet. Wow! I can't believe I just did that! Letting the music take over, I run my fingers through my hair and bite my lower lip.

I glance down at Tristan. The chick is off his lap, and he's standing. His eyes look so dark and carnal; he's breathing heavily. I love it! I continue to dance and sway my body while flipping my hair like the girls did in the '80s videos, but all of a sudden, I feel every drop of alcohol. I stop dancing just in time before the fog takes over.

I'm falling.

The last thing I see is Tristan running over to me with his arms out.

Chapter Thirteen

Beep beep beep . . . My eyes open slowly. The room is dark, and the sound of the alarm clock is in my ear. Noon, it says. Fuck! What happened? I blink my eyes as I reach over to shut the damn thing off. My head is literally going to explode! Why, oh, why did I do that to myself?

After I shut the alarm off, I lie back down, thankful for the blinds being closed. Weird. I don't even remember coming in last night. I'm hot and uncomfortable, too. I look down and realize that I'm still in my bra and jeans. I stare up at the ceiling, waiting for the strength to get up and take something for my headache. Damn. I have to be at the arena at two to get ready. How am I going to function? I fucked up last night. I fucked up real bad.

I lay there for a few more minutes before my phone goes off. I can't even find it. I pull myself up, listening carefully to hear where I may have put it. It's on the floor, beside the bed. I lean over and grab it. On the fifth ring, I answer.

"Hel-lo?"

Shit! Even talking hurts. I'm so screwed.

"Are you okay, girl?"

It's Cory. I'm so glad and relieved that he sounds okay. From what I remember, he was on some hard shit last night.

"Ah . . . I fucking don't know. I fucked up last night."

I hear him laugh a little.

"You'll be okay, girl. I'm coming over. Just stay put. I have a key to your room."

Everything I Want

I don't even say goodbye. I just push end and pass back out. The next thing I know, I feel a cool washcloth on my head and my eyes flutter open. It's Cory. He's sitting beside me with what looks like a glass of water in his hand. Just then, I realize that I'm in my bra and hurry to cover myself up. He laughs a little and looks away.

"It's okay, Sophia. I don't care. I don't look at you that way. You're like my sister. Here." He shoves pills at me. "Try and take these. I will start your shower. I ordered room service, too. We have to leave in an hour."

An hour! What?

I grab the pills and the glass of water from him and take them. The water is welcoming to me; the cool liquid runs smoothly down my throat. When I'm done drinking the entire glass, I hand it back to him. Leaning back against the headboard, I use the duvet to cover me by tucking it underneath my arms.

"Holy shit! What happened?"

I instantly regret asking. Cory's face lights up like a Christmas tree.

"You don't remember?" he asks.

I shake my head. I try to remember. Let's see. I was pissed at him for doing coke again; then, I was by the kitchen doing shots.

"Let's just say you would make any rock star proud to have you in their music video."

What the fuck is that supposed to mean?

"Huh?"

"You were giving 'er to 'Cherry Pie' on the countertop. Started taking off your clothes and everything. I thought for a second there, you were going to turn Frankie straight."

No, no, no! Please tell me he's fucking with me right now. He must've noticed my expression because he begins to carry on again.

"Don't sweat it. You rocked it! You had every guy and girl in there drooling. You danced amazing. You even beat Jared, but I'm sorry. Matt won."

Losing five hundred bucks is the least of my worries. I danced on top of the counter to 'Cherry Pie' stripping! Embarrassment courses through me.

"Everyone?" My voice barely breaks a whisper.

Cory grins.

"Everyone," he confirms.

I roll my eyes. I know I shouldn't make too big of a deal out of dancing in my bra. I do that kind of thing when I'm onstage performing. It's just that it's different in a more personal space, with a handful of guys around. Oh, my mistake. A few whores, too.

I start climbing out of bed when Cory gets up.

"I'll wait here until your food comes. Just go jump in the shower and eat something. You'll be okay, kid."

I nod to him slowly, making my way to bathroom.

Down at the arena, roadies are bustling all around us. I'm sitting offstage while Lux talks to one of the crew members. I just want to hurry my part along so I can go back into hiding. It's bad enough that I behaved like that last night, but getting high fives and whistles from everyone (and I mean everyone) is even worse.

Well, except from Tristan. According to Cory, he was the one who caught me falling off the island when I passed out and carried me back to my room. Out of all the people who could have done it, it had to be him.

Everything I Want

After another two hours of going over the sound check and setting up the equipment, we're done. I bend down to grab my water bottle and hurry my way off the stage with my eyes cast down. Just as I'm almost off, I crash hard into someone, losing my balance.

Strong arms reach out and grab me before I fall on my ass. I look up and it's Tristan holding me tightly to him. He's looking at me like he's kind of annoyed. I jerk myself out of his hold and push past him to go backstage. Out of all the people I really didn't want to see, it was him.

When I enter the back room, I go over to the refreshment table. As I'm picking through the sandwiches, Cory comes and stands beside me.

"Are you feeling better?"

"Yeah, getting there," I say to him.

I take my sandwich and head for my dressing room to meet up with Frankie. I know I should let the whole incident from last night roll off my back, but right now, I prefer hiding.

Taking a seat, I start eating my sandwich when Frankie enters the room. He's wearing his black leather pants with a tight, red V-neck shirt. His hair is bone-straight and he's wearing a lot of dark eye makeup. I like how his style is versatile. One minute, he's looking like his sexy Goth self; the next, he's wearing slacks and some of the nicest button-down shirts there are.

"Hey, Cherry!"

He waves at me, setting up his station. I blush knowing exactly what that means. I nod to him while taking another bite.

"Some little shindig last night, huh? Girl, you were cra-zy! But I liked it. So much fun."

I roll my eyes at him. Before the little stunt that I don't really remember, for most of the night, I had fun just hanging out.

"How bad was I?"

I really don't want to know. Yes, I do!

"What do you mean, hun?"

He's laying out his brushes. I swallow the last bits of food in my mouth and stare at him in the mirror.

"You know . . ." I flip my hand in the air. "The dancing thing."

My voice is quiet. He turns around to face me, grinning.

"I always said you were my rock goddess. Last night just proves how badass you are."

He starts laughing, and I give him a pleading look. Now he rolls his eyes.

"Oh, come on, girl! You weren't that bad. You were drunk and having a good time. Shit! It's not like you were giving away blowjobs to every Tom, Dick, and Harry."

He comes closer, kneeling in front of me, and continues.

"Honestly, you looked great dancing. If there was a camera filming, you would have been way hotter than any dancer that ever did that song. And besides . . ." Now he's only an inch away from me. I can smell the cinnamon gum in his mouth. "Tristan seemed to enjoy the show. Actually, that's why he was able to catch you so fast."

He pulls away, going back to organizing his makeup.

"He wouldn't let any of his guys near you. They were getting all excited, but one look from him and they backed off. He practically threw that one chick off his lap when you started dancing."

Everything I Want

I'm a little surprised hearing what Frankie just told me. I kind of hate to admit it, but I like the fact that Tristan was watching me with interest. The look I got from him today seemed to say otherwise.

It's finally seven, and I have successfully hidden from everybody all day. Suddenly, I hear Matt knocking on my door.

"Be there in a few. Just finishing up," I yell to him.

I stare at myself in the large glass mirror, I'm wearing what I call my 'Mad Hatter' outfit. It's a cami with a skintight bodice made up of aqua blue nylon. Black silk lines each side, with black nylon patches on the bust, too. A black garter belt holds up my sheer, soft black stockings.

Frankie did my hair and makeup the same as last time, but now I have a tiny aqua blue Mad Hatter hat pinned on top of my head. I slide on thigh-high black boots that are turned down at the top and make my way onto the stage, passing Caleb and Ryan, who stop dead in their tracks when they see me.

I take their looks as a sign that Frankie has done well. Approaching Lux, I nod to him and smile. Being up here and getting ready to go on, I don't feel embarrassed or hung over anymore. All I feel is excitement, and my adrenaline is shooting through the roof. This is what I love, and I cannot wait to go out there.

Roger comes up beside me and pats my shoulder.

"Ready?"

He smiles and I return it when I answer.

"Fuck yeah!"

After our set is over, we wave to the audience, which is roaring and cheering loudly. Roger tosses one of his drumsticks off the stage, and Cory shows off by doing a wicked little solo. This is the most amazing thing that could possibly ever happen to me and my band. The rush we get from performing and the high we feel is insane. We never want to come down.

When the lights turn out, I make my way off stage. The roadies instantly begin their work preparing for Undead Society to come on next. They start setting up weathered pillars and working on the fog equipment. The rest of my band decides to wait offstage and catch the next performance, but I'm just not into it. The last time I waited around, I was humiliated by Tristan in front of thousands of people. And I'm not going to lie to myself. My behavior last night surely doesn't help my mood today. I just feel too fucking good right now from just finishing my set to want my mood tainted by any negativity.

Gripping the railing tight, I make my way slowly down the steep stairs. I really should have a decent pair of shoes waiting for me when I get offstage because walking down a few flights of stairs in six-inch heels is freaking me out! A couple steps down, I hear his voice.

"Good job tonight, Sophia."

I stop and look over my shoulder and see Tristan standing there on the top landing, looking down at me with one hand holding onto the railing. He looks just like the rocker he is, wearing black jeans with a sleeveless white graphic shirt showing off his amazing muscles and tattoos.

"Thanks."

I smile quickly at him and turn around, continuing my way down the stairs. I didn't want to keep standing there for fear that he'd see right through me. Or maybe that he'd open his fucking mouth and ruin the compliment again. When I reach the bottom, I hear Undead Society starting up. Tristan's voice rumbles through the arena like thunder as always, sending chills down my spine.

Everything I Want

It's been five days since our show in St. Louis. We traveled by bus to Tampa Bay, then to Memphis. I'm totally pumped about our next stop, Detroit. I feel like Dollar Settlement will be on home turf there.

Since St. Louis, I've pretty much stayed in while the guys go out. We've been doing a lot of driving these past few days, but that hasn't stopped them from having a good time. They keep at it after every show. I'm starting to feel a little bad for their poor livers. Roger's always bugging me to let loose again, but I hide out in the only bedroom in the bus and lock myself in. I don't want them thinking I'm a loner or anything; it's just that it annoys the shit out of me when they keep bugging. It's better that I keep to myself for a few more days.

Chapter Fourteen

I wake up in the full-size bed I have been sleeping on and pull open the blinds. We're approaching our exit. I know this part of I-75 all too well; it's great to see a little bit of home again. All the time I was in LA, I was too busy working on the album getting covered and starting the tour that I really didn't have any time to think about home. But being back here, I realize that I miss it.

We arrive at our hotel. It's beautiful, overlooking the Detroit River. We have our show tonight at the Joe, then Lux is throwing us an after-party back here in one of the ballrooms. It's cool that we're not just jumping on another bus, even though they are very nice and not what I expected them to be. It's just that I miss having a real bed with my own bathroom, not sharing one with four dirty dudes.

Walking through the lobby, I first notice large windows showcasing the view of the Detroit River, looking on to Windsor. And of course, there is a shop right next to the front desk that sells Detroit Red Wings memorabilia.

Lux meets up with us, handing out our room keys, then goes to talk to a man in a suit. We really only have enough time to drop our things off because we have to be at the arena to set up for tonight. Tristan's band must already be there because I didn't notice any of them around when we got here.

Once I arrive on the twelfth floor, I search for my room. I find it at the end of the hall. I slide my card in and push the door open, then throw my bag on the bed and rest my suitcase against the wall. I pull the curtains open and stare out at metro Detroit. We are right next to the Joe.

Everything I Want

I walk over to the mirror that's resting on the wall behind the dresser. Once again, I look like shit. Being on the bus for eight hours after performing the night before really did one on me today. My hair is a little wavy and frizzy. Dark circles form around my blue eyes, and my light blue t-shirt is wrinkled from sleeping in it.

I know I have to leave soon, but I have to shower first. All I did today was brush my teeth, but that just isn't good enough. I grab a quick shower and towel myself off quickly. As I'm putting on jeans and a dark tank, my phone starts ringing. I step out of the bathroom trying to get to it before it stops. Shit! It's probably the guys waiting on me.

"I'm leaving right now," I answer before whoever it is can say anything.

To my surprise, it's Frankie.

"Hey, girl! I have the most fabulous surprise for you tonight before the party. Do you have a few?"

"Uh, no. Not really right now, Frankie. I have to get going. Sorry."

He starts pouting on the phone.

"It's really important, and I just can't keep it a surprise no more."

A surprise?

"Okay, fine. But hurry up, okay? I don't want to get chewed out for showing up late."

"Don't worry, my princess. I'm a few doors down. Be there in a few."

When I hang up with Frankie, I brush my teeth again. Almost right away I hear a knock at the door. I set my toothbrush down and go answer it. Frankie is standing in the hallway, holding a very expensive-looking garment bag in one hand and a black shoebox in the other. He is smiling hugely and his long, blond bangs are falling in his face and covering his eyes.

I push open the door, letting him in. He kisses me on my cheek and walks past me, putting the box on my bed and very carefully hanging the garment bag on my bathroom door.

"I was planning on keeping this little gem from you 'til your last show in New York, but . . . I just can't wait anymore. And besides, you're in your home state! I know you're really pumped for tonight, and Lux is throwing a fabulous party. Fabulous, I know, because I got to help plan it."

His grin widens. Frankie is so excited right now, and it's very cute.

He turns back around and slowly unzips the bag. I can only see a glimpse of gray. Once he is done unzipping, he gently pushes the bag off and pulls the fabric off the hanger and shows me.

"Ta-da!" he says proudly.

My eyes grow wide at the beautiful dress. I must say, it's stunning. It's short and dark gray, with very thin straps and a cowl neckline. It looks like it's made out of some pretty damn expensive silk. I reach out to trace my fingers on it, and it feels like heaven. It's absolutely soft and smooth. I usually don't get too excited about clothes, but this . . . this is different. My face hurts from smiling so much.

"Frankie, I . . . I—"

He raises his pointer finger to interrupt me.

"Shh. I have this friend back in LA who showed me this amazing, one-of-a-kind dress he designed right before the tour started. When I laid eyes on it, I just knew it had to be for you. I gave him your measurements to make sure it would fit absolutely perfectly."

I can't believe he even thought of this for me. I mean, we just met. And certainly, this piece looks like it costs what I would make in a year, or even two years, back at home.

"How much did this cost you?" I ask him nervously, hoping he didn't break the bank too much on my behalf.

His smile turns into a Cheshire grin.

"Oh, well. You know, it probably would've cost me much more if I didn't know the designer personally." He winks at me and continues. "But you, my dear, are going to be a little walking advertisement."

I don't even want to know any more details. All I know is that I can't wait for tonight when I get to try this on. I'm so excited that I jump into Frankie's arms, not realizing that he's still holding the dress. Thankfully, he's got quick reflexes. He lifts the dress up in the air with one arm as he wraps the other around me.

"Thank you!"

I kiss him on the cheek and pull myself away. Not only is the dress stunning, but also, I'm touched that he thought of me back in LA.

After he hangs the dress back up carefully, he grabs my hand and pulls me out of the bathroom and leads me over to the bed. He bends down and grabs the box and pulls the top off, showing me what's inside. I peer into the box, and I see these dark gray strappy sandals with five-inch heels. They sparkle back at me when the light from the room hits the straps. I rub my fingers along the straps to feel the sparkles, and to my surprise, they are not made out of plastic or sequins. But they feel like rocks, kind of.

"Swarovski," Frankie answers my unspoken question.

"Wh— *What?*"

"I saw these fabulous heels when we were in Vegas. I knew they would look perfect with the dress I was planning for you, but they were missing something. So I went to this friend of mine out there that works with Swarovski and had these little pieces put on."

Another friend. I quirk my left brow at him and smile. He starts shaking his head at me.

"No, no." He starts laughing. "Not that kind of friend, sweetheart."

I look back at the equally beautiful shoes and the straps that are made up of silver and dark colored crystals. Wow! Frankie so knows his shit when it comes to fashion. And I love that he's with me now because, obviously, I have no clue.

"Cinderella needs to have her glass slippers, right?"

"Right," I say, smiling and nodding at him.

After rehearsing for the rest of the afternoon, we take a break in the back. Roger is chain-smoking, and Cory and I are making a plate to eat. Jared and Matt are off wandering around.

"It's cool being able to finally play here," Cory says to me as we take a seat at the table.

"Oh, I know! I know it's not the biggest place we've played at, but it's not the smallest, either. It's so cool because I remember driving up here to watch Wing games back when I first started going to college."

Cory smiles.

"Yeah, I know. It's definitely crazy. But in a good way, of course."

Everything I Want

We're continuing our conversation about the tour when the heavy door slams. I turn around and see Tristan and Caleb walking in. Tristan comes right over and sits beside me, reaching over with his long arms and grabbing a pop from the center of the table. He takes a drink and then sets it down.

Cory nods to him.

"What up, man?"

Tristan just nods back and turns to face me. I feel my cheeks starting to burn. I hate that he makes me feel like some teenager that doesn't have her hormones in check. I'm also a little nervous, preparing myself for whatever shit might come out of his mouth. But nothing does. Like, nothing. He's not saying anything or doing anything. Good thing Cory, Roger, and Caleb start talking and don't notice this awkward stare/silence going on between Tristan and me.

I pick at my food slowly now, feeling extremely uncomfortable with his stare on me. What the fuck is he doing? I glance up at him, giving him an annoyed look, but he doesn't seem to crack. If anything, he pulls his chair closer and leans his body against the table. He starts chuckling a little. Okay, now I'm *really* getting annoyed. What? Do I have something on my face or something? I can't hold it in anymore.

"What the fuck is so funny?" I ask, trying to keep my voice down.

He turns to me again.

"You."

"Um . . . What do you mean, *me*?"

He starts laughing and I can't believe how pissed I'm actually getting, but I can sense shit vibes off of it.

"You're just funny, okay? Shit, I don't know. But you crack me up."

"Well, I must have done something to be so 'funny.'"

"Never mind, Sophia. Just forget about it. I forgot there for a minute that you're a bitch."

What? I was never rude to him in the first place, and he was laughing at me for no reason. And he has the nerve to call me a bitch? I don't think so!

"I'm not a bitch, Tristan," I say to him, setting my sandwich down and standing. "I think you forget that you have been nothing but a total douchebag to me since I fucking started!"

He's just looking at me. Not really looking up because he's so tall. His face is totally blank, and I can't tell what he's thinking or feeling. It's so frustrating! I shake my head in disapproval at him and walk away. I don't want to start raising my voice to him and to have him get the better of me, nor do I want any of the guys to hear us.

I find my way to my dressing room, and there is Frankie standing with his back turned to me and pulling items out of a bag. He must've changed his clothes since the hotel, too, because now he is wearing skintight dark blue jeans and a very tight long-sleeved shirt. So tight, in fact, that you can literally see his pecks and his um . . . his nipple piercings. His long, blond hair is pulled back into a half-pony.

"Hey! You ready now?" I must have a pissed-off look still on my face because Frankie's smile fades. "What's wrong, girl?"

He steps closer, holding out his hand.

"Nothing. I'm okay."

I make my way over to his bag of tricks, but he grabs my arm gently and stops me.

"Something is bothering you." He stares at me with these puppy dog eyes now. "Tell me," he demands softly.

I roll my eyes and shake my head.

"It's nothing, really. Just easily annoyed right now, that's all. I'm fine."

Instantly, Frankie lets go of my arm.

"Uh-hum," he replies, and walks with me over to his bag.

I peek over his shoulder.

"So what look are we achieving tonight?" I ask.

My wardrobe has all been fun, sexy, and edgy. I love what he's been planning so far. He leads me over to the table and points.

"Tonight we're covering more, but it's also going to be one of the sexiest yet. And it also gives you that badass chick look, too. After all, we are in Detroit."

He laughs a little. I look at the table and nod in approval.

"It looks pretty sweet, actually. Let's get to it."

And with that, he tosses the outfit at me and begins to prep his station.

We are about to go on in ten minutes. I decide to crack open a beer to relax myself. For some reason, I'm more nervous now than I have been since Vegas. Checking myself out, I'm totally feeling it. I'm wearing very low leather pants with a chunky belt that hangs loose on the right side of my hip. They're so low, in fact, that if I bend over, people will definitely be seeing back cleavage. The pants flare a little at the bottom, and underneath the leather bottoms, I'm wearing a sexy version of biker boots.

My top is very short, too. It stops just below my breasts. It's a leather vest and unbuttoned to reveal the black bra Frankie picked out, which is pushing me up even more than usual. I'm already well-endowed in that department, so wearing a top like this is almost dangerous . . . but I love it!

My hair is sleek and smooth and hangs to the middle of my back with slight waves in it, not the usual full hair that I was rocking in previous shows. I also have pale lips and dark gray smoky eyes with fake eyelash pieces at the corners.

I slide a couple of metal bracelets onto my right wrist and a chunky silver ring on my left middle finger. My nails are freshly painted black, and I feel like I belong on that one show. What's it called? Oh, yeah! Sons of Anarchy! I feel like that.

Exiting the dressing room, Frankie tells me he will be in my hotel room when I'm done to prep me for the after-party. I give him a quick hug and go find my boys.

"Holy shit!" Caleb walks up behind me. "Damn girl! Looking good!"

I blush and look down.

"Ha ha! Thanks, Caleb."

"Do you just use the music to give yourself an excuse to prance around half-naked all the time?"

Tristan walks up holding a beer, staring at me again with dark eyes. He starts to walk by me, but instead of getting upset, I decide to tease him a bit.

"You know it! I really don't care about the music at all. I just love being a cocktease."

Everything I Want

He stops dead in his tracks, and I hear Caleb burst out laughing. I give Tristan a devilish little smirk and wink. I push past him, making my way to the stage, but damn it! It backfired on me, because touching his hard arm sent that intense hot and cold sensation running through me as always. Thank God he doesn't realize it. He's still standing there glaring at me, nothing at all coming out of that cocky mouth of his. Good.

The stage is dark, and the crowd is chanting. People are clapping their hands together, ready for the show. I know we're not big yet, but I can't help but imagine that they are here waiting for us and not Undead Society.

I step up to the mic and grab it off the stand. Tristan and Caleb are now standing next to Lux. He hasn't been in that spot since our Vegas show. Even though Tristan can't see me, I smile at him and flip him off. I turn back to face the crowd, and purple lights illuminate the stage.

"How's it going, Detroit?" I yell into the mic. The audience is getting even louder now. "Before Undead Society graces you guys with their presence, we would like to have the honor of jamming for you guys."

I gesture toward my band, and Roger does a double bass riff, getting them going even more.

"I would like to introduce ourselves. We are Dollar Settlement! And it feels so fucking good having the honor to play in Detroit tonight!"

Screams pierce the arena. I laugh a little into the mic, walking closer to the end of the stage.

"You see, we are all from this great state, and being back home to play for all of yous is surely going to be one of the best fucking shows I think we will ever do."

The clapping is getting in sync now, and it's pretty wild in here. I haven't felt a vibe like this at any of our shows so far on tour. My cheekbones are getting a little sore from my huge grin. Even my eyes feel a little moistened.

"This one is called, 'Damage.'"

Cory starts shredding the beginning of one of our old songs from back in the day. It's personally one of my favorites. Roger kicks in with double bass followed by Matt and Jared. I hold the mic tightly to my lips, humming softly into it, singing softly at first then going deeper the further the song progresses.

When the chorus comes up, I jump on top of one of the smaller sound boxes on the front of the stage. It's something that I've always wanted to do but never could because I was always in heels. Leaning over the audience and running my fingers through my hair, I began to wail into the mic. And they fucking love it. The energy tonight is phenomenal.

When our set comes to an end, I don't want it to be over. These people are simply amazing. I go over and set my mic back into its stand, then lean down into it.

"Thanks for giving us an awesome time tonight. You guys are the fucking best!" I shout.

They start cheering and chanting for more, but we've already gone through all of our material. Hmm . . . Maybe I have one more trick up my sleeve. I don't even care right now what Tristan, Lux, or even the roadies think. I jog over to Cory and whisper my little plan in his ear. He smiles and nods and walks over to Roger. I let Matt and Jared know my plan, too.

The roadies are waving for us to exit so they can get Undead set up. I gesture one minute with my finger and I walk back over to the mic as the audience continues to chant for more.

Everything I Want

"Okay, okay! We will do one more, but we can't take credit for this next song. You see, it's not ours. But it's done by one of my favorite bands. It's a newer one, too, so some of yous may have heard it. So here it goes . . . 'Scarlet' by In This Moment."

Jared starts strumming on the guitar, then Cory comes in playing. Keeping the microphone on the stand, I hold it with one hand and close my eyes and sing. I use my other hand to rub softly up and down my upper body. Roger begins playing now with Matt, and I start swaying softly.

Using two hands now, I grip the mic tightly and sing harder as we lead into the chorus, tilting my head back when we get there. Now looking back at the crowd, I point toward them with both hands; then facing my hands palms up, I raise them high in the air. I sing with all of the power that I have left in me. When the final chorus comes on, Cory walks over to me and begins his solo. As I turn to face him, I arch my back, singing forcefully on these final notes.

As soon as the song finishes, I bow before them. Everyone in the entire audience is whistling, cheering, and clapping. I press my hand to my lips and blow them a kiss as we walk offstage. The lights go out, and the entire arena is pitch-black for only a moment until the giant screens start playing Undead Society footage while the roadies do their work.

When I arrive backstage, Tristan is just standing there with his arms slumped to his sides, his lips slightly parted as he breathes deeply. His eyes are wide, almost as if he were in shock. He looks completely lost right now.

Chapter Fifteen

Wow. He's either really pissed that we took up some of his time, or because I fucking rocked it. I'm hoping for the second, but knowing him, it's probably the first. Lux suddenly stands in front of me.

"I don't know what you were thinking!"

He grabs both sides of my face and kisses me hard on the forehead. He pushes himself away and walks over to one of the crew members again, just grinning.

As the guys from Undead pass by us to make their way onstage, they all pat my shoulders and congratulate me. Tristan is the last one, and this time, the look in his eyes has me hypnotized. I can't move. There is no hate, no glares, no look of disgust; but confusion, or even pain. Between the high from my performance and the audience's reaction, and then the instant crash brought on by Tristan's gaze . . . I feel like I might just lose my balance. Fucking eh.

I know I'm supposed to go right back to the hotel for Frankie to do his thing, but I can't seem to pull myself away from Tristan right now. I turn around to watch. He grabs the mic, his hand so big that it swallows the entire thing. He breathes hard into it, then he begins to speak.

"How's everyone tonight?"

The band starts playing behind him, and lights flash all over. The audience answers him back with screams and roars. They're going absolutely insane, but in a very damn good way. He starts singing—well, screaming—into the mic. That's the thing with him; we both kind of have the same singing style. I call them "pretty" and "screaming."

Everything I Want

And he knows how to work both.

Eventually after the third song, I have to pull myself away. As I start backing up to leave, Tristan's gaze turns and locks with mine, and once again, I cannot move. His singing is so intense right now that I feel like I may just lose it and combust right here, right now. Once he faces the crowd again, I know it's my only chance to be able to leave. I say goodbye, telling everyone I have to get ready and that I will meet them at the party.

"Don't get lost."

Lux smiles at me. I know he's joking because the party is in the same freaking building.

"Oh, I won't," I reply, then I'm off.

Frankie is finishing up on my hair. I'm sitting on the edge of the bed nursing a beer while he wrings the curling iron through my hair. The makeup was easier; he cleaned up my face a bit and made touch-ups to my foundation. The good thing is that I have good skin that doesn't require a lot of work.

I had on heavy, dark gray eye shadow for the show, but it weakened by the end my performance. Frankie used a brush to remove some of the excess and touched it up with a little darker nude coloring on my brow bone. My lips are just wearing sheer nude gloss. Most of the work has been on my hair, which he made a little fuller than the flat look I rocked earlier tonight. With my naturally thick hair, it was easy to achieve.

"Voila!" Frankie kisses his thumb and first two fingers like a chef in a restaurant would. "Cinderella is ready for the motherfucking ball."

He snaps his fingers. I start giggling at him; he's so funny. I stand carefully, getting comfortable in the shoes. Surprisingly, they don't hurt my feet as badly as I thought they would. But the dress .

. . it is very beautiful, but, like I've seen on the hanger and in Frankie's hands, very short. It hangs down to about ten inches above my knees. One of the comforting things is that it hugs me, so I don't feel like it's riding up or going anywhere.

"Hold on, Cinderella. I have to pin your hair up on the left side."

I stop and he steps in front of me. Even with these heels on, Frankie is still a tad taller than me.

"I want it out of your face on the one side and cascading over to the other side. Very old-school pin up. And very mysterious."

He winks at me as his fingers busy themselves in my hair.

"I just love your fucking hair so much. Gawd! And your fucking body, too, for that matter. I mean, your skin is flawless. Did I ever mention that I want to skin you and wear you?"

We both start laughing.

"Yeah, I think you mentioned that once before."

He grabs my shoulders and turns me to the mirror, and my mouth drops open. Frankie was right. With my hair pinned up on the one side and done in full waves, I do look like some pin-up model.

"I love it!" I exclaim. Turning around, I give him a hug. "Well, I better get down there."

"I will be down in a bit," he says as I head for the door. "I have to put my suit on."

"Okay. But please don't be long. I don't want to be hanging around by myself," I say desperately.

"Oh, honey, you won't be by yourself for too long. Trust me."

I guess he was right. Approaching the ballroom that Lux reserved for us tonight, I already notice that I'm getting a lot of stares. It's making me feel a little self-conscious. I should have had a stronger drink than just a beer before coming down here.

As I push through the doors, the next song instantly starts playing. Talk about perfect timing. I laugh to myself. It's the Cardigans' 'Erase and Rewind.'

I begin to feel a little paranoid. People—men, and women—when they turn to see who came in, stop suddenly and stare at me. Okay . . . now I'm shitting myself inside. My cheeks feel like they should be red right now, but with my tanned skin, they can't tell.

I take a quick glance around to find the bar and see it just off to my right. Thank God! Sitting at the table right in front of me, though, is Tristan, and he's staring just like the others were. But he's still staring. I can't help but stare back for a moment.

He looks devastatingly handsome. He's wearing a dark suit with no tie and the first few buttons undone, showing off his collarbone and skin so fucking well. His hair is pushed back from his face and falling to the sides. Someone taps my shoulder, pulling me out of my Tristan trance. It's Lux.

"Would you like some champagne?' he asks, holding a flute in his hands.

"Yes, thank you."

We smile at each other, then I take the drink from him and press the flute to my lips, sipping it slowly. It tastes sweet, but not too sweet. I've never really drunk the stuff before; just some cheap shit a long time ago, and it was horrible. This, here . . . this is actually very good. Maybe I will stick to this for the night.

The ballroom Lux reserved for us tonight looks amazing. It's red and black everything; red linens, red flowers, and red lights casting their glow throughout the room. The crystal chandelier reflects thousands of rainbow lights over the place, too. It looks like an upscale gothic wedding is being held here. I'm relieved that Frankie gave me this dress now, and to my surprise, everyone is in the exact same attire. Well, not Roger, but that's okay. He did take the time to clean up bit, though.

After talking with Lux for a few more minutes, Cory walks over with another drink for me in hand. That is, unless he's drinking both, which actually wouldn't surprise me at all, but he hands it to me and smiles, showing off his beautiful facial features. Damn. He looks like he could be Eminem's impersonator.

"That was fucking epic tonight!" he says to me.

"I know, right? I couldn't believe it. Everything was so amazing!"

As we continue talking, my body suddenly reacts in the familiar way it always does whenever Tristan is close by. I peek over Cory's shoulder and there he is, standing by the bar with a drink in his hand, watching me. I feel myself getting slightly turned on.

Wait! What am I thinking? I can't have these feelings for him. I must say, Tristan Scott is one of the biggest assholes I have ever met. But then, the look on his face and in his eyes after our performance tonight makes me think and feel otherwise.

I slam the rest of my drink to try to forget about my thoughts.

"All right!" Cory exclaims. "Want another one?"

I nod, handing him my empty glass. Cory waves down a waiter and grabs one off the tray and hands it to me.

"Thanks."

This must be strong stuff because it's only my third, and I'm feeling a little lightheaded. Or maybe it's because I've drunk two within half an hour. Oh, well! I'm celebrating!

Everything I Want

Roger and Jared walk up to us. Roger has his arm around some woman. She looks decent, but there's a 'groupie with class' vibe coming off of her. We exchange a few words before they continue to the bar. I decide it's time to start mingling.

An hour and four more drinks later, I'm feeling pretty good. Every time I realized Tristan was nearby or staring, I would get another drink and walk away. He is just making me so uncomfortable tonight. I can't put my finger on it, exactly. Maybe I need him to say hateful things. When he's quiet or nice, it throws me off.

I'm good and drunk now, and decide it's time for me to make my way to the nearest restroom to relieve myself. I make sure to walk very carefully so I won't trip. I push open the door out to the hall. The bright lights instantly blind me, and I use one hand to shield my eyes. Damn heels. I can feel my legs wobbling a bit in them, trying to keep balance. That's it! When I get back, I will order one more drink and sit down before calling it a night.

Walking on carpet is almost like going through an obstacle course; carpet, heels, drunk. Fuck me! Not good. I finally see the doors to the restrooms, and I move a little faster. Yes!

After I'm done fulfilling my needs, I wash my hands in the sink and peer into the mirror. I still look great, just a little flushed. It must be from the booze.

Or Tristan, I think to myself.

No! Not him. I'm drunk, and my drunk thoughts and hormones are running away with me again. Damn it!

After I finish up, I step out into the hall again, but suddenly I feel a strong hand grip my shoulder firmly—but not enough to leave a bruise—and push me through the corridor leading to the elevators.

The wind is almost knocked out of me when my back hits the cool, smooth wall. What the fuck?

I'm getting ready to scream when all of a sudden Tristan's lips come crashing down on mine, his tongue invading my mouth. His hard body pushes mine up against the wall, trapping me in. He rests his arms on either side of my head; then, with one hand cupping my face, he tilts my head up to give him better access to my mouth.

I know I should stop this right now, but I can't! He tastes so good. The salt on his lips and the whiskey on his breath are intoxicating me even more than I already am. He's breathing heavily, his chest crashing up and down on mine. My nipples soon become hard, rubbing against the smooth, delicate fabric of my dress.

Something ignites inside my core. Tristan's other hand starts rubbing up and down the silky material on my side, gripping me tightly at my waist. A voice in the back of my head screams at me to stop doing this, so on instinct, I react. I pull my swollen lips from his, and using my free hands, which had been gripping his shoulders, I place them on his hard chest and try to push him off of me.

He licks his lips slowly, shaking his head.

"No, Sophia." he threatens, trying to catch his breath.

He crashes his mouth down onto mine again. I take him in only for a moment before breaking the kiss again. He looks angry now and pulls my hair tightly with one of his hands, using his pelvis to pin me against the wall.

"Fucking stop, Tristan!" I say to him in a loud whisper.

"No."

Using his other hand now, he begins to caress my full breasts, only the sheer, thin layer of silk separating his hand from them. I try to wiggle my way free of him, but all I end up doing is turning myself on even more. While I'm moving against him, I can feel how hard he is for me, pushing against my stomach. He grips my hair tighter, causing pain to my scalp, and forces me to look at him. He comes closer until his face is only an inch away from mine. His other hand is fondling my breast tenderly. His hand slowly glides down my stomach, feeling every inch of me.

"You fucking want this, Sophia. I know you do."

I'm forced to stare into his eyes. He is truly the most gorgeous man I have ever seen. With my hands still firmly pressed against his broad chest, I start shaking my head. Well, I try to. His grip has my head restrained pretty tightly in place.

"No! No, Tristan. I don't."

He gives me a sexy smirk.

"Yes, you do," he states.

"Fuck off, Tristan! Let me go."

I can't even think straight right now. I'm so turned on, but I know, deep down, that this isn't right. Just then, Tristan's hand moves from my stomach and starts gently rubbing my inner thigh, while his other hand maintains its grip in my hair, forcing me to look at him. His hand inches its way higher, bunching up my dress as he makes his way to exactly where I think he's going.

"You want this. You want this just as bad as I do, Sophia," he growls. His hand grazes the fabric of my panties, rubbing softly. He's grinning at me now, and all of a sudden, I hate it.

"Fuck you!"

I try to sound forceful, but it comes out sounding almost like a plea. He tugs my panties aside with his forceful fingers and begins to rub up and down the length of me, feeling how much he is turning me on. It's so fucking good.

Suddenly, he pulls his fingers out and steps back a little, still holding my head in place to keep me still. He puts his fingers in his mouth and swirls his tongue around them slowly. I want to look away at such wantonness happening right in front of me, but he won't let me. His groans when he tastes me on his fingers are going to make me break.

"It tastes to me like you're ready to fuck!"

"Fuck you Tris—"

He swoops down on me again, swirling his tongue around in my mouth so I can taste myself on him. I know this is wrong. Very wrong. I mean, we're in a fucking corridor, for fuck's sake! But I can't stop this now. The ache inside me is too strong, and deep down, I want this badly.

While we are engaged in our passionate kiss, he manages to spin me around, slamming us up against the opposite wall, and hits the elevator button. I moan quietly into his mouth, rubbing myself on him as he does the same to me.

When the elevator arrives, he shoves me inside. I lose my footing and begin to fall before he crushes me to him again. Once the doors close, he punches the button for the top floor and turns back to ravage my mouth, jaw, and neck.

I can't help but try to feel every single part of him. My hands run through his soft hair, pulling hard as I do, and fumble to push his jacket off so I can better feel his chest against me.

"I'm going to have you now, Sophia. And I'm going to have you again in my fucking suite. I'm going to fuck your sweet pussy all night. I want you thinking of me tomorrow, and the next fucking day . . ."

Everything I Want

Oh shit!

Chapter Sixteen

As soon as those words come out of Tristan's mouth, I feel myself getting wetter.

"Grab onto me," he commands, using his foot to kick the button to stop the elevator.

I do as he tells me and hold on to his shoulders, wrapping my legs around him.

He starts biting softly at my neck then sucking the bites.

"You don't think I fucking know what you were doing to me tonight out there on that fucking stage.?" he snarls at me, lifting me up higher on the wall and pushing up my dress so my ass is exposed to him. "Fuck!"

The last part comes out in a feverish yell. Suddenly, with one strong tug, he tears my black lace panties off. I'm in such a heavy daze that I didn't hear him unzip his pants. He positions the head of his cock at my entrance while the other hand wraps around me, holding me in place. He assaults me swiftly, not giving me any time to adjust to him.

"Ah!"

My head falls back as I try to take him in. He stills only for a moment so I can get acquainted with his enlarged cock. He breathes heavily on my neck, then he thrusts the rest of the way into me, piercing me as he does. It's both pain and pleasure . . . I just wish it was more pleasure right now than pain.

I feel him stretching me as he begins to piston his way in and out of me. I'm biting my lip hard, trying to keep moans of pleasure from escaping my mouth. All I hear from him are deep, raspy breaths.

"Your pussy is so fucking tight."

Everything I Want

He uses both of his hands now to grip my ass, his fingers so close to the back that I feel them almost penetrating there as well. The straps of my dress fall from my shoulders, baring the tops of my breasts even more. Tristan begins to lick and suck them. He keeps pushing me up higher and harder. Licking, sucking, and biting me.

"Look at me, Sophia," he demands, and I open my eyes to him.

Everything around me right now seems cloudy with the intensity of our fucking. He's looking at me with his full lips tucked into his mouth as he's pressing down on them. The tendons in his neck are bulging, and he's grunting as he pushes even faster. I can hear my arousal on him, smacking with every thrust he gives me; then, suddenly, I can't hold back any more.

Releasing my lip from my teeth and throwing my head back, I come loudly, scratching at Tristan's shoulders. He thrusts into me a few more times before stilling, breathing loudly in my ear as I slowly try to come down from my impressive orgasm.

Shit! I've definitely never come like that before!

Tristan releases me and pushes the button to continue on our way. As he buttons up his pants, I notice that I actually ripped his shirt. Shreds of black fabric line the elevator floor. I hold onto the railing for fear of falling over. My legs feel like jelly, and my head is light. I'm trying to get back to breathing regularly. When the elevator stops, Tristan scoops me up into his arms and carries me down the hallway toward his suite.

"Let me down, Tristan!" I slap at his chest. "I'm an adult! I can walk!"

"I told you, I'm not done with you yet."

When we approach his room, his bodyguard quickly opens the door. If I wasn't so drunk right now, this would be embarrassing.

Once we're in the suite, the only light comes from the glow of the city and the moon shining through the window. Tristan puts me down, and I quickly turn to him. He looks absolutely desirable, his chest rising and falling with every breath he takes. His jaw clenches, and his hands are at his sides in fists. I gaze up at him and realize that I still crave more. He just watches me for a moment before I step closer to him, rubbing my palms up and down his entire chest.

I slowly lick my lips.

"What the fuck were you thinking back there?" I whisper.

As I study him, he gives away nothing, grabbing me firmly by the hands but remaining silent. Instead, he takes hold of the hem of my dress and pulls it off of me in one swift motion, just like he did with my panties. Thank God he didn't tear the dress like he did them. I'm left completely bare to him, standing there in the soft illumination in the darkness with only my heels on.

He takes his time devouring me with his eyes. Slowly licking his lips, he unbuttons his shirt, pulling it off and dropping it onto the floor. I know I should feel self-conscious standing here in front of him like this, but I don't. I need and want more. He steps closer to me and pulls me forcefully against him. Already, I feel him hardening again.

My hair is falling down out of its pins, and he pushes it away from my face. Using one hand, he tilts my chin up higher and bends to me. I feel his full lips feather against my own.

"You're so fucking beautiful, Sophia."

He then kisses me hard, and I wrap my arms around his neck, my fingers twining into his thick hair. He picks me up, and I wrap my legs around him as he carries me into the bedroom. He gently lays me down on top of the bed and pulls away. I lift up, resting my weight on my elbows and panting. His gaze is still on mine as I watch him undo his pants and pull them down with his boxers.

My eyes adjust to the dim light peeking through the curtains as his erection springs forth. No wonder it hurt so badly in the elevator! I never really got a chance to see it, but he's huge! He crawls onto the bed and flips me over. I'm pressed against the mattress as his body rests heavily on top of mine. He reaches down and starts caressing my ass, his touch a mixture of gentle and firm as he strokes me. Then, his fingers find their way to my most vulnerable part and slide in. I'm already wet again; Tristan groans at feeling it.

"I know you love this. I'm going to make you come so many times tonight that you will be begging me to stop, you hear me? You will never want another dick inside of you besides mine ever fucking again."

I'm panting harder now, trying to push myself up into his palms. His laughter is low and almost villainous.

"You greedy little bitch. Hold on!"

He continues his slow torture of my body, feeling me from the inside while his other hand strokes the entire length of my body. I'm clawing at the sheets and trying to hold my grip to keep from grabbing him. I know I should be pissed that Tristan is talking to me this way, but all it does is turn me on even more. Suddenly, I feel a sharp bite on my ass cheek. He lifts me suddenly and uses his free hand to grab me by the waist and flip me over to my back before crawling on top of me again.

I can feel his rigid cock pressed against my stomach. He grabs my face tightly with both hands so I can't move.

"Don't tell me what to do to you, got it? Tonight, you're mine and I fucking own you! And I will do whatever I want!"

His deep voice rumbles dominantly through me, but I still try to maintain my dignity.

"Fuck me or let me leave. I'm not playing here, Tristan."

I try getting him to move, but he slams me down again and roars.

"What did I just say, bitch? You've been nothing but a fucking cocktease since I met you. Well, you're not teasing my cock no more. You fucking got it?"

His mouth finds my breast and starts sucking and licking the tip of my nipple while squeezing it. I lick my lips and bite down, trying to rub myself on him to get some relief. He knows it, too, because his other hand finds the ache and starts to softly rub in between my folds. My head falls back on the pillows as I reach up and grab the headboard. Tristan, again being the tease that he is, lifts up and leaves me lying there panting again. He grabs the back of my head, hard, and pulls me to him.

"I want you to taste my cock, Sophia. My cock that's already been inside that sweet, sweet pussy."

He slams my face down onto him. Bending over on the bed, I grab him firmly with both hands and stroke him as I take him into my mouth. Shit! I can't even fit his entire length in. I close my eyes and relax my throat as best as I can and start sucking, stopping each time at the top and flicking my tongue over the head before going back down.

He lets go of my head and rests his weight on his arms behind him, pressing down into the mattress with his legs outstretched. He's groaning louder now, and it turns me on even more. Taking one hand, I gently rub his inner thighs and over his balls, while the other strokes the entire length of his velvety cock.

I can taste a salty substance at the tip now. I lick the length of his dick slowly, laying a soft kiss on the tip. Tristan grabs my shoulders and pulls me away. His eyes are full of lust and need. He grabs my hips and pulls me onto him. I reach underneath me and position him right at my entrance, then lower myself onto him, trying to take him in less painfully than in the elevator. With my lack of pervious partners and with how endowed he is, it's not an easy fit.

He shows his teeth suddenly and grabs me, impaling me again. I can't help but scream at the top of my lungs, throwing my head back. Tristan moans loudly, too, closing his eyes. Then he starts making me work on top of him, but right now, all I can think about is the sharp pain inside of me, and I don't want to move.

After taking a few moments to collect myself, I slowly rub myself on him and get used to the fullness inside of me. Looking down at him, seeing him like this, makes me even hotter. I hold onto his chest and glide myself up and down. Feeling brave, I lean over him and whisper in his ear.

"Is this what you wanted, Tristan? My pussy wrapped around your hard cock?"

With that, he growls and flips me over suddenly, pressing his entire weight on top of me. He starts to really move, slamming into me harder. It's as if he's punishing me for my words, but I don't care. I grab the headboard again and take all of him in, screaming lustily now.

"Fuck you, bitch," he says as he continues his rhythmic strokes.

Just then, I feel I'm there again. I close my eyes tightly to try and control it, but my body stiffens as my orgasm rips right through me. I see fuzzy spots when I close my eyes, so I open them again. A tingling sensation rushes through every vein and nerve. Tristan finds his release next. I can feel him pulsate inside of me as he moans quietly into my ear, breathing heavily. Darkness starts to creep over me, and the last thing I remember seeing is Tristan's eyes staring down at me.

Chapter Seventeen

My body is tight and sore everywhere. My head is pounding. I slowly open my eyes. The room is mainly dark, but I notice through the window that the sun is starting to rise. I try to stretch out, but I can't. I feel a warm and heavy body on top of me. I jerk my head over to see what's stopping me. Tristan! What in the fuck?

I stop for a moment and remember what the fuck I did last night; Tristan grabbing me and pulling me into the corridor; our passionate kiss; him feeling every inch of my body; him tearing my panties off and fucking me senseless in the elevator and in his room! Oh, my God! I even sucked his dick!

My free arm flies to my mouth to cover it when I realize what I've done. My eyes are huge as I examine the room. It's lovely. Tall windows overlook the same view as I have downstairs—the Detroit River. The bed is spacious, too, with very soft linens. Tristan's hard body is wrapped around mine. His arm is sprawled across my stomach. His face is buried in the nape of my neck. Feeling his hot, heavy breath on my sensitive skin right now is only making me feel even more suffocated.

I slowly peel myself from underneath him, inching my way to the edge of the bed. Tristan's arm slides away from my chest, and suddenly, his head falls from my neck onto the pillow. He stirs for a second and I pause. Shit! Shit! Shit! Please don't wake up. Please don't wake up. When I notice that he's still sleeping, I pull the rest of myself away and jump out of bed.

I rush around the room looking for my dress. Glancing down at my feet, I see that I'm still wearing my heels.

What the hell? I slept in my heels all night? Well, no time to think about that now. I need to get the fuck out of here. I stop and try to remember where I took off my dress last night. Wait! He

Everything I Want

pulled it off of me. In the living room, I think. I scurry out of the bedroom into the living area, where I see the expensive dress lying on the floor. I hurry over to it and grab it, hastily pulling it over my head before heading straight for the door.

Gently squeezing the handle, I turn it slowly, trying not to make any noise. Once I see the bright lights of the hallway, I'm gone. I sprint down the hall and to the elevators, pushing the same button over and over again. Like it matters; it's not going to make it arrive any faster.

When it finally arrives, I hustle in, pushing the twelfth floor. Relief floods over me when the doors close. I fall back onto the wall, holding the railing tight, and blow out the deep breath that I must have been holding in since I got out of Tristan's bed.

I cannot believe I just slept with Tristan Scott! Twice! And he was fucking unbelievable! The doors open to my floor. I step out, heading straight for my room, when I realize that I don't have my room key. Great. It's not like I can go back and knock on Tristan's door and ask for it. Actually, come to think about it, did I even leave my key there? Shit! I don't want to go downstairs to the lobby and ask for another one. I must look like shit right now. My hands run through my hair and it's a tangled mess. Yep. Definitely not going down there. Wait! Frankie. I'll go to Frankie's room. Yes. That's what I'll do. I know he said he's a few doors down from mine, so I start counting.

I walk up to the one that I'm hoping is Frankie's and knock.

"Frankie!" I whisper/yell. "Frankie, open up!"

I press my ear to the door and hear footsteps. Please let this be the right room, or I'm gonna die. I hear the handle click and see Frankie's sleepy face peeking out, looking like he's sleepwalking. He rubs his eyes delicately.

"Sophia? Is that you?"

I push past him just to get myself out of the hall. He shuts the door and turns toward me, still rubbing his eyes.

"What the fuck is going on?"

"Shh!" I don't know why I tell him to be quiet. It's not like anyone can hear us. "Frankie, I need you to do me a really big favor. Please. I'll owe you."

He steps closer, eyeing me.

"You look like you just got hit by a truck. Or a big dick . . ."

My mouth drops. How can he be so blunt? The look on my face gives me away.

"I take it, it was the big dick."

"Please, Frankie! Go down to the lobby and get me another key."

"What? It's . . ." He grabs his phone off the dresser. "It's six fucking thirty!"

"Please, oh please! I can't go down there like this."

I point to myself. Frankie checks me out from head to toe, smiling now.

"Well, girl, I guess I can, but . . . who were you with last night?"

I shake my head. I don't want him to know. Or anyone, for that matter! That was a very big mistake. 'Big' being the key word here.

"Well, I guess you can go down and get it yourself, then. No one should really be down there at this time . . . besides the men in suits, you know. Business."

He's laughing to himself now and I hate it. I roll my eyes and look down at my feet, which are killing me from having these damn heels squeezing them all night. I blow some of the hair out of my eyes and stare at him. His face is warm and his smile fades.

"Oh God! I think I know."

He presses his hands to his mouth. My eyes bore into his, pleading him not to go further.

"Tristan?" he whispers.

All I can do is slowly nod, unable to look him in the eyes right now.

"Fuck, Sophia! Damn!" he exclaims. "I'll be right back."

He grabs his shirt off the dresser and pulls it over his head. Still wearing his pink, zebra print silk pajama bottoms, he leaves the room.

I plop down on the bed, holding my head. What did I just get myself into? A little over five weeks left of my first tour and I blow it by sleeping with the lead singer of Undead Society. Who is a prick, by the way! I reach down and cup myself. Fuck! He wasn't joking when he said I would feel him the next day!

Then, another thought occurs to me. Tristan didn't use protection either time! I'm on birth control, so that doesn't bother me, but what about STDs? Oh, God! What have I gotten myself into? I will have to have a serious talk with him about that matter, but I don't want to think about when that will be. Not any time in the near future. Damn me for being drunk and needy!

Minutes pass before I finally hear the door opening. Frankie! He comes in slowly, yawning, and tosses me the key card before flopping back down on the bed.

"It's all yours, sweetheart," he says to me.

I hold the card tightly in my hand and bend over to kiss him on the top of his head.

"Thank you," I whisper.

Getting up from the bed, I head for the door when suddenly he stops me in my tracks.

"Don't think you're getting off the hook that easy. I want details soon."

With that, I step out and close the door behind me. Damn. I almost thought I had a clean getaway.

Once I'm in my room, I go straight for the bathroom. Turning the shower on, I strip out of my dress and heels. For some reason, I feel that if I scrub myself hard enough, then last night never happened. I stand there soaking under the spray, not moving, just letting the water cascade over me.

Images of Tristan race through my mind. I didn't realize I was doing it, but when I started thinking of last night, I began to touch myself. Shit! I hate that Tristan has such power over me. I hurriedly wash myself and get out. Without even brushing my hair, I wrap the towel around me and lay down on my bed.

I fall asleep again, only being awakened by my phone going off. I get up and reach over to grab it. It's Matt, so I pick up.

"Hello," I say alertly.

"Hey, we're leaving in an hour. You ready?"

Shit! I thought I would take a short nap, but I fell back asleep for four hours.

"Yeah. Give me ten, though."

With that, I hang up and go in search of my brush.

Everything I Want

After I'm all dressed and ready, I collect my things from the room and make my way downstairs. Once again I'm wearing ripped blue jeans and a white tank top. My hair has more waves than usual from falling asleep on it wet, but I don't care. I put some frizz serum in so at least it wouldn't be frizzy. I didn't bother with makeup since we are going to be on a bus to Cleveland for tonight's show.

I'm holding my breath the entire way to the bus, hoping not to run into Tristan. Thankfully, I don't. I give my belongings to one of the roadies and climb right on. Roger and Jared are already there.

"Just waiting for fucking Cory to get back," Roger says to me as he's rolling a joint.

"Where is he?" I ask.

Jared looks at me then back down to check out what Roger is doing.

"We don't know. Lux got a hold of him, though. He said he's on his way," Jared says.

"Fucking great."

I didn't realize I said it out loud, but I know where Cory is. He's out scoring more coke. I hate it! Matt climbs onto the bus, putting his phone in his front pocket. His long dark bangs hang in his face. Normally, even in the morning, he has his hair styled to perfection.

He looks around at us.

"Cory's here. We're leaving in ten minutes. The other buses left half an hour ago." He laughs a little and says, "Lux is pissed. Apparently, we all should have left over an hour ago. Now there's less time to prepare for tonight so . . . I take it Cory will be chewed out."

"Good!"

The word comes out of my mouth before I can even stop it. All of the guys look up at me.

"I— I . . ."

I'm searching for excuses for my remark, but Roger lifts his hands up, stopping me.

"Don't. We've all been thinking it lately. Shit. We've been on the road for almost three weeks now, and that boy been doing this shit almost every time we leave."

Roger reaches in his front pocket to grab a lighter and pulls it out to light the joint. After he exhales, he continues.

"Cory needs a good ass chewing. Maybe he'll get his shit together. Let Lux handle it."

I don't want to stand out there anymore, nor do I want to see Cory get on the bus, so I make my way back into my own little room and close the door. I lay down on the bed and put my headphones into my ears and press play on my iPod. Slipknot's 'Before I Forget' comes on, and I close my eyes to forget all about the shit with Cory. And Tristan.

Chapter Eighteen

I wake up around five o'clock in the afternoon. We're in Cleveland now, and it's time to get ready for tonight. Great.

I pull myself out of the bed and bend over to grab my shoes. Just what I needed; to be around you-know-who shortly after we had sex. Twice. And not the innocent kind, either. Straight up fucking, something I've never done before. I've always been in a relationship with the guys I've had sex with, so to me, that made it okay.

We're at the arena now; the roadies are doing their thing and we're doing ours. Thankfully, no one from Undead Society is around. Once my part is done, I leave to find my little private concrete room to hide in.

Taking a seat in the room, I blow out another breath. What am I doing? Eventually, I will have to face him. How is it going to be? What will he do or say? Maybe he'll be like me and pretend it never really happened. I hope so.

Frankie comes in twenty minutes later with his things for tonight. Bringing the bag over to the vanity, he starts emptying the contents, humming softly as he does. I walk over to him to see what he has planned, and he looks up at me and smiles.

"Hey, girl."

He's acting like this morning never happened. Good.

"Hey," I reply.

"I have this sexy dark plaid skirt with buckles on the side for tonight with this black silk top. I thought maybe we can undo some of the buttons to show off this fuchsia bra I picked up. What's one without a hint of color, right?"

Everything I Want

I scan the outfit he has laid out for me. Normally, I wouldn't mind. Shit. Normally, I would be wearing a corset and panties. But now I just feel too exposed from what happened last night.

"Um . . . Isn't this a little, 'Smells Like Teen Spirit-ish?'" I ask him.

Don't get me wrong. That was a pretty sweet video. I just didn't expect to be wearing something like that for my performance. Looking at Frankie's face, I suddenly feel bad about what I said. Frankie's face drops a little.

"What do you mean?" he asks.

I quickly try to recover myself.

"Nothing. It's just that . . . a plaid skirt? Isn't that like high school, or something?"

He shakes his head at me.

"No. Well, I mean, yeah, I guess. But these are blacks and grays. Even your top is black. It's very form-fitting, so a couple of the buttons undone showing your bra is sexy. I have these knee-high socks with a pair of 'Phat' shoes to bring edge. You said last night that you liked wearing the boots because you could move more freely around the stage."

I smile at him. Aw, my. Frankie is trying to find more comfortable outfits for me to wear. And the outfit is cool. I realize that it's just my sudden urge to try and cover myself up that is the cause for my judgment of the outfit. Besides, it's my stage clothes—my other half—so I shouldn't give a shit. I pull him into an embrace and hug him hard.

"Yes, I did say that. Thank you."

He pulls back a bit and studies my face.

"It will look good, girl. I wouldn't send you off on that stage looking not. Yes, it's a little Britney Spears-ish. But a darker, sexier side."

He pulls out this all-black ball cap with the rim bent.

"I was going to add this to it, too. Maybe off a little on top. Your hair wavy, but not thick. And the sleeves rolled up. Kind of badass, right?"

I look at all the pieces together. They are nice, so I nod to him in approval. He smiles at me and starts laying out his makeup.

"Shit! I forgot my brushes!" he exclaims. "I'll be right back."

With that, he rushes out of the room. Standing there, I look at myself in the mirror. My hair is hanging loosely, falling off my shoulders and onto my back. My sapphire blue eyes peer back at me through the reflection. I adjust my tank a little to cover more of the tops of my breasts when I suddenly hear banging at the door.

Did Frankie forget something? The banging continues, but I freeze. It's not Frankie. This has way more power than Frankie's delicate hands could create. I have a very good idea who it is, but I'm frozen where I stand, scanning my eyes around the small room for a place to hide.

Then, the door bursts open. Tristan! He comes barreling into the room. Glaring me down, he reaches over to grab my arm; but I jump away, running behind the table.

"What the fuck are you doing?" I yell at him.

He's still glaring, and his hands are now in fists. He grabs the table and pushes it out of his way. I scream a little at the action.

"Why did you just walk out?" he asks me calmly, almost chilling.

What? I don't answer, so he repeats himself.

"Why did you just walk out? And why are you hiding? Fuck, Sophia!"

I roll my eyes at him.

"Tristan, why would I tell you I was leaving? What the fuck is wrong with you? And I'm not hiding, either, so don't flatter yourself."

Now it's my turn to glare at him. He glances over at the busted door to see what damage his massive body has done to it, then he looks back at me.

"I didn't know if you made it back to your room okay. You don't have security. I don't give a shit about cuddling in the morning, but for fuck's sake, let me know you're all right!"

Tristan closes in on me. His tight t-shirt looks like it's about to rip right off of him with how hard he's breathing. He pins my arms to my sides and holds me tightly. I try to squirm away, but his hold is too tight.

"You could've texted that you were okay, bitch, instead of making me worried about you and having to ask Lux if you made it on the bus."

What?

"Why would you even do that?"

I press my hands hard against his chest, trying to push him away. He steps back and combs his hands through his hair, looking aggravated. He scowls back at me.

"Maybe because we were in a fucking city? And you leaving my room dressed the way you were . . . I don't know. I thought something might have happened."

He grabs both my wrists and pulls them together in front of him.

"Or, maybe it could've been that I wasn't done with you yet."

He leans in and assaults my mouth with his. I pull away from him, and before even realizing it, I slap him hard across the face.

Oh, shit! The look in his eyes goes from near concern to anger in an instant. Tristan makes a low groan in the back of his throat before he jumps toward me. This time, I'm not fast enough to escape. He uses one of his hands to grab both my wrists again and lifts them above my head, using the other to crush me into him.

"You fucking hit me again, I will put those hands to good fucking use. Got it?"

He bends over and starts kissing me again. His tongue licks my lips, then he sucks my bottom lip out and bites it. Hard. I moan into his mouth and he takes full advantage, invading my own mouth with strong, fervent strokes of his tongue.

I can't fight this anymore because deep down, I want it, too. I kiss him back, using my tongue to massage his slowly. Now it's his turn to moan. He spins us around, then breaking free, he reaches behind him and grabs the back of his shirt, pulling it off. I see the muscles in his arms and chest flexing as he does this, and it's making me wet.

After he undoes his belt and the top button of his jeans, he leans against the vanity station, using his arms to hold himself up. Wow, does he ever look like some hot fucking model right now! Like Calvin Klein or something.

Tristan licks his lips and points at me using his chin.

"I know you love being the little cocktease that you are, so here's your chance. Strip."

Everything I Want

I have a feeling that he's not asking. Why am I even considering this? I should bolt out of the room right now, but I won't. I'm panting from our kiss, and my core is on fire just at the sight of him.

I look down at myself, rubbing the white hem of my tank top between my fingers. I can't stare at him right now. The look he's giving me will make me break down, and I want this. Yes, I want this so fucking bad.

Breathing out slowly and blowing a piece of my hair that's fallen into my face, I grab my shirt and pull it over my head. I close my eyes when I do, so I can't see him. After I'm done with my shirt, I undo the top button of my jeans and slowly unzip them, fingers trembling. I tug slowly, working them down my thighs, exposing my white cotton panties. Hell, I didn't know I would be doing this today, so my undergarments are modest.

"Good girl," Tristan says in a low voice as I step out of the jeans, eyes still downcast. "Now turn around and take off the rest. I want to see that tight ass of yours."

I jerk my head up and glance at him. He looks so dangerous right now. His eyes are darker-looking than I have ever seen before, and his mouth is set into a hard line.

"Now!" he barks at me, making me jump.

"Calm the fuck down," I say, turning around for him. "I'm doing it, aren't I?"

Rolling my eyes, I face the brick wall. I love this, sick as it is. No man has ever taken control of me the way Tristan's doing right now. I reach behind me, unclasping my white bra and letting it fall to the floor.

"Is this what you wanted?" I whisper, peeking over my shoulder.

With that, I face the wall again and grab the sides of my panties, bending completely over as I pull them down. Slowly.

"Fuck," Tristan says so softly that I have a hard time making out what he says.

Good! I'll shut that cocky son of bitch up.

I carefully step out of my panties, breathing a little heavier now. Feeling the moisture between my legs, I wait for his next command, but he doesn't say anything. I'm just left standing there, feeling the chill of the room on my hot body, making my nipples harden.

"Come here, Sophia."

I turn around, showing off my full body. With no alcohol in my system, I feel a little timid. But my arousal outweighs my embarrassment. My breasts are heavy, and my thighs are wet. I need him to touch me now.

I walk over to him, checking out his torso as I step closer. When I reach his side, I stop in my tracks and look up at him, biting my lip. He reaches over to me and uses both hands to cup my face, his thumbs circling my cheekbones.

"You're so fucking perfect."

He kisses me hard, like it's the first and last kiss we'll ever have. He pulls my tongue between his lips and gently sucks it. I rest my hands on his chest, feeling every firm inch of him, his chest hair tickling my palms.

I glide my fingertips slowly over his lower abdomen, feeling the deep outline of his V. Tristan takes one of his hands and cups my ass firmly, crushing me into him. I suddenly feel his hard cock bulging through the rough fabric of his jeans. I stop and push him off, taking a few steps back, trying to catch my breath.

"What the fu—" Tristan tries to yell at me, but I interrupt.

Everything I Want

"Shut the fuck up!" I say quietly but forcefully, pointing my finger at him. "You. I want you to undress now. And let me fucking enjoy it."

A small smile dances across his face, and his dark eyes crinkle again at the corners.

"You got it."

Completely unhurried, Tristan unzips right in front of me, never taking his eyes off mine. He's so confident, and it's sexy as hell. In one smooth motion, he pulls down his jeans, leaving him standing there in front of me with only his boxers on.

Fuck! My eyes grow wider. His thighs are so muscular that they stretch the fabric of his shorts. And the way his cock is stretching through the thin layer of his boxers . . . oh, my! His deep laugh awakens me from my trance. He grabs the sides of his boxers and yanks them off.

Sweet fucking mother. I knew I had a hard time fitting it in my mouth, but I was drunk last night. Seeing it here, now . . . that's exactly why I'm still sore and very excited. His cock is like nothing I've never seen before. Well, except in porn.

I grin at him.

"Good boy."

Tristan checks me out leisurely and makes his way closer.

"Lie on the table," he commands.

I look over at the table on which Frankie has laid out my outfit.

"Now, Sophia!"

I glare back at him and make my way over to it. Climbing up, I carefully turn myself over and sit at the edge.

Tristan stalks over to me, grabs my thighs, and pulls them apart violently.

"I've always wanted to eat that sweet pussy of yours. The taste of you I got on my fingers last night just teased the fuck out me."

Tristan kneels between my parted legs and gently kisses my inner thigh, gradually working his way up and tracing his tongue over the areas he just kissed. I can't watch this. I lean back on my elbows, getting comfortable. Tristan's mouth is right at my entrance now, and he lays a soft kiss right on me.

Using his fingers, he gently pulls apart my folds and starts sucking and licking my swollen clit. Soft whimpers escape my throat. My eyes roll up and my head falls back. He licks right up the length of me, beginning at my entrance and working his way up to my clit. Every time he reaches it, he pulls it gently into his mouth and sucks before releasing it and continuing his slow torture.

He moans into my pussy, sending vibrations straight to my clit, making me gasp. He slides a finger inside of me, stretching me as he begins to lick me up and down again.

"You like this, baby?"

Feeling his lips rub against me makes me start quietly moaning even more. Reaching over, I grab a handful of his thick hair and press him to me, rubbing myself on his mouth. His cackle on me just sends even more vibrations on my swollen clit.

"Fuck, Tristan!"

"I know, baby. I know."

And he continues to lick and adds another finger inside me, preparing my pussy for his cock.

Releasing his hair, I lay completely back on the cold table. Pulling at my nipples, I'm aching for relief; suddenly, Tristan brings it to me. My body quickens and my head gets light. Loud cries escape my lips as Tristan slams into me.

His hands are at my waist, pulling me into him with every stroke. My heavy breasts heave as he does this. Tristan's mouth is around my nipple now, sucking hard while his other hand kneads my other breast. His moans are probably the sexiest noise I have ever heard; it makes me even more turned on and I moan louder myself.

Tristan stops and pulls me up by my wrists onto him, then carries me over to the vanity. I can't stop grinding on him as we make our way over. Just then, Tristan pulls out of me and sets me down.

"I want you to ride my cock here."

He points to the chair. He takes a seat on it, and I climb on top of him. When he grabs me by my wrists again, he shakes his head.

"No. I want you facing away."

He turns me over and I grab him, positioning him beneath me. I am slowly gliding up and down on him when he tugs my hair hard, pulling my chin up.

"Look, bitch!"

My eyes fly open. I don't know what has shocked me more; the assault on me, or his words.

"See that?" He points to the mirror as he plunges in and out of me. "I want you to watch me fuck you."

I moan again. How much hotter can he possibly get? So I do as he says.

Keeping my eyes open, I rest my palms on his muscular thighs and work myself up and down on him. Every time I'm down, I make sure to rub myself on him, stimulating my clit even more. We both start breathing heavier. Tristan is grunting in my ear with every thrust. I can't take watching his eyes on me anymore, so I close them. Getting close to my ecstasy again and pulling even harder, Tristan growls in my ear.

"Fucking look, Sophia! I want you to see yourself come on my cock. And I want you to see me come in that fucking sweet pussy of yours."

He starts licking my neck, his eyes still on mine in the mirror. He's pounding harder now. And watching myself on him with my breasts bouncing harder than ever, I let go. I close my eyes tightly and let my second orgasm flood over me.

I twitch slightly in his lap as I try to still myself. An explosion is going off in my core and making its way through my entire body, just leaving the aftershocks behind as I come down. My skin is tingling everywhere as if my entire being is full of static.

I open my heavy eyelids gingerly, trying to adjust. Tristan grips my waist firmly, and with one last hard thrust, I feel him pulsating inside me, his cock jerking as he finds his release.

We're both just sitting there now, our breathing hard and raspy. I feel Tristan starting to soften in me. Holding onto his thighs, I lift myself off of him, wincing as I do. Shit, I'm so . . . Leaning on my hands in front of the vanity, I look at my reflection in the mirror. My hair is just-fucked-looking, and my face is flushed. My lips are wet, and my bottom lip is raw from biting it when I found my release both times. Shaking, I try to still myself.

Tristan gets up and walks over to the table. He leans down and picks up his jeans, not saying one word to me.

I peer at myself again and shake my head a little. What the fuck did I just do? Again!

Chapter Nineteen

Shit! Fuck! Shit! I turn around abruptly, scanning the room for my clothes. Tristan is just in his jeans, casually bending over to retrieve his shirt from the floor. For a man as massive he is, his movements are graceful.

I'm standing here naked, panicking. Frankie! He was supposed to be right back! He probably came up to the door and heard me screaming. I blush at the mortifying thought. I make my way over to snatch my panties off the floor, and slide them on. Not looking at Tristan, I take my top and pull it on over my head. It doesn't matter if I don't have a bra on, I'm changing into my stage clothes, anyway. Slipping on my jeans, Tristan tries to suppress his laughter, causing me to glare up at him.

"What?" I yell at him as I'm doing up my jeans.

"Nothing," he denies, raising his hands defensively.

"No. What the fuck is so damn funny, Tristan?"

He just grins at me and saunters toward the door.

"This will never fucking happen again!" I yell at him.

"Okay, Sophia," he says sarcastically.

I'm so pissed at myself and at him at this moment that I grab my shoe and throw it at him. He blocks it with one fluid movement, causing it to drop to the floor. He storms over to me, backing me up against the wall.

"Don't ever do that to me again. The next time I fuck you—"

I cut him off.

"There won't be a next time!"

Everything I Want

Maneuvering my way around him, I head over to the table—the same table he just fucked me on—and pick up the pieces of clothing Frankie laid out for me.

Tristan doesn't say anything back, but stomps his way out the door, slamming it behind him.

I slump down onto the floor, cradling my head in my hands. I don't know what's gotten into me. First of all, I never just sleep with anyone. Only boyfriends, like committed relationships! Second, not using any protection at all! I feel some of his release starting to leak out of me. The third and final thing- he's a dick!

Why have I even considered sleeping with him when he is such an asshole? I don't feel disgusted with myself, but I feel like I should be. And that's what pisses me off the most. What's happening to me?

"Sophia?" I hear Frankie calling me outside the door.

Oh boy, here we go. I rise to my feet, holding onto the table as I stand. He knows. I know he knows.

"Yeah?" I reply to him, trying to inject my voice with a 'nothing just happened' tone.

He slowly opens the door, peeking his head in. He notices me by the table and makes his way in, closing the door behind him. Oh shit! The look on Frankie's face tells me all I need to know. He's strutting toward me, smiling so big that I can't even see his eyes. When he approaches me, he puts down the brushes that were in his hand. He's not saying anything, though. He turns on his heel and saunters over to the vanity. He starts singing to himself.

"I smell sex and candy, here . . ."

Oh, my God! I want to die!

"Frankie, please . . ."

"What, love?" He's giggling as he's playing with one of the brushes in his hand. "I'm just singing."

Rolling my eyes, I walk over beside him by the vanity.

"No. You're not just singing. Did you, by any chance, hear anything?"

My voice is small. Even I had a hard time picking the last of it up. Frankie looks over at me. He gently cradles my face in his delicate, bony hands, and smiles.

"Yes. Well, kind of. I was walking up to the door and heard faint noises. So I backed away and went for a walk."

Frankie takes his hands off of me and continues doing what he was doing.

"Frankie, I fucked up."

I try to explain myself to him, but he just lifts one hand up to me.

"Girl, you don't need to explain shit. I'm always here for you. I don't judge people, okay? As long as you're happy, do whatever the fuck you want. You're a woman. You can make your own choices."

"But that's it, Frankie. After every time I've slept with him, I feel like shit and regret it."

Frankie stops what he's doing again and crosses his arms. With his head tilted to the side a little, he presses his lips together. Kind of like those duck face poses you see everyone doing nowadays.

"So why do you keep doing it? Does he force you?" he asks sarcastically.

If only he knew!

Yes, Tristan is kind of possessive. But the sick part is, I got off on it. Just thinking about that makes my face burn. Good thing my tan skin covers that up.

"Sophia, you think too much. You just have to go with it, you know? If you enjoy having him, take him. If not, then tell him no. But like I said, just from what I saw of you two together at the shoot back in LA, and then again in St. Louis, I could feel the sexual tension between you. It is so obvious."

"I guess I'm just scared, but I don't know why. I've never really done anything like this before."

Frankie's jaw drops.

"Please tell me you weren't a virgin?"

I give him a 'don't be stupid' look.

"No, I wasn't a virgin. It's just that, normally, I would be in a relationship first. This kind of feels dirty or something."

I shrug my shoulders, not really knowing how to explain it. Frankie's mouth turns up at the corners. It reminds me of the Grinch when he smiles at his wicked ideas.

"Honey, that's the best fucking kind."

His remark makes me laugh. Yeah, I guess he does have a point. I'm a woman and I have needs. And yes . . . all three times were unbelievable.

Entering the backstage area before the show, I'm so nervous. I notice Lux in the back, talking to Matt and Jared. So I walk over there to see what's up.

When I close in, Lux nods to Matt and turns away, facing me now. I think I must've startled him because he jumps.

"Oh, Sophia! Shit, you're quiet. I didn't even see you there." He starts laughing, shaking his head. "Almost ready? You guys go on in five. Roger and Cory just stepped out."

I look him over, and he seems nervous or something. What's going on?

"Are you okay, Lux?" His face drops and he starts rubbing his hands on his expensive suit.

"Yeah! Yes. Of course. Why wouldn't I be?"

He stutters a little and I give him a puzzled look, but he just bends down and hugs me quickly.

"Good luck tonight, kid."

And with that, he walks out.

I turn back to Matt and Jared. They're both just standing there, staring at me. Jared looks away quickly, too, playing with the chains on the side of his belt. Matt runs his hands through his styled black hair, laughing. I quirk my eyebrow up at him.

"What's funny?"

Matt shakes his head, looking at Jared. Jared being pale, I can see his skin starting to turn red. What the fuck is going on?

"Can someone please tell me what the hell is going on?"

I raise my voice a little, not in anger, but more concerned, if anything. Matt strides over to me. He bends down to whisper in my ear.

"Um . . . I don't know how to say this to you, Sophia, but . . . the next time you um . . ."

Everything I Want

Matt pulls away and gives Jared another look before turning back to me. Oh, shit. I think I'm going to be sick. Matt blows out a breath and shrugs his broad shoulders.

"Next time I what?" I say almost inaudibly.

"Sophia, shit, I don't know how to say this, but . . . Everyone heard you."

I want to die. I want to die now! Fuck Tristan for barging into my room. Damn. My face falls and my skin color pales like I've just seen a ghost. Matt notices my discomfort and pulls me in for a hug.

"It's cool. It's just sex, right? You'll be fine."

He pulls away, and suddenly, I feel like I'm going to pass out. Just then, I hear Roger and Cory come in. I turn to look over my shoulder, and Roger pulls his aviator shades down his nose and smiles.

"Sophia. Damn girl. Damn . . ."

The next five minutes feel like I'm living an out-of-body experience. After Roger teases me with what I have done, I somehow manage to coast my way through to the set. I've seen all the guys from Undead Society, but didn't pay attention to them or to their stares. I think even Tristan was standing with them. But at the time, I really didn't want to see the look on his face. I blocked everyone out. It's bad enough that I still feel the physical effects of Tristan and me, but now . . . Now I'm feeling the mental effects, as everyone knows and is talking about it.

Once I'm on stage, I feel safer. I walk over to the mic and grab it, but my mind goes blank. Where are we again? Cleveland? Toledo? I really don't care right now. I just need to start singing.

"Hey!" I shout into the audience and wave my hand at them.

Their excitement starts relaxing me. A smile makes its way on my face again. I feel confident. I'm wearing the skirt set Frankie set out for me. I have the black silk button-down shirt on with only a couple buttoned in the middle. The rest of the shirt is hanging loose and open. My sleeves are rolled up to my elbows, and my black knee socks are pushed up at uneven lengths on each of my legs with the skater shoes I'm wearing. I will really be able to move around the stage tonight.

I'm also kind of glad that Frankie picked out the black ball cap. The rim being bent and pushed down on my face more makes me feel like I have a shield up or something, which already came in handy earlier.

My hair is down and in soft waves with the same makeup as most nights; I have on heavy, dark eye makeup with a nude lip.

Looking over my shoulder at my boys, I see they're ready, so turning back around to face the audience, I begin with our set. I'm not really in the mood to chat with them tonight. I just need to release.

"We're Dollar Settlement!"

Hearing them roar feels so good.

"But I'm not going to talk your damn ears off all night. Yous wanted to jam, so let's get fucking to it!"

Everyone in the arena is screaming and chanting for more.

"This is, 'Done With!'"

Matt starts off with Cory before Roger and Jared join in. I move around, pointing at the audience. This is a good song to kick off with tonight. I feel all my frustrations leaving my body. During the heavy solo, I bang my head to the music. I grab the hat off my head and throw it into the crowd. I don't really need it anymore, and it's kind of getting in my way.

Making my way across the stage, I peer down at the crowd, my hair covering my face. I take my hand and brush it away. After 'Done With,' the boys go right into 'Boss.' Yes! Another good one to let go to. And I sing my lungs out.

We've just finished our whole set. I'm out of breath and totally exhausted from our performance tonight.

"Thank you!" I yell into the mic at the audience, and bow for them.

Dropping it onstage, I begin to walk off. Cory comes to my side and drapes his arm over my shoulder. I rest my head on it 'til we're off.

Tristan is standing there, just offstage. He is wearing the exact same clothes he was wearing when I saw him earlier. Even in just jeans and a t-shirt, he's still sexy as hell. Especially now that his hair really has that just-fucked look. His dark eyes glance over at Cory then back at me. He doesn't say anything, but walks right past us, making his way onstage.

For a second there, I thought I was going to have a heart attack. He must know that everyone knows what happened between us, but he still comes off with the same attitude as before. The one wherein he doesn't give a shit about anyone or anything. I can't even stand around to watch them play tonight. I just want to get on the bus and hide in my own little cove. It seems like I've been hiding a lot, but the 'Cherry Pie' incident has nothing on what happened today.

I brush my teeth and slip into my sleeping shorts and tank top. I wash the makeup off my face and pull my hair up into a ponytail. I just want to crash.

I settle myself on my bed, placing pillows behind my back, and pull out my iPad to go on Netflix. Yes, going to bed and watching a movie seems perfect right now. Also, knowing the guys, they will be all drunk and loud when they come in after Undead's performance tonight. Having earphones in will help drown that noise out.

Scrolling through the list, I decide on Wayne's World 2. Perfect. I need something with humor in it right now. I'm about thirty minutes into the movie when I feel my eyelids get heavy, and I let go of trying to fight off sleep.

Chapter Twenty

I jerk up, waking to a loud thump. What? Leaning over to stick my fingers through the blinds, I notice that we're still in motion. The sun is starting to rise, and the scenery is nothing but rolling grass hills and a few houses scattered around. If I had to guess, I would say Wisconsin, or maybe Iowa, depending on which route the driver decided to take to Minneapolis. I lay back down and shut my iPad off. I wonder what made that loud thumping noise.

Rolling over to my stomach, I quickly fall back asleep.

A few hours pass and I hear the noises going on again, waking me up once more. I reach over and check my phone. It says nine-thirty in the morning. I climb out of bed, making my way out of my room to investigate.

Cory is up and sitting on one of the sofas, fidgeting. I slowly walk over to him, realizing that he looks like shit. I don't think he slept at all last night. And that pisses me off.

"Cory?" I say groggily, rubbing my eyes.

He jerks his head up.

"Soph— Sophia!" He hurries and starts rubbing something off of the table into his palms. Looking down, I notice it's probably coke. Son of a bitch. I bend over and gently grab his wrist. He looks up at me, but this time, he kind of looks pissed.

"Cory, what the fuck are you doing?" I ask him, trying not to piss him off, but he certainly just pissed me off. Tugging his wrist free, he continues cleaning up.

"Sophia, just go back to bed."

Everything I Want

He gets up, making his way toward his bunk, but I grab him by the elbow to stop him. He turns swiftly, almost making me lose my balance. I grab the edge of the sofa for support.

"What in the hell, Cory?" I scream at him. "This isn't like you. What are you doing to yourself?"

His eyes look clouded and glazed over. He drops his head a little and walks back over to me. Just then, Roger yells from his bunk.

"Fucking eh! Trying to sleep here!"

Cory looks over that way before meeting my gaze again. I feel my eyes water. What is happening to my friend? But Cory says nothing. He just hugs me for a moment and walks over to his bunk.

I don't think talking to him now will help. I know some of the other guys do the shit too, but not like this. Cory's been different since St. Louis. I'm going to have to think of something to help my friend before he's too far gone.

After taking a really quick cold shower, I dress myself in ripped jeans and a burgundy long-sleeved thermal. The hot water must be out again on the bus, but I can't complain. At least I'm not washing myself in the sink of a rest area like I used to have to do when we had to caravan to play at festivals.

I blow-dry my hair, leaving it feeling soft and wavy. The hair dryer feels so good right now since I caught a chill from the shower. I put on a little mascara and eye liner and go in search of my boots. I love how the nineties are coming back strong. These Timberlands I have are comfortable and waterproof, so they're nice to wear on fall days like today.

The bus parks around noon at the location in Minneapolis. I walk out of the bathroom and see Jared eating a bowl of cereal at the table, wearing only his boxers. His frame is smaller than the rest of the guys. He's tall but lean; very lean. His hair is all matted and pushed into his face. I go over to sit across from him.

"Hey, Jared."

"Hey," he says back to me, before shoving more cereal in his face.

"You want to come out with me when you're done? We don't have to play until tomorrow, so I want to go exploring."

"Sounds good. Just let me get ready first."

Oh, boy. Jared takes forever. He even irons his hair to make it spike up a certain way. He takes longer than I do to get ready.

"Well, make it quick, okay? I'm bored in here."

"How about I meet you somewhere for lunch, Sophia?"

Assessing him, I think that would probably be the better idea.

"Yeah, that's cool. There's this one place I heard of on that TV show, Diners, Drive-Ins, and Dives that I always wanted to check out. Let's meet up there."

"Sounds good. Just text me where when you're ready."

"Cool," I say to him before grabbing my I.D. and money out of my bag. I push it into my front pocket and take out my phone.

As I'm leaving, I turn back to Jared.

"Don't forget, or I'll kill you."

I wink at him and step out of the bus.

Walking through the parking lot, I notice a black SUV there. It must be for one of the guys from Undead Society. They have way more perks than us. I pull out my phone, getting ready to call a cab, when I hear that deep familiar rumble again.

Everything I Want

"Where you off to?"

I turn on my heel quickly, finding Tristan standing there behind me. He's wearing jeans, of course, and a black zip-up hoodie. His hair is falling into his face a little, and he must've trimmed his facial hair a bit because it's not as thick as it's been the past couple days. Staring down at my phone, I look up at him.

"Uh . . . I was just going to check out Minneapolis."

He stares at me, then smiles.

"Can I join you?"

His request throws me off guard. He's either being nice or fucking with me. Nothing really in between. I tip my head to the side and check him out. He crosses his arms, tilts his head back, and waits for me to answer. Well, I guess it wouldn't hurt. And I would feel a little more comfortable with someone with me than without, so . . .

"I guess you can."

His deep voice chuckles, almost like he's up to something.

"All right."

He rubs his hands through his hair and shrugs.

"Did you want to walk or have Phil over there drive us?" He gestures behind him at the SUV.

It's kind of cloudy and cold out, so having a ride would be nice. And besides, all I need is some crazed fan to spot him.

"We can go with Phil," I say to him, not waiting for his response as I head toward the SUV.

I get to it before he does and climb in. Tristan walks around to the other side. When he enters, I instantly get the chills all over my body again. How awkward is this? We are actually hanging out. His body is huge next to mine. I stare down at his muscular thighs. The weathered old jeans he's wearing make me want to feel him. He blows out a breath and turns toward me.

"Where did you have in mind?"

I look up quickly from his leg that I was staring at and look toward the driver.

"I don't really know. I just wanted to check out the city. I heard of this place I wanted to try here. I think it's on 14th Avenue?"

He nods at me then tells Phil to go to there, without me giving him the name. How does he know what it's called? It's probably because he's been here many times before.

We drive to the restaurant in silence. I'm staring out the tinted window, and Tristan says nothing, either. He stretches out his long body, resting his left arm on top of the seat behind me. Feeling the warmth of his body this close makes me squirm in my seat. Damn it, body! Get it under control!

We pull up outside the restaurant, and Phil gets out to open the door for me. I thank him as I step down. Tristan is already at the door, holding it open for me. Entering the establishment, I notice it's dark with one wall showing off its bricks. It's small, too, but I like the vibe I'm feeling in here. Customers seat themselves, so Tristan puts his hand on the small of my back and leads us over to a table. The simple contact ignites my body. I feel myself starting to weaken under his touch. Just that gesture already sends electric waves to my core. Get it together, Sophia!

He lets go of my back, and I suddenly feel cold. I hurry and sit down. Tristan takes a seat across from me. Normally I would prefer a booth, but with Tristan being as big as he is, this is probably more comfortable for him.

Everything I Want

The waitress brings us our menus. She looks like she's in her mid-forties, with short, blonde hair and a thick frame. The tag on her uniform says her name is Molly.

I grab my menu and start looking it over. Being around Tristan, I don't really feel as hungry as I did this morning when I woke up, but I know I need to eat something. I peek over the menu to see him. He catches my eyes and gives me a closed-mouth smile. I glance back down at my menu then back at him.

"Aren't you going to look at your menu?"

I tilt my head at his menu, still folded up on the table. He shakes his head at me.

"I don't need to. I already know what I want."

Somehow, I feel like he is talking about more than food.

"Oh," I say, looking back down at the menu.

Molly comes back ready for our order. Tristan laces his fingers on the table and looks at me. Okay, Sophia, just pick something.

"I'll have the Eggs Benedict with an orange juice, please."

Handing the waitress my menu, I grab my water to take a sip.

Tristan looks up at Molly and proceeds with his order.

"Steak and eggs. I would like my steak rare and my eggs over easy. And I'll just have a black coffee."

Molly scribbles his order down and reaches for his menu. When Molly leaves, Tristan clears his throat and leans back in his chair. He stares at me and then, every once in a while, looks down at his hands, which are resting on the table. I bite the bottom corner of my lip and look out the window.

"This is kind of weird, isn't it?"

I really shouldn't have said that, but it's the truth; and I have to try to do something to break the ice. Tristan slowly looks back up at me with confused eyes.

"What's weird?" he asks, shaking his head.

"Ah . . . you know. This."

I gesture between our bodies with my hands, but Tristan still looks deadpan. He leans toward me with his arms resting on the table so he's even closer to me. I suddenly squirm in my chair. With the look that he's giving me, he instantly makes me feel a hundred different emotions, the prominent ones being nervousness, fear, arousal, and excitement.

Molly arrives with our drinks and places them on the table.

"Just a few more minutes on the food," she says and walks away, greeting new customers that have arrived.

Tristan's still sitting there the exact same way he was before the waitress came over. But now, instead of looking confused, he has this cocky half-smile on him now.

"Sophia, I'm not quite sure I know what you mean. Eating breakfast?"

He damn well knows what I mean. He starts laughing a little and leans back again. His quiet laugh is a turn-on, too; low and deep in a way that makes my stomach flip. Shit!

Rolling my eyes, I grab my orange juice to take a sip. After I place my glass down, I square my shoulders and look him dead in the eyes. Wow.

"No, Tristan, not eating breakfast. Well, maybe a little . . . It's just that, I don't know. You don't really like me, and now we're here trying to have breakfast like—"

"Like what, Sophia?"

I lower my head. I can't really seem to look him in the eyes anymore.

"Like we're friends or something? I don't know. You hate me, remember?"

I look back up at him when I say the last part.

His face is blank for a moment, but then he shakes his head. He leans over again, whispering in my ear.

"I don't hate you. I thought I made it pretty obvious that I like you."

My mouth drops for a second as images of him fucking me, taking me in the dressing room, in the elevator, and in his suite come to mind.

"Here you go, kids."

Molly is back, setting our plates in front of us. How am I supposed to eat now? I stare down at my food. It looks delicious, but I just can't seem to dig into it. I look back up at Tristan, and he's cutting up his steak. Calm and cool.

Picking up my fork, I begin cutting into my eggs. I take a bite, and it tastes just as good as it looks. The hollandaise sauce is creamy and rich.

"Mmm . . ."

I close my eyes and take the flavor in, not realizing that I just moaned out loud. When I open my eyes, Tristan is staring at me with his fork midair.

"It's, ah, really good."

He just looks at me for a minute then goes back to eating his breakfast.

We eat most of our meal in silence. When I am almost done eating, I start up conversation again.

"So you've been here before, huh?"

Tristan stops eating and takes a drink of his coffee, nodding.

"Yeah, about five or six times."

He goes back to finishing the last pieces of his steak. Seeing him cut up the meat like that with the tendons in his forearms flexing makes my mind wander again.

Damn it! I have to yell at myself. Is everything about sex now? Well, when it's as good as it is with Tristan, then yeah. I shake the thoughts from my head, sipping on my orange juice. Molly brings us the bill and smiles before walking away. I reach out to grab it, but Tristan's hand seizes my wrist.

"What are you doing?"

"Uh, I'm taking the bill. What the fuck does it look like?"

He shakes his head at me and, with his other hand, pulls the bill out of my hand.

"It's on me."

He lets go of my wrist and lifts up a bit to reach for his wallet in his back pocket.

"Tristan, I can at least get my share of the meal. After all, it was my idea to come here."

He ignores me. He pulls out some bills and throws them onto the table. He takes one more sip of his coffee and stands, reaching his hand out to me. I'm sitting here wondering what just happened. I don't want to keep thinking, so I do what feels right. I place my small hand into his. It's firm and rough. He clamps it around mine and pulls me up.

"Come on."

He tugs me behind him, still holding my hand as we walk out of the restaurant, moving so fast that I have a hard time keeping up with him. Once we're outside, I abruptly stop in my tracks. Tristan realizes it and turns around to face me.

"What are you doing?" he asks me.

I let go of his hand and cross my arms. Okay, I still have more to get off my chest before any sort of friendship can occur. Blowing out a breath, I just go for it.

"Tristan, what is it that you want?"

He stands there looking confused again. Damn. Even his confused look is sexy as hell. I must learn to control my emotions—or I should say body—better around him.

"Sophia, what the fuck are you talking about? Let's go. It looks like it's going to start raining."

He reaches for my arm, but I pull my body away.

"No! I need to know some things first. You just can't be a total dick to me one minute then fuck me the next, and then expect friendship from me. I don't switch gears that fast."

He steps in closer to me, looking down to where I have to tilt my head back just to look at him. His body is so close to mine and smells so good that I instantly become lightheaded. Breathing heavier now, I stare up at Tristan. He takes his one hand and gently caresses my cheek.

"I'm sorry," he says.

Sorry for being a dick, fucking me? What? What exactly is he sorry for?

"Tristan, I just need to know what I did that pissed you off. It's not like I did any shit to you on purpose."

He stops caressing my cheek and places his hand at the small of my back again and leads me over to the SUV. Tristan holds the door open for me and helps me inside. The gesture is so not like his usual asshole style. He climbs in after and shuts the door.

"Phil, take us back. Lux is setting us up with our rooms."

I'm just staring at him, waiting for him to elaborate. Phil takes off into traffic, and Tristan is just staring ahead, almost ignoring me.

"I never hated you, Sophia. I was annoyed."

What? What did I do to annoy him?

He goes on.

"I was annoyed that the last band before you guys, the ones that were supposed to come on tour with us, fucked up. I was annoyed that Lux signed a new group and brought them on tour without discussing it with me first or even letting me know. And I was annoyed at how beautiful I thought you were when I first laid eyes on you, knowing damn well that I couldn't have you."

Sitting there stunned at his confession, I just look out the window at busy Minneapolis passing by. I'm flattered, but I'm also pissed. None of that gives him the right to be a douchebag. First of all, it's not my fault what happened with the last band. Second, it's not my fault that Lux didn't let him know. And third, well, I guess it's not my fault that he thinks I'm beautiful.

I can't lie. It did send butterflies through me when he said that. Looking back at him, I don't want to keep going on with this conversation. I have bigger fish to fry, so to speak. He's just sitting there with his arms resting on top of the seat. He's so huge that he pretty much takes up the entire space.

"Tristan," I say to him all quietly. I'm kind of embarrassed at where my next question is going. "I have to ask you something."

He tilts his head to the side, waiting for me to ask away. Licking my lips, I look down at my fingers, which I now notice that I'm twiddling in my lap.

"We didn't use condoms . . . at all. So I w . . . was—"

Tristan places his hand on my fidgeting leg to keep still and answers my unfinished question.

"I'm clean, Sophia. I get checked regularly, and besides—" He shrugs and settles back into the seat. "You're only the second person I have ever been with without a condom."

What? No way! Well, for my vagina's sake, that's good. But how can I believe him? He's a musician, for God's sake! He knows I have doubts and smiles at me. Not in his usual teasing way, either, but more genuinely.

"I know, right? I've been with a lot of women. I knew some were probably rats, so I've always used a condom. I do have some standards, Sophia."

I feel a little guilty when he says that, but I had to ask for my own well-being.

Peering over to him I smile.

"I know you do, Tristan. I had to ask, though, for my own safety. I've never done anything like that before," I say, gesturing between us. "You know. Sleeping with someone that wasn't. Well, wasn't—"

"Your boyfriend?" he finishes for me, and I'm embarrassed again.

Biting my lip, I nod my head. I can't keep my eyes on him right now, so I turn to gaze back out the window.

I can tell we're getting close to where the buses are parked, and I still have one more question for Tristan before everything is lifted from my chest. Tristan is resting his chin on his knuckles as he gazes out his window. Clearing my throat as lightly as I can manage, I turn to him again.

"Tristan?"

He looks up at me. His face has no emotion on it, but his eyes seem like he's been deep in thought about something.

"What's going to happen now? I don't mean boyfriend or girlfriend shit, but . . . I just don't want your attitude all the time. It would be nice if we could have some kind of friendship on this tour."

I give him the most innocent smile I possibly can, batting my eyelashes at him and trying to pull the sweet card because he's only seen two sides of me. One I wasn't going to pull out unless I had to, and the other, well . . . If I say I hope it never happens again, I would be lying.

Tristan studies my face for a moment but doesn't smile back. Oh shit. This probably won't be good, but he simply shrugs his shoulders at me.

"Whatever you want, Sophia."

Chapter Twenty-One

Walking back to the bus, I'm confused at Tristan's last words. Whatever I want? What the hell is that supposed to mean? I just don't want him being a dick to me anymore, which I'm pretty sure won't be the problem. And I don't want him thinking that I want to be his girlfriend or some groupie, either.

I can't believe I'm even thinking about this, but if he by any chance wants to be—oh, I don't know—"friends with benefits," then I'm definitely down. I'm only a woman—a woman with long pent-up desires, as a matter of fact—so maybe screwing around with him and having a little fun on the side while on tour wouldn't be that bad, right?

Oh, God! I can't believe I'm even thinking like this, but my body is overruling my mind on this one. After the tour, I will go back to busying myself with the album, and Tristan will continue touring in Europe. It will be like this thing never even happened. I'm grinning on the inside right now at my devilish little plan. Right when I approach the door, it swings open. Roger is standing there, looking down at me.

"Where the hell have you been? And why was your phone turned off?"

Shit! I forgot I shut my phone off when Tristan and I got to the restaurant. I pull my phone out of my back pocket to check.

"Well?"

Roger keeps pushing for more information. I look back up to him, trying to explain myself without giving away that I was with Tristan.

"I told Jared I was going out sightseeing. Calm the fuck down."

Everything I Want

I push past him, making my way back to my little cove. Jared is standing in the hallway, all dressed up in his best; dark jeans, white t-shirt, and perfectly styled hair. It looks like he took about half an hour on it, at least. He speaks softly to me so that the other guys won't eavesdrop.

"Um, Sophia, I tried texting you when I was ready. But when you didn't text back, I got kind of worried. So I woke up Roger."

The face he makes reminds me of the same face Jim Carrey did in the movie Dumb and Dumber. You know, the "find a happy place" look. I stop glaring at him and pat him on the shoulders.

"That's all right, Jared. Thank you for your concern, but I was fine. After all, I'm a big girl, remember?"

"You're a hot chick in a city wandering around by yourself. It's not cool, Sophia," Roger chimes in from behind me.

I roll my eyes. I don't want to keep fighting about this. At least they don't know that I was with Tristan. They would really think that I was falling for him then. First, everyone heard us . . . you know. But then to catch us having breakfast together? No. It is way better for them to think I was out on my own.

Just then, we hear a knock at the door. Lux enters the bus, again wearing a nice suit, and takes a look around at us.

"Good afternoon, everyone. Got a room for you guys tonight, downtown. It's a real nice place and close to entertainment, so you guys should be able to unwind before tomorrow night's show." He looks over at Cory before continuing. "But not too much, though. You guys have to be at the arena at two o'clock tomorrow. Then after that show, we start making our way out west again, stopping in Seattle by the end of this week. So there will be a shit-ton of travel coming up in the next few days."

Lux strides over to me and hands me a packet.

"Here are the keys to you guys' rooms. I actually have to fly out tonight, so I won't be at your show tomorrow, but please get there on time!"

He stresses the last words again. Great. What Cory did in Detroit is making all of us look like we're immature or irresponsible or something. I will make damn sure that everyone gets their asses in gear tomorrow.

Taking the packet from him, I tell him everything will be fine and that he has our word.

"Good. Now kick ass tomorrow. The internet is starting to buzz about this 'new band' they've been hearing of who's touring with Undead."

Oh, shit. I haven't been on any social site since the tour started. I was nervous at first, but then just totally forgot about it. I'm going to have to check it out later. We say our goodbyes to Lux, and I head back to my area when the bus starts up.

"Fuck yeah!" Roger says excitedly. "Let's rage tonight, boys!"

I shake my head at his remarks; I know that they're just going to do what they're going to do. My only concern is Cory, but hopefully, our little spat this morning knocked a little sense into him.

"Sophia!" I hear Roger yelling my name. "Sophia, get your little ass out here!"

What does he want now? I climb off my bed and peek out into the narrow hallway.

"What is it, Roger?" I snap, kind of annoyed at him right now.

"Girl, don't give me that attitude. You're coming with us. We must party."

"No. You guys are fine—"

Everything I Want

"Oh, shut the fuck up! When we get to the hotel, you have thirty minutes to get dressed. Jared, you have forty-five because you're a bitch."

Roger looks toward Jared, smiling at him.

"I'm already ready, man. By the smell of *you,* though, I would say you could take up to an hour on your ass."

We all laugh at Jared's little comeback. Well, everyone but Roger. He just flips Jared off and heads to the table next to Matt.

"Sophia, it will be crazy tonight. And hey, if we start early, we end early, so . . ."

I know that's not entirely true, but I could go for a drink; and we are in Minneapolis, so I'm down.

"Okay, I'll go. But sometime tonight, I want to swing by somewhere," I say to them as I take a seat next to Cory on the couch.

"Sure. Where do you wanna go?" Roger asks me.

My smile splits my face in two, and I know he's probably not going to like it.

"I want to go to First Avenue. You know, like in the movie Purple Rain. It's supposed to be a good music place."

Roger now rolls his eyes, and Matt starts laughing. Cory leans over me and grabs his guitar and plays the opening bars of 'When Doves Cry.'

I clap my hands together, bouncing excitedly in my seat. Oh, yeah, that gets me in the mood to party. We start discussing our plans for the night.

It only takes me twenty minutes to get ready since I already showered and blow-dried my hair. I decide on wearing the same jeans as earlier, but change my top to a dark gray strapless corset.

It's made up of cotton blend with boning in it. The top folds over, creating a black V on top.

Sitting on my bed, I grab my compact mirror. I start applying more eyeliner, smoking out the corners of my eyes. When I'm done with my eyes, I dig around in my makeup bag for my lip gloss and stick it in my front pocket. Getting up from my bed, I search for what I can wear on my feet tonight. I don't want anything too comfortable because it won't go with my top, but I don't want to be falling over easily when I'm buzzed, either. I will wear the boots that I wore in Detroit. Frankie gave them to me after the show because I fell in love with them.

After lacing them up, I grab my black belt and pull it through the loops of my jeans. I slide a few bracelets onto my right wrist and walk over to check myself out in the mirror. Cool. I like it.

So will Tristan, I think to myself.

Damn it! I hate that the thought even crossed my mind. But I couldn't help it. Normally, I would just wear a t-shirt going out with the boys, but there is a chance that Tristan might go, too, so . . .

I pick up my phone and text Roger.

Ready.

After I press send, I spritz my wrists with perfume, then rub them together and dab them behind my ears. I know those perfume ladies at the shops tell you not to because it loses its scent or whatever. But I never find that true and always do it.

My phone bings and I look down, thinking it's Roger. But it isn't.

What you up to tonight?

It's Tristan! How did he get my number? I'm sure he had to ask one of the guys, or Lux.

Everything I Want

I bite my lip, staring down at the text. I was hoping to run into him tonight, not to hang out with him. Well, that wouldn't really be that bad, either, because he seems cool when he's nice. Deciding on whether or not to reply, I hear a bang on my door. I jump at the noise. Oh my God. If Tristan is out there, I'm going to shit.

Slowly walking up to the door, I close my left eye and lean onto it, peeking through the peephole. Roger is standing there, running his tongue over his teeth. Gross! I let out a breath of relief and open up.

"See, I knew you'd be ready. See, Matt? Wrong again."

I look over Roger's shoulder at Matt, who isn't paying attention to us, but rather to his phone. I know, though, that Roger is just screwing around.

"Where we off to first, boys?" I ask as I shut the door behind me.

I feel my front pockets for my I.D. and my room key. Yep, have them both. I then feel my back pockets and pull out a couple fifty dollar bills and two fives. I'm all set. I push the money down into my front pocket, though. A little safer there. I really should buy a purse or something, because one of these days, I'm going to lose shit.

Cory walks over to me as we head for the elevator.

"There's this pub we're going to swing by first. You know, if you're hungry?"

"Sounds good," I say to him, nodding as we wait. "I should have something in my stomach before tonight starts, anyways."

After we're downstairs, I scope out the lobby. Lux was right. This is a real nice place. Its decor is all modern-like, almost like a museum. When we're outside, I see the usual SUV parked out front.

"Are we getting in there?" I ask, pointing over at the vehicle.

"Nope," Matt, laughing a little, mocks me. "We're not special enough, yet."

Roger butts in.

"We're on foot, sweetheart. But the good news is, this first place is only a couple blocks from here. Later on, we can always use a taxi."

Following them down the street, I notice that it looks like it's going to rain. The sky is dark and there is a chill in the wind that lets you know that a storm is coming.

"Shit! I forgot my jacket!"

Tristan's text asking me what I was doing threw me off. I rub my hands up and down my arms, trying to warm my skin up.

"You want to wear my hoodie?" Cory asks me.

"If it's only a couple blocks, I should be okay. But I will probably take you up on that later, if you don't mind?"

"Not at all, Sophia."

Cory then kisses the top of my head and wraps his arm around me. I don't feel uncomfortable at him doing so. It's not like that with us. Cory holds me close as we make our way down the street.

Roger looks back at us, laughing again.

"She'll be so drunk off her ass, she won't need it later."

We arrive at the pub, and from the outside, it looks small with only two windows that you can glimpse through, but when we walk through the doors, it opens up. It has very high ceilings where you can see the duct work. It also has brick walls and wooden floors. It's

Everything I Want

kind of dark in here, too, but not nightclub-dark. More like mellow-dark.

"Jared, wanna find us a table?" Cory asks him. "I'll go up and get our first round. Roger, come with me."

Cory lets go of me, making his way toward the bar. He doesn't ask me what I want, but he doesn't have to. He knows that a beer is always my drink of choice, followed by a gin and tonic. I follow Jared and Matt to a large round table in the corner, by a pool table. I take a seat in the back since I'm smaller than the rest of them. Jared and Matt take a seat on either side of me. Matt looks over at me, smiling at me knowingly.

"So, this should be fun," I say to them, looking around the bar.

"Oh, yes," Matt grins.

I look back over at him, but now, he wiggles his eyebrows at me. Jared laughs but quickly covers his mouth with his hand to stop himself. I look back at each of them before crossing my arms and resting them on the table.

"Okay. What's so funny?"

Matt shrugs his shoulders. He's covering up something, but I don't know what it is.

"Nothing, Sophia. I just have a feeling that tonight will be fun, is all. I'm already a little buzzed."

I really don't believe him, but I don't want to spend my night doing the guessing game thing, so I drop it. Cory and Roger come back with our drinks, and I see that Cory has a platter in one of his hands.

"Beer batter dip and chips. Thought it would be good to start the night off with some grub," he says, placing it on the center of the table.

"Of course, Roger had to pick out something with alcohol in the name."

"Hey, Cory, this is a night to party! So if we're going to puss out and eat, then it might as well be something that's beer-battered."

I'm thankful that Cory got the appetizer. I pick up a chip, swirl it around in the dip, and take a bite. It's very rich and creamy. So good. I lick my lips and reach for another.

After the dip is finished and I'm on my third beer, we start talking a little louder. It always happens when we're all together getting drunk. It's only around five now, so there aren't many people in here yet. I glance at the pool table beside me, and I kind of want to play. Even though I suck, it's still fun.

"Who's up for a game?" I ask, pointing my chin over toward the pool table.

The guys are all listening to a story Matt's telling about the last city whore he fucked.

"Well, I'm going to rack them. Whoever's down, join me."

Jared nods and uses his finger to tell me to wait one minute. Before I set up the rack, I decide it's time to get a little buzz on first. The dip really filled me up. Leaning on the counter by the bar, I wave to the bartender. He is a short man with long hair pulled back into a ponytail. He has on these little round glasses pushed down to the end of his nose and a button-down shirt that looks kind of wrinkly.

"What will it be, doll?" he asks me while wiping the counter down.

"I'll have a shot of tequila and a gin and tonic, please."

The bartender nods at my order and busies himself making my drinks.

Everything I Want

I won't drink like this all night, but I'm too damn full to drink any more beer right now. He places my shot and drink down in front of me and he pushes over the salt. I pick up the salt and lick the top of my hand and start shaking the salt on it. I place the salt down and grab the lime wedge that he placed on the side of my drink. I lick my hand and grab the shot. After I'm done with the shot, I hurry and bite into the lime.

"All right, Sophia!"

Roger is standing at the table, clapping a couple of times. He must've seen me do the shot. I peel the lime wedge out of my mouth and grab my other drink, lifting it in the air at him. He did want us to party, so here I go.

Making my way back over to the pool table, I set my drink down on the ledge. I start placing the balls in the rack, moving around in the order of where I think they have to go. Think, Sophia. I've seen Matt and his friends back home do this plenty of times before. I'm too preoccupied with my task at hand to even hear the guys at the table clap. I'm concentrating on which order these stupid balls have to go in when someone from behind me grabs my waist.

I jerk quickly to see who touched me, but stop suddenly when Tristan's body is rubbed up against mine. He looks down at me, smiling and showing off his gorgeous mouth and those full lips of his.

I step off to the side a bit to escape his nearness. He leans his back against the table, crossing his arms. He tilts his chin up to me.

"You play?" he asks.

I can't stop staring at him. His jeans hang off his hips slightly, and he has just a black t-shirt on. With how muscular he is, the shirt looks like it wants to rip off of him. Damn . . . He bites his lip as I see him checking me out from head to toe; then he turns toward the table.

"Wanna play?"

Play? Play what? With him? Oh, shit, he means pool! I look back over at the rack I was setting up, and Tristan is switching around some of the balls I had placed in there. Correcting me, I guess. I walk over to the wall, not saying anything to him, and reach for a cue. When I turn around, he's staring at me again.

I grab the white ball and place it in front of the others that are set up. Tristan brushes past me as he grabs his cue. Grabbing some chalk, he quickly rubs the tip of it on his cue a couple times before placing it on the ledge of the table.

"Break?"

He points with his cue stick at the rack, asking me if I want to go first. Nodding to him, I walk over and position myself on the table. Lining up the stick with the cue ball and using my thumb to rest on the table, I take a shot. Balls go clinking around and a couple stripes go in. Smiling, I walk over and take another shot. Unfortunately, I miss this time. Shit! Tristan is smiling at me then studies the table for his shot. He gracefully leans in and takes his shot. A couple balls go in as well. He strides over to the other side, and again, a couple more go in. I can already tell that this will be over soon.

He misses his next shot. Thank God; he only has a few balls left, and I still have most of mine. All my stripes are in awkward positions now, though. I lean in but I can't get a good shot, so I walk over to the side and rest my hips up on the table, stretching out for my shot. I know this move is really not allowed, but it's the only way I can stay in the game with Tristan over here.

Everything I Want

When I hit the cue ball, it pushes my stripe into a pocket. When I climb off, Tristan's eyes are alight at watching me crawl and stretch out on the table. I didn't really think about it, but it must have been a sight.

Tristan is grinning but still silent. He takes his next shot, which drops all of his remaining balls in. Fuck! He's good. The only one left now is the damn eight ball. And before I can blink, he sinks that one in, barely tapping the cue stick on the white ball.

He tosses his stick on the table and looks over at me still holding tightly on to my own stick.

"Want to get out of here?"

Yes! I mean, I should stick with the boys tonight, but . . . I look over at them and they're all over the place, drinking and mingling.

"Let me just let Matt know."

Tristan smiles, and I walk over to Matt and tap him on his shoulder.

"Hey, I don't feel so good."

Matt looks at me in concern, making me feel awful about lying to him.

"Are you okay?"

"Yeah, I think that dip got to me, is all. I'll be fine."

I give him a reassuring smile.

"Let me take you back."

"No, no. I'm fine really. Stay."

I hug him, and then I walk out the door. Tristan is outside in front of the SUV, waiting for me. I can't help the nerves of excitement that I feel.

Chapter Twenty-Two

We drive in silence for thirty minutes out of Minneapolis. I have no idea where we're going. Every once in a while, Tristan glances over at me. The little buzz that I did have is fading now.

Finally, we pull up to this little shack outside of the city. It kind of reminds me of a bar back home. I don't mean in Ann Arbor, where I've spent the last eight years, but home where I grew up in northern Michigan. There are a few pickup trucks parked out front and even a couple of bikes. Some people are hardcore, still riding them around in the middle of October, especially in these colder states. One day it could rain, and the next it could snow.

Phil pulls up to the door.

"Do you want me to wait around awhile, Tristan?" he asks.

Tristan, grabbing the door handle, shakes his head.

"Nah. I'll call you when we're ready."

I wonder what Phil will be doing while we're inside. And how long will we be inside? I scoot across the seat and Tristan reaches for my hand. I shiver on the inside at the sweet gesture. Taking hold of it, I jump down from the SUV.

"Where the hell are we?" I ask, covering my upper arms with my hands, my forearms crossed over my chest.

"It's cool. Just this little place I know. Only locals, usually. Not like the crowd you get in the city."

Tristan places his hand on my lower back and leads me to the door. Suddenly I feel self-conscious. If I would have known we were going to a small town bar, maybe I would've just put a t-shirt on and not some corset with the tops of my breasts bulging out.

Everything I Want

Tristan uses his other hand and swings open the wooden door. Music is blaring in the background. I know it must only be around six, seven at the latest. To my relief, they're not playing country. Stepping inside, I scan the room; a few men sit at the bar, a couple plays pool, and only one of the tables has a group.

"What do you think?" Tristan grins at me.

Smiling back, I shrug my shoulders.

"It works."

He shakes his head, grinning, and leads me to a table that's in the center of the tiny bar. It's pretty "hills style" in here. The walls are made of cedar, I think, with different kinds of beer paraphernalia decor on them. There are mounted deer and bear heads, and some fish. The bar wraps around the perimeter in a U shape, with one side having some tables laid out and a jukebox sitting in the corner. The other side of the bar has a few more tables with foosball and pool tables pushed off in the corner.

Grabbing a hold of the chair, I pull it out from underneath the table. A couple of men turn to look at me. Yep, I might have to grab Tristan's jacket later. Oh wait! I think he left it in the SUV. Shit!

Well then, I need a drink. Besides, I doubt anyone will try anything. I showed up with the sexy version of Paul Bunyan, so I should be okay. Tristan bends down, holding the table.

"Going to get us a round. Beer good?"

Nodding to him, I smile and turn my face away. This is so insane; I'm having a casual night with Tristan.

I watch him stalk over to the bar. There're no servers in this place, just one little old man. Tristan slides some money across the bar at him and looks at me as he speaks.

The little old man grabs a pitcher from the shelf and goes over to the tap and begins to fill it. I doubt it's Coors Light, but I don't really care right now. Being around Tristan when he's not being a jerk, or um . . . fucking me, is different, but I like it. I have so many butterflies in my stomach right now from anticipation of what tonight will bring. I'm down with having a good time and getting to know him, and I'm also anxious to see what tonight will bring after we're done here. The smile on my face is huge now, starting to make my cheekbones hurt.

Tristan carries over the pitcher, smiling back at me.

"What?" he asks, as he sets the pitcher down. In his other hand, he has two glasses clasped between his fingers.

Peering up at him, I shake my head.

"Nothing."

"Don't lie to me, Sophia. What?"

He sits down in the chair next to me and starts pouring our drinks.

"Nothing, I swear. It's just nice being in a place like this. Reminds me of home."

I kind of lied, but hey, I'm not going to say, "Hanging out with you and possibly fucking later."

"Oh, I know. I hate the city scene sometimes. Dave and I came across this place the last time we were touring through Minneapolis. The best part is, you can get hammered and someone will take you back where you need to go."

His smile spreads farther across his face.

"Are you saying you want me to get hammered?" I quirk my eyebrow up at him, teasing.

Everything I Want

He laughs, rubbing his hand over his scruffy face.

"Well, that's up to you. I'm just saying, it's nice to let go and not have to worry about the people around. I don't know if you know this, but eventually photos of you will start getting out everywhere. When you're at a low-key place like this . . ." He leans back with his arms out. "You don't usually have to worry about that bullshit."

"Yeah, I guess. I really haven't been thinking that far ahead. I thought it would take years for it to come to that."

Grabbing my beer, I take a long drink. When I place the glass back down, Tristan is staring at me. He shrugs and leans toward me, resting his forearms on the table.

"You may think that, but you guys are killing it. I don't think it will be that long. Your voice is very compelling. Shit, haven't you been reading what they've been saying about you?"

Oh, yeah . . . I forgot to check that out. Shaking my head, I reach for my beer again.

"No, not yet," I say after taking another sip. I shrug my shoulders and glance down at the table. "I guess I was too scared."

Peering up at him through my lashes, I see him sitting there with wonder and amusement in his eyes. Tristan reaches over to take a drink of his beer and mumbles something to himself.

"Well, believe me. It's mostly good shit," he says.

Mostly? I jerk my head a little. What the fuck does that mean?

"Huh?"

"Oh, you know. Some people are gonna hate. I mean, you got talent and your looks are drop-dead gorgeous."

He gestures his hands up and down my body. The butterflies are now storming around in my stomach.

"Give yourself some credit. A lot of people can't sing that well naturally with all this computer shit they have going on nowadays. Just jealous, is all."

He presses his lips together and glances over at the jukebox. I follow his stare and wonder what kind of tunes they have on that thing.

I reach into my front pocket. It's time to play DJ. Pulling out a five-dollar bill, I point at Tristan.

"I'll be right back."

Getting up to my feet, I make my way over to the jukebox, feeling Tristan's stare on me the entire time. This feels good. Tristan is showing another side of himself that I never knew existed. Before, I was intimidated and pissed. Now, I actually like hanging out with him. Plus, he's some good fucking eye candy. And just knowing that, maybe later, something might happen . . . Damn. It's awesome.

Flipping through the songs they have to offer, I see a lot of nineties and big eighties music on here. Not really a whole lot of modern. That's okay, though. I love nineties music, so I select bands like Bush and Stone Temple Pilots.

After I'm done with my selections, I twirl on my heel and see Tristan leaning back in his chair, watching me and smiling. Once I get back to the table, I pour myself another beer.

"What was on there?" He nods over to the jukebox.

"Shouldn't you know? Weren't you here before?"

"I never paid attention."

He licks his lips before polishing off his drink. We sit there for a while laughing about casual shit and joking around. Finally I notice my music starting to play. First choice: Bush's 'Mouth.'

Everything I Want

This song sends tingles through me, especially with us sitting so close to each other right now, and knowing exactly where his mouth has been . . . And mine, too. The images of us together make me feel carnal.

The little old man bartender is on his game tonight. He must have noticed that Tristan finished the last of the pitcher and comes right over, taking it away to pour us another round. Staring at Tristan's full lips as he runs his tongue over them makes me want to do the same. Only with my own tongue.

"So," Tristan pauses and gazes at me.

"So," I say in return, kind of mockingly.

The little old man sets down the beer and gives me a quick smile. Feeling pretty good right now, I smile back, showing all my teeth. Taking hold of the pitcher, I pour myself another drink.

"You're a good little drinker, aren't you?"

Tristan starts laughing and grabs the pitcher from me.

"What do you mean?"

"I've been watching you every time we go out. For how tiny you are, you sure can hold your booze."

Tristan takes a drink but stares at me as he does.

"This coming from the man that bet against me a few weeks ago?"

I quirk my eyebrow at him, puckering my lips a little. Maybe it's a little Zoolanderish, but, oh well! I'm drunk!

"I only did that to piss you off."

He gives me this cocky grin. Son of a bitch. I knew it!

"Well, I hate to admit it. But it did. Just a little."

Tristan starts laughing, and he rests his hand on my thigh. Instantly, the touch does things to me. Electricity runs through my veins, making me feel hot everywhere. Just a simple touch, I know; but when it's Tristan's hand on me, I only crave more. When he removes his hand, the area suddenly becomes cold. His eyes grow a bit darker when he stares at me, but he still has that half smile of his on his lips. I better start up another conversation, or we'll probably end up fucking right here on this damn table, I just know it. Taking another drink, I clear my throat.

"So . . ."

What to say, what to say? Being kind of fuzzy-headed right now, I blurt out the first thing that comes to mind.

"I know you said before you were pissed about the previous band, but that still doesn't give you an excuse to treat me like shit." Holding my glass, I stick out my index finger, pointing toward him. "I mean . . . It's not like I'm a bad person or anything."

Shit! I really have to start focusing a bit. The alcohol is starting to consume me, right after he just told me that I can pretty much hold my own.

Tristan rolls his eyes, shaking his head. Taking a drink from his beer, he sets it down and gives me a hooded gaze. He pulls out his cell and texts someone. Placing the phone back in his pocket, he takes another drink, not saying anything.

"What?" I ask.

Did I say something wrong? Damn booze confidence. Maybe I crossed some stupid line or something. Tristan looks right at me, not showing any emotion but the dark look in his eyes.

"No," he growls sharply.

Um . . . okay. Whatever. I'm just going to brush it off. I thought we were becoming friends, at least while on the tour, so I should be able to speak my mind comfortably. It's funny. Stone Temple Pilots is playing now. And the lyrics to that song go, "Time to take her home, her dizzy head is conscience laden."

I kind of feel like that right now. I giggle to myself at the thought. Tristan sits up straight.

"What's funny?" he says, almost agitated.

The tone in his voice kind of throws me off guard. Using my thumb, I point toward the jukebox.

"The song," I blurt out, sitting up straight.

Tristan looks at me funny.

"What about it?" he asks, almost like he's intrigued.

"'Time to take her home,'" I say, laughing again. "I'm pretty buzzed and it just seemed funny, I guess."

I shrug my shoulders and take another drink.

Just then, Tristan's phone goes off. He reaches down and pulls it out of his pants, not looking up at me.

"Let's go."

Chapter Twenty-Three

Okay. I take it that he must've texted Phil earlier when I saw him on his phone.

Standing up too quickly, I feel a rush spread over me. It could've been from the beer, or it could've been how dark Tristan turned while ordering me what to do. Or at the fact that I'm actually following along.

I move and instantly have to lean on the table. Damn it! I'm really buzzed. What the hell? As I'm laughing at myself, Tristan says nothing and puts his arm around my waist so that I'm leaning against his hard body. Mmm . . . I like this.

Tristan bends down to whisper in my ear.

"Are you okay?"

"Of course," I reply, nodding back at him.

He finally smiles again but it fades quickly. Leading me through the door, he helps me into the SUV, and I feel his hand directly on my ass when he does. Oh my God! He's not playing coy at all. Climbing in after me, he scoots right up on me. On the way here, he put a little distance between us, but now, he's holding me close to him with his one arm and using his hand to tuck a piece of my hair behind my ear.

I look up at him and I see that he is just staring down at me with his mouth in a tight line, breathing hard.

My body reacts, feeling hotter than it did moments ago and tingling where he is touching me. My core is starting to throb a little at the anticipation of what maybe, hopefully is to come.

Tristan notices my squirming when I press my thighs together to dull the ache.

He licks his bottom lip slowly and all I can think of is how his tongue would feel on my most delicate area again.

I'm breathing heavier now, too. It's hard to do wearing such a tight top. I see his eyes go from my face down to my chest, watching my breasts move up and down with my breathing.

Suddenly he bends down and slowly licks the top of my left breast. Holy shit! I know I should be thinking about Phil being right there, but all I can think about is Tristan. Tristan touching me, licking me, and hopefully soon, fucking me.

I press my lips to his neck and slowly lick up toward his ear, every once in a while stopping to lay a gentle kiss along the way. He growls in my ear and reaches up to tug my hair. Pulling my lips away from him. Ouch! What the fuck?

He leans down and whispers on my lips.

"Don't!"

Then he gives me a brief kiss before softly growling at me again.

"I didn't say you could do that."

Huh? Okay. My spinning head is a little confused right now. My body is aching to touch and kiss him everywhere, and he doesn't want me to? But he can lay his hands all over me and expect me to just calmly sit there?

I try to pull out of his arms but he just pulls me closer to him, crushing me into his firm chest.

"Don't!" he says to me again, then crashes his full lips down onto mine, kissing me hard as if he's starving for me.

I taste the sweet taste of beer on his breath and the salt on his lips. I open my mouth up, partially letting him in. He uses his tongue forcefully and plunges deep into my mouth. He starts caressing my body and I let him feel every inch of me, his hand cupping my breast and gripping it as we make out here in the back of the SUV. With Phil right there.

But I don't care. I'm too keyed up right now to even give a damn. I hesitantly press my hands against Tristan's hard chest, thinking he might pull away again. But he doesn't, and I caress his chest, feeling every hard inch of him. His chest rises and falls heavily.

Now it's my turn to be a little tease. I pull away a bit, removing my hands from him. I feel my swollen lips and see his in the hints of light that we pass by as we make our way back into the city. He lunges for me, but I pull back. I don't know why I'm doing this, but seeing Tristan's reaction turns me on even more. I lazily peer up at him through my lashes and bite down on my lower lip. That's all it takes to shove Tristan over the edge.

"Pull over!" he yells at Phil.

Phil instantly obeys, dirt and rocks flying behind the vehicle as we hastily pull off on the side of the road. What in the hell is he doing?

"Come back in twenty," Tristan commands, and then yanks me out of the SUV by my arm, hard.

Shit, it feels like he pulled it out of socket. Phil tears off; the last thing I notice is the headlights fading away in front of me. We're not in the city yet, but on the outskirts. There are only a few street lights around, and warehouses. Tristan grabs my arm tightly and pushes me into an alley. My back collides with the cold concrete wall. The chill of the October night cools my already on fire skin. Tristan grasps my neck with one hand and the other firmly pushes my chin upward.

"What the he—"

Everything I Want

He slams his entire body into mine, stopping me dead in my tracks, then rips away from me with a carnal look his eyes.

"Shut up! Just shut the fuck up."

His lips find mine again, massaging them with his, roughly. I know part of me, the feminist part, is screaming for me to stop this, but I'm way too hot right now from Tristan's dominance to give a shit. Whatever I did to send him over the edge was well worth it as of right now.

Tristan grabs the top of my corset and rips it open, sending buttons flying everywhere; they clink as they hit the pavement. My breasts are fully exposed now and Tristan groans before he leans down and takes one nipple his mouth, sucking forcefully. His other hand has my right breast cupped in it. The chill in the air and my internal heat make my nipples like pebbles right now, and my breasts feel heavy with need.

My head falls back and I moan, stroking my fingers through Tristan's thick, soft hair.

I'm letting him take me like this. And I don't care.

Suddenly I feel brave and a little cocky. I want to wind up Tristan even more to see where it takes me. I tilt my head down to where my lips are grazing his scalp.

"Why did you tell him only twenty?" I whisper to him.

My breathing picks up as Tristan's mouth clamps around my nipple.

"You can't handle my pussy for longer than that," I smirk.

Tristan rips his mouth away, causing a little pain at the suction being released. Using his hand on my throat, pushes my head tightly against the wall. His gaze is dark and intense. His voice is deep and dangerous.

"Your pussy is mine now."

He releases his other hand from my hair and unbuckles my jeans, sliding his hand down, cupping me.

"This is mine."

He slides two fingers in, causing me to jump.

"I can have it whenever, wherever. Don't test me, Sophia. I'll fuck you all goddamn night just to shut your smart mouth up. And I don't give a fuck who comes out to watch."

He pulls his fingers out and in an instant undoes his zipper.

"Pull down your pants and face the wall," he barks at me.

I don't hesitate. I'm so ready for him to be inside me. I slide my jeans down to my thighs so I can only separate my legs by a couple of inches. I press my palms up on the ridged, cool brick wall, scraping them a bit from Tristan's force behind me.

I feel the head of his cock at my entrance. He's much larger than any guy that I've slept with before. I'm anticipating the feel of his cock tearing my insides. With a low noise coming from his throat, he places one hand firmly on my hip with the other twists my hair tightly in his hand. He thrusts ruthlessly inside of me.

"Ahh!" I moan loudly, but I don't care.

His cock is stretching me; I feel him tear through my delicate flesh. Being like this with my legs only a few inches apart, his size makes me feel almost virginal. I buck back at him, meeting him thrust for thrust.

"Mmm . . ." he groans, and starts slamming into me harder and harder.

Hearing him breathing heavily makes my pussy even wetter. The slapping sound of our bodies is turning me on. He must notice it too.

Everything I Want

"You're so fucking wet," he grits out. "And that pussy is tight. Mmm . . . Fuck!"

He bends over me and starts licking and kissing the nape of my neck. I move my head back and out of the way to give him easier access.

"Fuck! Tristan!" I start moaning even louder.

I can't help it, my body begins to feel the tightening sensations deep within its core, and I know it's coming. Hearing him grunt in my ear as he pounds into me is about to send me over the edge.

"I . . . I . . ." I gasp, breathlessly, but I can't say any more. I feel my body constricting and my core on the verge of explosion.

"Ahh . . .!"

I come hard, shuddering over him. He gives me a few more deep thrusts before I feel him pulsate inside me.

"Fuck!" he whispers, his head falling down on mine.

I feel like I've just lost all strength. I'm spent.

Tristan wraps his arms around me and pulls me close to his chest.

"I. Can't," I say with no breath, trying to grab my jeans to pull them up.

Tristan notices and in seconds, pulls my jeans up for me. But I don't think he buttoned them.

I feel a breeze blow across my chest. Trying to pull my top together, I realize that the buttons are gone. He must have pulled off his shirt because I feel him slipping it onto me. I'm drunk and I just got hit with an intense orgasm. I can't move. My head falls back onto Tristan's shoulders and I feel him pick me up and cradle me.

Part of me is saying, "Get your ass up!"

But I can't.

He takes a few steps, his breathing slowing down, and I hear a vehicle pull up. My eyes are so heavy; I try to open them, but I can't. All I can focus on at this moment is taking in air.

I can feel the heated leather of the seat on my back as Tristan lays me inside the SUV, but I don't say anything. Neither does he. I close my eyes and the last thing I hear is the door closing and Tristan saying something to Phil; then everything goes dark.

Tristan is lifting me up out of the SUV. We're in a parking garage. My head is heavy and my body feels weak. I can't even lift my head off of him. Nestling my head on his bare chest, I fall back to sleep.

I awake on a soft bed. I'm hot. I look down and notice a comforter on me. I press my legs together and realize that I have no pants on but I'm wearing a huge t-shirt. It smells of Tristan. I inhale deeply for a second, taking in the scent. I stretch out and my feet bump into Tristan legs. I didn't forget how he took me out in the alley. Good. I wasn't too drunk to forget, but everything afterward is a blur. I know I should get up and make my way back to my room, but I still feel too weak.

I roll over to my side to get more comfortable and Tristan mumbles something in his sleep and reaches over to me, pulling me close. My eyes grow but I don't try to break away. This isn't so bad. Right? Last time I would be running for the hills, but now I feel content being here with him. I like it. Adjusting myself to be more comfortable, I exhale and close my eyes again with Tristan's arms wrapped around me, holding me close.

I awake to soft fingertips gently rubbing up my thigh. My eyes pop open and the sun is shining through the blinds. I feel Tristan's scruffy face on my neck as he begins to nibble under my ear. Turning my body over slightly, I rub my eyes with my wrists.

Everything I Want

He gently kisses my lips and pulls away. He places his hand on my stomach and softly begins to stroke circles on it.

"Good girl," he whispers.

Opening my eyes, I stare back at him.

"Wh— what time is it?"

My voice comes out in barely a whisper. He smiles down at me and glances over to the bedside clock.

"Nine-thirty," he says.

Shit! I can't believe I'm still here! I sit up quickly and he stops rubbing me. Placing my hands on my head, I blow out a long breath.

"Shit, Tristan . . ."

He sits up now, too, with his back resting against the headboard. I turn to look over at him and he's just sitting there, his eyes warm and soft but I can still see some tension in them.

"Why?" is all I can get out.

He raises his eyebrow at me and grunts while shaking his head. He rubs his hands over his face then drops them in his lap.

"Why what, Sophia?" he asks, staring ahead at the blank wall.

Grabbing the comforter, I pull it close to me.

"Why do we keep doing this?"

"Doing what? Fucking?" he says casually.

Looking away out the window, I nod. Tristan lets out an enervated breath.

"I can't stop."

He uses his index finger and thumb and gently holds my chin, turning my face toward him. He stares into my eyes for a moment before he continues.

"I don't think you can, either. I've never had anyone before that I couldn't get my fill of."

His words make me feel like melting into his touch. I say nothing and he leans into me, kissing my lips lightly, and I let him. Nothing as intense as last night, but almost . . . caring, or something. I don't break away, but take him. Parting my mouth slightly, he eases his tongue inside.

We kiss each other gently before I pull away. His breathing had picked up again, but instead of what he might have done last night, he lets me pull away. I say nothing else to him. I swing my legs over the side of the bed and stand, scanning the room for my jeans.

Tristan just watches me as I slide them up my legs. I know I can't take off his shirt. He totally destroyed my top. I feel my nipples rubbing against the fabric. I give him apologetic eyes and look down at my hands.

"Tristan," is all I can say.

I don't really know what my mind or my body is feeling right now. I'm so confused.

Looking up he gives me the same stare back, and I know. Know to just get out *now*.

I feel my pockets to make sure I have my room key this time. I feel the key through my back pocket and know I'm good to leave.

As I make my way to the door slowly, I look over my shoulder, seeing only a part of him, shirtless, leaning against the headboard.

"Um . . . See you later?" I say hesitantly.

What do I say? Thanks for hanging out with me? Thanks for the fuck?

He doesn't say anything and I open the bedroom door to make my way through.

Closing the main door to the suite behind me, I rest against it. There's no one in the hallway, which I'm thankful for. Pulling my key card out, I have to figure out where my room is again. It says that I'm on the ninth floor. Okay . . .

I walk down the hallway, holding myself tightly. What in the hell am I doing to myself? Should I just be civil with Tristan, or keep playing this fucked up game of soirées?

Chapter Twenty-Four

It's almost two o'clock. I climb out of the bathtub, wrapping a towel around me. My body is sore. Partly from what happened last night, but this morning when I got back, I decided to take Matt's advice on the workout after drinking, to cure my hangover.

Drying myself off, I slip into dark blue jeans, and a thin, dark, long sleeved, cotton shirt. I pull my hair back into a loose, low, sideways ponytail. I put on a little mascara and lip gloss after I brush my teeth. Simple and clean. I love it.

Walking out into my mini suite, digging for my socks, my phone buzzes. I texted the guys before my bath that I would meet them down in the lobby at quarter to two. It's only one-thirty right now.

I don't even bother to look at it once I pick up my phone. Instead I sit on the edge of the bed and pull my socks up, then lace up my shoes. My phone goes off again! Rolling my eyes, I pick it up as I zip up my bag to take downstairs.

Shit! Two texts from Tristan. The first one reads,

Lux just called. We're flying out tonight instead of the bus. Broken or some shit.

Then the second one says,

Hey!

We're flying now? I wonder if Lux has said anything to rest of the guys yet? Sitting back down on the bed, I text Tristan back.

Okay.

Is that all I could think of? I'm sure I will be hearing more of the details when we get to the arena today. I hope.

Everything I Want

Sliding my phone into my back pocket, I pull my bag over my right shoulder and head out. Walking through the lobby, I notice all of the boys, even Cory, thank God! waiting for me.

"Did you know that we're flying out tonight?" I ask, going up to Roger.

He gives me this odd look and shakes his head no. Hmm . . . That's weird.

"Oh?" I say, looking around at the other guys.

"Why?" Roger gives me this questioning look.

"I thought one of the buses was down or something."

I didn't want to bring up Tristan's text just yet.

"Maybe one of us should call Lux and see."

Matt joins in as we walk out of the lobby.

"Yeah I will, after we get set up for tonight." I reassure them.

All of the crew is at the arena. The techs, roadies, and all. Undead doesn't have to be here yet, because all of the techs and roadies do everything for them. My band on the other hand, has to be here. We work with the roadies, but still have to do a lot of our own tune and set up.

When we're done, it's around five. Before I meet up with Frankie to get ready, I go into the restroom and call Lux. It rings only twice before he picks up.

"Please tell me everyone is there?" He sounds annoyed.

I place my hand on my hip.

"Yeah, everyone's here. I just wanted to know, what's going on with the buses? Are we flying out now?"

"Buses are fine," Lux quickly says. "Some little glitch came up earlier, but everything is taken care of now."

What? I was getting ready to ask why Tristan would text me about flying out then, but Lux continues.

"Some of the guys from Undead have a few days off. I told them that they can chill on the road with you guys, or maybe wait around in Seattle and rest 'til the next show. You see, they go right over to Europe after this leg of the tour, so I try to give them a little break."

Right now my mind is blank. Why would Tristan tell me that we're flying? Maybe because he's trying to scheme a way to be around me more? I try to shake the idea out of my head, but why else would he text that?

"Oh, okay. I thought I heard that we're all flying. Never mind."

Lux jumps back in.

"I'm sorry, Sophia. With expenses, it's easier for you guys to go by bus. They bring in more to the company. Obviously. But—"

I cut Lux off. Shit! I don't want him thinking I'm pissed or something. I was just trying to figure out Tristan's text, which I know now was set up by him. Sneaky fucker. I start laughing a little, to ease Lux.

"Hey, don't worry. Someone must have misheard, that's all. That's why I called you. No worries. We're cool. And everyone here is on their game."

Lux breathes out a sigh of relief. We say our goodbyes and I hang up. Hmm . . . What am I going to say to Tristan? Like, how am I going to ask him about lying? Because that's pretty much what he did, didn't he?

I guess I'll have to figure this shit out after the show. I really don't know what to think about it. Part of me is flattered at Tristan actually wanting to be with me. But another part is like, why would he do that?

I turn around the corner of the hallway, heading to where Frankie is. I notice that down a bit farther, Tristan and one of his techs are talking. I suddenly stop. I'm not ready to ask him about the flying thing. Whatever. I pick up my pace again, not looking at him, but at the door where I need to go, acting like I'm not really paying attention. Tristan nods to the guy and starts walking up to me.

Not saying anything, I keep my pace. He looks so incredibly good right now, too, clouding my head and the questions I need to ask him. But I'm only thinking about him being with me right now. Focusing on me.

We walk together silently down the hall for a few more steps before he gently grabs my elbow, making me come to a halt. I love and hate how he treats me forcefully. I jerk my arm away, glaring now.

"Why did you fucking lie about the buses? Are you psycho or something?"

Wow. I didn't mean for it to come out so harshly, but Tristan doesn't blanch. He just starts smiling at me, slowly. That sexy, cocky smile of his.

"I was going to explain more, but all you said was 'okay' back."

"What is it that you want from me?" I demand, crossing my arms, it's time to figure some things out!

Tristan looks at me confusedly, taking a step back.

"Nothing. It's just that . . . Well, shit, Sophia! I like this." He gestures his hand between us.

"I know the text came off shady. But you left my room today so casually that I . . . I guess I panicked."

Oh my God. Staring up at Tristan, his eyes look genuinely concerned. No more glaring or dominance. Instead it's like he's scared, or lost. That instantly makes me feel a little wet. I don't know. Something about how powerful he is, and how crazy sexy he is too, and wanting to be around me, a 'plain Jane.' I shake my head, trying to grasp the concept.

"Wh— Why didn't you just talk to me instead?"

He now looks a little irritated, rubbing his hands up and down on his face.

"Fuck, I don't know. I just know that I can't get your fucking ass off my mind. And it's pissing me off. I'm not used to this shit, Sophia. I don't know."

Okay, please take me now. Never would I ever have imagined this shit right now. I go on, trying to play it cool.

"Well, Tristan, maybe if you would've just said, 'Hey, fly with me out to Seattle for a few days,' then maybe I would've."

His cocky smile is back on, and he steps in closer to me.

"No, you wouldn't."

Actually, I think he's right. Gawd! He's so right. This pull between us is so intense and raw. I've never felt anything like this before. I look away from him again, staring down at the floor.

"I can't," I whisper.

I peer up at him and see his jaw clenching, but he doesn't say anything, so I go on.

"I mean, this is my band's first tour. I can't just fly out and stay at a hotel while they're on the road. This has to be all of us, together."

Everything I Want

I think Tristan understands, but is a little disappointed. He nods and backs away from me. He starts walking away in the other direction. I turn around to watch him. Shrugging my shoulders, I let out a long breath.

I feel kind of lost right now. I mean, should have I taken him up on his offer to join him? Part of me wonders all the things that we could be getting ourselves into for a few days. But I know to keep my distance from him. This is just a tour. He *is* Tristan Scott, after all, and ladies are what he knows. Just the thought of how many would be jumping at his offer blows my mind at how I just turned him down.

Pushing open the door, I see Frankie applying mascara on himself in the mirror.

I step inside and sit in the folding chair by the table. He doesn't look away from what he's doing.

"Hey, doll face."

I look over at my outfit for tonight, hanging on the rack. Leather shorts and a leather strapless corset top. It looks pretty fucking cool.

When Frankie is done, he turns to me, leaning against the sink.

"I came out last night, like around nine or something," he says, waving his hand around in the air. "But the boys said you weren't feeling well and went back to the hotel."

He pushes himself off the counter and slowly strides over to me. Panther-like.

"So . . . I took it upon myself to check up on you. After all, what are friends for?"

I think back quickly in my head. I don't remember receiving any texts or calls.

"I got a key from the front desk."

Lifting his hands up defensively, he turns his nose up in the air.

He looks back down at me, and squats down right in front of me. Raising his eyebrow, he places his hands on my knees.

"You weren't there . . ."

I'm shocked right now. Why is everyone suddenly in my shit? But I can't lie to Frankie. A smile creeps over my face, but I say nothing.

"Uh-huh. Just as I suspected."

He pushes himself off of me, twirling around on his heel.

"Let's get ready," is all that he says to me.

I'm thankful that Frankie knows when to drop something.

After I'm all done getting ready for tonight, I walk over to grab the joint I had stashed away in my jeans. Pulling it out, I light it up and exhale slowly. Fuck, this feels so good right now. My head begins to feel light, and all of my nerves about Tristan and the performance tonight fade away.

Frankie leaves the room to take a call, and after a few more tokes, I turn toward the mirror. Short leather shorts with a leather vest crop top, which makes my breasts look ginormous. I also have on these black, thigh-high boots. My hair is laying long and thick, with waves cascading down.

My makeup is done in a more extreme style than the last few shows. Frankie always does heavy eye makeup and lashes, but tonight, I have more of a clean face. I have much redder lipstick than usual going on, though. My wrists are covered in bracelets and my fingers covered in silver rings. I look like some bad-ass biker chick, ready to take on anything.

Everything I Want

When I'm done with the joint, I feel calmer, but more anxious at the same time. Anxious in a good way. I'm ready to get out on that stage and show Minneapolis a good time.

But my mouth is dry. Not the best thing before performing, so I grab a water and put a piece of gum into my mouth, to help saliva form. Shit! I'm pretty stoned right now. I laugh at myself; I don't really care. I feel pretty damn good.

I decide it's time to round up the boys. Making my way down the hall, I keep my ears open for any of them. There aren't a lot of rooms around here, so it shouldn't be that hard to find them. Right when that thought crosses my mind, I hear Roger's obnoxious laugh. That laugh tells me he's already buzzed, too.

Not caring, I swing open the door to where I hear his voice. It's a large room with a beverage table in the center. Everyone is in here; I mean, everyone! Tristan's band included. They all literally stop and look at me, with some mouths dropping.

I take it that Frankie did another great job tonight.

They must know that I'm stoned, because Caleb covers his mouth to hide his laugh.

"Shit, girl. Have any more?" he says, lifting his hand away.

I give him a smile and tilt my chin up at him, shaking my head.

"Nope."

We're about to go on in a few, so I want to round up the guys and get out of here.

Tristan's eyes are on me, scanning my body from head to toe. He's wearing jeans and a black sleeveless shirt again, showing off those delicious muscles and tattoos of his. His hair is pushed back out of his face, but curls slightly around his ears and neck.

"Just letting you fuckers know it's almost time."

I wink at them. What has gotten into me? The tendons in Tristan's neck flex at my wink, and Roger gets up.

"Fuck, yeah!" he exclaims. "I fucking love this shit."

He slaps his hand on Cory's shoulder, making Cory stand. I turn away from them and start making my way out the door.

I don't pay any attention to the laughs or whispers behind me. Good or bad . . . I don't give a fuck. I'm ready to do this. The tour is already halfway over with, and I'm going to make the most of it.

I hear my guys behind me as I start walking down the hall. Lux isn't here, but I see one of the crew members with a clipboard, standing in front of me as I approach the stage.

"You're all set in three," he says, then he's off walking past me to another guy.

I'm not even going to look back right now. Rubbing my hands together, bouncing from one foot to the next, I'm just ready to get out there. Shit! It's almost as if I didn't smoke pot; instead, it feels like I'm on something else, with my behavior right now.

Honestly, it's not just the pot. It's being on tour, the fans, and Tristan actually liking me that's getting me off right now.

I hear the crowd chant more and more, and our introduction is being announced through the speakers. I can feel my band's presence behind me as I slowly inch my way off the sidelines and toward the stage. Hearing our cue, I stride over to the mic, waving to the crowd.

We're not big enough to have all the fancy effects when we perform. I admire Undead. They're not sellouts. I remember reading an article about them a few years ago, and it was Tristan that was saying they did that stuff for the fans that pay the money. He wanted them to have a good time and enjoy a show. *'It's all for them. I'll gladly pay any amount for them.'*

His words, even then, touched my heart. Especially when it comes to performing.

Taking the mic into my hands and raising one hand to quiet the crowd down some, I shout into the mic.

"What's happening, Minneapolis?"

They scream.

"You may not know who in the hell who we are, but we're Dollar Settlement. New to this shit. And I can't wait for us," I turn behind me slightly, gesturing to my band. "For us to start you guys off right!"

"Wooo!"

I hear screams and whistles come from audience. I glance quickly over my shoulder, letting Cory know that I'm ready to begin. I hear a cryptic melody play through the amps, and I know exactly what song we're starting off with. 'Chills.'

That's a good one. I know it's not very professional to start each show not really knowing how we're going to do it. But I like how we've been just doing a guessing game with the first songs.

Leaning down into the mic while my other hand runs up my side, I softly sing into it.

I start slowly, swaying my hips from side to side. The crowd is eating it up. Yes! I fucking love this feeling. Once the rest of the band breaks out into the song, I traipse upstage, eye fucking a few different audience members, feeling a connection with them. I love it! As the song progresses, I make my way over to Roger on the drums. Pulling my hair back off my scalp, I shove the mic right in my face and let it all go.

My lungs almost feel like they're about to give way with all the force I'm singing right now. But I don't care. This feels so good, always has, and I'm pretty sure it always will. And I will never get sick of it.

We're almost done with our set. Just one more song left. Breathing hard, I'm a little winded. Usually I do these techniques to help me get to that level of singing without hurting my voice, but tonight's adrenaline just took me over. I'm so glad that we have a few days before our next gig.

The lights dim into a soft haze of orange and white. Licking my lips to get some moisture back, I glance over at the side of the stage. All of the guys are there waiting, but I can only focus on Tristan. His arms are crossed, but he has a playful smile on his face. No glare, no emotionless expression, nothing bad; almost as if I have a friend or something waiting for me. I can't help it when I feel my own face give the same smile to him.

Looking back at the audience, I feel completely Zen now. This couldn't possibly get better. Our show was fucking insane, and feeling Tristan's now new presence like this, is overwhelming.

I breathe into the mic, feeling my chest rise up and down. I use one hand to grip my waist.

"Last one for the night, folks, so we're going to slow it down for this one. This next one is 'Lullaby.'"

Roger starts this one, and soon Jared, then Matt and Cory join in.

At the end of the song, the lights go out and we hear everyone chanting and whistling. I drop the mic on the stage and turn on my heel and walk off. The crew are busying themselves again, getting ready for Undead Society.

Chapter Twenty-Five

I peer up at Tristan as I step offstage. He's still standing in the same exact spot, his right shoulder perched on the wall right in front of him. He leans forward and with his other hand, he grabs mine and pulls me in, trapping me to him. I can't believe he's doing this in front of everyone, but I can't pull away, either. Being in his presence after a show and taking him in like this, feels amazing. He smells amazing, too, a clean, musky scent and something that I can't put my finger on. It's wonderful and instantly sends liquid heat to my core.

Saying nothing to each other, we just stare.

"You guys are good to go," announces one of the roadies, and I can see out of the corner of my eye, his band making their way over.

Still, Tristan doesn't move. Doesn't take his gaze away from mine. His smile is gone now, but his face still shows genuine appreciation. I try to move away to let him go on, but he just stills me in his grasp. What is he doing?

"Tristan you have to go," I whisper-yell at him, trying to free myself again. Again he stops me.

"Come on, man!" Dave yells over at him, and I'm starting to wonder what in the hell is going on his head.

Tristan leans into me and brushes his lightly scruffy face against my cheekbone. His soft lips tickle my ear as he whispers into it.

"Tonight."

Then he lets go of me quickly. I suddenly feel cold without his body near mine.

Everything I Want

I turn back around and watch him make his way onstage. Caleb is laughing and shaking his head. Dave says something to him, but Tristan ignores it.

Tonight.

I have a feeling that, that wasn't a request, and I'm excited about it. Being with Tristan, no matter what mood he's in, is completely addicting. I can't get enough.

Right about now, I would normally go find Frankie and get ready for whatever party we're doing after. This time, however, I decide to stay. Leaning on my right side, pushing against the wall, I cross my arms like he did and watch him.

His voice rumbles through the entire arena and it's hot as hell. He didn't do an introduction this time, just got right to it. Seeing his hand grip the mic and the tendons in his arm flexing underneath the dim white lights brings back visions of how his arms were wrapped around my body when he took me, and I suddenly grow hotter.

I can't move, but I sit there watching him, song after song. I'm in a trance seeing him like this. Before I met him, I used to watch videos on the internet of his performances, thinking he was so good. But now, being on tour with him and actually being *with* him brings something incredibly more to the table. I feel almost powerful right now.

Finally they're almost done. They always do the same set, except for that first show when he threw 'Harlot' in there. I'm still not going back to get ready yet, though even my band has taken off to do whatever they do during this time. Tristan looks over at me and notices that I've been watching the entire time. His look is carnal. No smile dances on his beautiful lips this time, but his eyes are dark and sensuous. The smile I did have on my face from watching him perform disappears. My body begins to ache for his when he looks at me like that.

Tristan moves toward the front of the stage, but doesn't take his eyes off of me.

He then speaks to the crowd, who by the way, are freaking the fuck out right now. Tristan finally breaks our gaze.

"Everyone good tonight?"

They all reply back to him, some chicks even throw their bras and panties toward the stage at him. But he doesn't notice. Or maybe just doesn't care.

"That's good. Well, I don't really want to waste time bullshitting, so are you guys ready?" He laughs into the mic. They start chanting and clapping. "I dedicate this one to my favorite . . . 'Harlot.'"

Screams blow through the arena. My face drops and Tristan looks over to me and winks. I'm not a freaking harlot, that son of bitch! Of course when things were actually starting to go good, he throws some shit out there like this. He starts singing, but instead of standing there waiting for him to look at me to flip him off, I turn quickly on my heels and make my way out.

"Dick," I mumble to myself as I make my way around the corner.

"Who's a dick?" Cory's voice says from behind me.

I turn around to see him leaning against the concrete wall, holding a beer. His eyes are a little red and bugged out. But he seems to still be acting like his usual self.

Caught off guard, I have no time to question him on what he was just doing. Shaking my head at him I turn back around, stomping to my room, acting like some spoiled brat. Cory starts to follow me, trying to keep up with my pace.

"Hey wait!" he says, sounding alarmed. "Sophia, stop!"

Hearing him say that makes me realize that maybe I was acting childish back there.

"What is it?" I ask, rolling my eyes, but not looking at him.

Cory moves around so that he's now facing me. Gripping his beer with one hand, he rubs my shoulder for a second with the other one.

"Is it Tristan again or some shit?"

I cackle at him for a moment, looking down at the floor. I can't hold back anymore.

"I just thought the asshole was actually turning in a human being or something. I was wrong. Again."

Cory smiles at me, lifting my chin.

"Sophia, I don't know much about this kind of shit," he begins, letting go of my face and taking a drink of his beer. "But I do know that Tristan must have something for you. Who fucking cares if he dedicated a stupid song to you. It's not like he wrote it for you. And look at it this way; he did say, *my* 'Harlot.'"

His grin grows into a full blown smile and he takes another drink. What the fuck did he just say? Gawd, he doesn't make sense sometimes. But I do think it's very cool of him to try turning this into a positive. I smile back at him, shaking my head from side to side.

Cory glances behind me suddenly before looking back down.

"Speak of the devil," he leans down and whispers in my ear, and with that, he walks away.

Damn it! I'm not really in the mood to be lashing out at Tristan right now, so instead of looking back at him, I take the five steps to my room and once I push through the door, I quickly lock it behind me.

Frankie is sitting down sipping a drink and filing his nails. His eyes grow big at seeing me hurrying my way into the room as if I were running from zombies or something.

"Damn. What's going on out there?" he asks before going back to his nails.

"Nothing. Just forgot about changing for tonight. Where're my clothes?"

He uses his nail file and points to the small attached bathroom.

"In there, sweetheart."

As I make my way to the bathroom, I hear a couple of pounds at the door. Frankie's eyes grow big again, and so do mine. Damn that fucking caveman psycho. More blows rain down.

"Please, Frankie. Stay in here with me."

"Who the fuck is that?" His voice comes out in a squeal.

I just have to give him one look and he knows.

"Damn, girl. Your pussy must be very addicting for him to be coming at the door like that."

"Please, get rid of him," I beg, and then I'm in the bathroom behind another locked door. Thank God.

I hurry and undress. Completely naked, I scramble to find my panties. I hear Frankie walk over to the door and yell through it.

"She'll be out in a bit."

Everything I Want

Then I hear Tristan yell something, but can't make out what he's saying. The door clicks and I hear the lock going off. Damn fucking Frankie. Fuck!

"Oh, hey Tristan," Frankie says all casually. "She's just getting dressed. Would you like something to drink, or maybe an herbal refreshment?"

I can't believe what I'm hearing! Frankie offering him drinks and shit . . . he was supposed to get rid of him! I'm scared shitless right now. Not so much of Tristan going off on me, but of him fucking me senseless. I really don't need that right now since I have an after party tonight.

After I pull up my jeans and slide on a black tank top, I slip on my shoes. My face still has its full blown stage makeup on, and since I didn't come back right away, Frankie has no time to fix it. Whatever.

Blowing out a deep breath, I grab the door handle and yank it open, giving both of them a glare from hell. Frankie is just sitting back smiling, playing with his damn nails again, and Tristan is sitting on the chair, leaning forward with his arms resting on his knees. He looks up at me and stands, tucking his hands into his back pockets. Damn him for being so fucking good looking! It really makes it hard to stay mad at him.

Not giving in to my attraction, I walk right by him, heading for the door, but Tristan catches my arm. He's gentler this time than usual. Not looking at him, I try to tug free.

"Let go of me," I hiss through clenched teeth.

Surprisingly, he lets go. I'm actually shocked that he listened to me. I don't look up at him, though. Instead, I walk through the door, leaving him and Frankie in the room. Tristan doesn't follow me, and now I'm kind of wondering why. Oh, well. I see the room that they have reserved for our after party tonight. Everyone is in there; my band, his band, roadies, crew techs, and some sharply dressed men that I assume work for the label. Oh, and let's not forget, there are quite a few groupies lounging around in here, all big boobs hanging out. I can practically see their cooches.

I walk up to Jared and grab the drink out of his hand. Swigging it back, I instantly feel the burn of bourbon shooting down my throat.

"Damn girl, that shit was straight." He starts laughing and I wince at the grossness of it. "I just sip on it here and there, but I definitely wouldn't have pounded it like that."

"Because you're a bitch, Jared," Roger says.

He's grinning, and has some skank under his arm. Wiping my mouth off with the back of my hand, I nod to him.

"That a girl," he says before walking away.

Just then, Tristan walks in and all the groupie whores flock to him.

Tristan is staring at me, but all I can see are all the whores. Rolling my eyes at him, I flip him off and turn my back to him.

"Jared, get me another, please."

Jared's eyes now look like they are going to pop out of his head, but he nods and grabs my empty glass from me.

The music is low in here, which I kind of like tonight. It's mellower yet more crowded, all at the same time.

Since Jared's not here, I'm pretty much just facing a wall, but I don't want to turn around and see Tristan all over some groupies. But then I feel that flare of heat, and I know he's behind me. I'm trembling on the inside right now, but I still don't look. Now I feel his chest to my back and he leans down.

Everything I Want

"Sophia, I'm sorry."

His voice sounds cryptically causal. Turning slowly, I look up at him. I can't really say anything at the moment. I'm just lost in his face. His beautiful face.

Jared comes back and hands me my glass. He must know that right now is not a really good time to chat, because he's out of there as soon as he hands me my drink.

Tristan steps in closer, and I don't back away. He starts to smile now and that smile is my undoing. I start smiling back, too.

"Motherfucker," I say to him, batting my eyelashes.

"What?" he says back, with that playful edge in his voice.

"You know fucking what. Don't act dumb. I'm not your harlot!"

It comes off kind of sternly when I was trying to add a joking tone to it, but Tristan doesn't care. He shrugs his shoulders and bends down to whisper in my ear.

"I know. But that's the only song I have that I can sing to you right now. The point you're missing is that I said *my*."

He pulls away from me, staring. Wow. That right there was my complete undoing, for sure. My center starts to fill with liquid heat at his dominant words.

The next two hours, I mingle with my band and his. We keep coming up to each other every so often, and I'm pleased to say that every groupie that tried to come on to him was quickly dismissed. He had no attention to give them. Only me.

I'm walking with my band toward where the buses are parked. I didn't take Tristan up on his offer to go with him. The heavy doors swing open and to my surprise, there's about fifty to seventy people outside waiting, screaming as they see us. Well, more like Undead.

The bodyguards and bouncers go to work. Roger and Cory are right by my side; but when their names get called to sign this tit or that, they were gone.

"Sophia! Oh, Sophia!"

I hear my name and I see this young woman with short hair holding a picture of our shoot in LA. I smile to her and walk over. She hands me a sharpie and starts smiling.

"Oh, thank you, thank you. You fucking rock! I caught your act in Chicago, too."

My smile now shows off my teeth.

"Really? Cool. Thanks."

It's so awesome that we do have some loyal fans from the beginning. I hand her back the photo and sharpie, and someone else throws one at me to sign. Inching my way toward the bus, I keep stopping to sign.

"Hey, Sophia! Me!"

I hear a man's voice and right when I turn to sign the next thing, I feel a strong blow to my gut, instantly taking me to my knees. My vision becomes blurred from the excruciating pain. Roger comes to my side, wrapping his arms around me for protection. I can barely make out the guy who hit me, but I see Tristan on top of him, pounding him to the ground.

Bodyguards and bouncers push the crowd back as Caleb, Dave, and Gunner try to pry Tristan off the dude. There's a pool of blood underneath Tristan's body; he's kneeling over the guy and he won't quit hammering him.

Finally they are able to get him up. The dude that hit me is unrecognizable; his face is just blood and flesh. Tristan turns over his shoulder and notices me in Roger's arms. He strides over and picks me up, cradling me like a baby. I wince at the pain in my stomach.

Tristan carries me over to the bus, and now I hear sirens in the background. He takes me back to my room and gently lays me on the bed. He's breathing hard and his mouth is in a tight line.

"What in the fuck? Fuck!" I hear someone yell out in the front of the bus.

My head is too clouded from the blow and booze to pay any more attention. I curl up on my side and hold myself. Tears sting the back of my eyes. Tristan doesn't say anything and walks out. I don't know how long I lie there, but then I hear a knock on my door.

"Miss Sophia, this is Pat with EMS. May we come in and check you over?"

I'm too tired and sore to say anything, Cory opens the door slowly then nods behind him. He walks in first, then two EMS workers follow. They press on my body and shine light in my eyes, checking all of my vitals. The woman asks if she can lift up my shirt and the other EMS worker and Cory turn away. She feels around, and again I wince when she hits the certain sweet spot right below my ribs.

"You should be fine, dear, just some bruising. You will probably feel some discomfort for the next few days, though, so please take it easy. Maybe take a couple painkillers."

She gets up and I am able to get a look at her face. She looks like she's around my age. She has very warm, kind green eyes, and her dark hair is pulled into a tight bun. She and Pat, I think his name was, exit the room.

Cory blows out a breath and shakes his head. His eyes look like he's been crying, or wanted to.

"I'm so sorry, Sophia . . . Shit, I'm sorry," he says in a raspy voice.

I lick my dry lips.

"It's not your—" I manage to get out.

"Yes, it is! I shouldn't have left you alone like that. I'm so fucking sorry."

It's quiet in the room now and Cory comes over to the bed and kisses me on the top of my head, taking the duvet and pulling it on top of me. He walks out of the room hanging his head as he shuts the light off.

Holding myself tightly again, my body is ready to shut down after everything that has happened tonight. And I let it.

Waking up I wince again as I stretch my legs. I'm in my panties and tank top. But I still feel hot. I don't remember removing my jeans. Just then, my leg runs into Tristan's strong thigh. I blink my eyes open to see him sleeping peacefully beside me.

Chapter Twenty-Six

Oh my God! I blink at him again. He's in a deep sleep with his mouth parted slightly. His face is absolutely handsome. His curls are a mess that stick out all over on the sides of his head and face. He doesn't look anything like the seductive, mysterious man I have seen before. And nothing like how dangerous he looked last night when he was on that guy. He looks absolutely, breathtakingly beautiful. And he's here with me. His band was supposed to fly out last night and have a little break before the next show. Instead, he's lying next to me on a very uncomfortable bed. My heart aches at the sentiment. I just can't believe it.

I study his features a little more. I have never gotten a really up-close look like this. On the other mornings that I've woken up beside him, I felt panicked and would only think of how to escape.

I want to kiss his soft lips so badly right now, and graze my tongue along the stubble on his jaw. My core is starting to ache slightly at the thought.

I can't resist.

Leaning my face over his, I can feel his hot breath blow out on my skin.

Licking my lips to moisten them, I bend down and gently lay them on his, molding my lips to his. I raise my left hand and softly run his thick, untamed hair through my fingers, while the other is holding me up over him. His eyes are still closed but I feel him starting to slowly kiss me back.

He brings one arm up and wraps it around, causing me to moan in discomfort. His eyes spring open and he releases me.

"Fuck! I'm sorry."

He's looking at me as though he's done something to me. Crawling up closer to his side, I shake my head softly.

"It's okay. I'm fine."

With that, his hand gently starts rubbing delicate circles on my belly, raising my shirt up even more. His eyes fall and harden. When I look down, I notice the black and purple bruise taking place on my abdomen. It really looks worse than what I feel right now. But Tristan just clenches his teeth and looks up at me. I hope he's not mad. I mean, everyone was signing autographs. I wasn't the only one.

Taking a hold of his hand that has now stopped rubbing me, I raise it up slowly, pressing gently on my skin through my tank, and rest it on my breast. Still holding on to his hand with mine, I place my other hand on his pectoral muscle and lean in to kiss him again, lightly brushing my lips in feather like kisses against his. Tristan groans in my mouth, and begins to kiss me back with a little more force.

I don't know how long we lie here like this, kissing each other. But it's wonderful. No pushing, no force, no angry, pent up frustration. This feels more intimate; the hazy morning sunlight peeking through the blinds; the sound of our breathing and the low moans coming from each other.

I grab the hem of my shirt and, not taking my eyes off Tristan, I gracefully pull it over my head. I'm only wearing a black lace bra and matching panties. His eyes greedily take in the sight of me. I don't feel embarrassed or ashamed, but grateful. Grateful for Tristan sticking up for me, grateful for him being here with me right now, when he could've easily just hopped on a jet. And grateful for him wanting me this much.

He pushes back my hair on my shoulders, exposing my chest to him more, and I reach around behind me, undoing the clasps. The bra slowly slides off my shoulders and he inhales deeply.

"You're so fucking beautiful."

He lifts his body up, leaning his back against the wall, and pulls down his boxers. His impressive erection springs free. I lean back as he eases down my panties, exposing every part of me.

Tristan is getting ready to get on top of me when I wince again at his hard chest pressing against my bruised abdomen. His eyes look angry again, but I react quickly. Gently placing my hands on his chest, I lay him back down on the bed and climb on top of him.

Straddling him, I lift myself up and take his firm cock into my hands. My body already feels the hot moisture pooling beneath me. I press the head of his cock to my entrance and work my way down on him, feeling him stretch my passage the deeper he goes. I can feel more of him this way.

Placing my hands on his thick thighs, I let my head fall back. I can feel my long hair tickle the base of my spine as we move in sync with each other. He takes hold of my hips and slowly but forcefully starts rocking with me. My swollen clit rubs up against him as he takes control. I feel his warm, moist mouth close around my nipple. He gently takes it into his mouth, sucking and kissing and licking, while his other hand kneads my other breast.

I whimper quietly as he moans around my nipple. The vibration of the sound over my sensitive skin makes my body quicken and I feel my core tighten around him. My breathing becomes heavier and our bodies move a little faster against each other.

Tristan's hand wraps itself in my hair. I really can't even feel the dull pain of my stomach. My body soaking in all this pleasure has taken over. Suddenly, I tighten around his cock and my vision blurs.

Everything I Want

I hold my breath as my orgasm rips right through my body, trying to diminish the intense pleasure. Crushing my lips to his, his tongue forces its way in and out, then back in again as I cry out my orgasm inside of his mouth.

He pulls his head away as I come down, kissing and sucking and biting gently on my collarbone. Moments later he starts thrusting deeper and deeper inside of me, then he stills and lets go of his own release.

Holding me in place on top of him, we lie there like that for I don't know how long. I feel the warm ooze spilling out as he softens inside me.

He falls back onto the bed with his arms stretched out on either side of him. His eyes are closed, but he has a huge, satisfied grin on his face. I gingerly try to lift off of him, cupping myself the best I can so I don't get this shit all over him or the bed. Once I'm off, I bend over and grab a hand towel off the hook on the wall and wipe myself with it. I'm so sensitive down there right now that I wouldn't be able to stand any more stimulation.

Tristan perches up on his forearms and checks me out.

"That was a fucking nice way to be woken up in the morning. I think I might be in your bed every night from now on with that kind of wake up call."

He's teasing me right now, so I take the towel and toss it at him. He dodges his head to the side and misses being hit with it.

Pulling out the sleep shirt I had laid out on my bags, I slip it on.

"Yeah, that was okay, wasn't it?" I smile at him, teasing him back. Pulling up some sweats, I grab for my toiletries bag. "Um . . . I think I should go take a shower."

He smiles and crosses his arms behind his head, lacing his fingers together.

"Sure. Do you want company?" He raises an eyebrow at me.

"No. No, that's okay. I think it would be, um, well . . . Better if you just stay in here for now."

"What do you mean, 'better?'"

His tone is still playful. Holy shit, I can't get over this right now. It's like our friendship or whatever you would fucking call it has just done a complete 180. And the thing is . . .

I like this.

"You know damn well what I mean, Tristan." Placing my one hand on my hip, I try to seem serious. "We go in there together, the guys will probably wake up to us—"

"Fucking in the shower."

Wow, he's so blunt and says it so casually. I can feel my cheeks heat up. Once again, thank God I have tanned skin.

"Yeah, I guess you could say that."

He starts laughing.

"Yeah, I suppose you're right. After all, you can't keep those tiny hands off of me."

I roll my eyes at him.

"Oh, okay. You're so right," I agree jokingly, then I turn and walk out of the door, tiptoeing my way down the tiny hall.

I take a quick shower, because first, the bus doesn't hold water hot for very long, and second, doesn't hold too much water at all, at that. I'm pretty sure the rest of the guys won't even shower. Well, maybe Tristan and Jared will. Yes, definitely Jared.

When I climb out, I hastily dry myself off and dress in jeans with no holes in them this time. Wow! I can't believe I actually own a pair like this. But they're nice and make my ass look great. Then I pull over a thin, long-sleeved heather gray thermal. Simple, but it makes me feel cozy and the color goes nicely with my eyes.

I grab my hair brush when I'm done brushing my teeth and just comb through once. No need to do anything with it today. I have no idea when and where we're stopping. For that matter, I don't even know what state we're in right now. Which reminds me. I should ask Tristan why he's here, anyways. I mean, I know why; obviously me. But I really want to know more about it.

Tristan is still gloriously naked when I return to my little cove, sprawled out on my bed. He's still wearing a full blown smile though. I can't help but feel a little shy, and turn away.

"Are you, um . . . going to shower or something?" I ask.

He chuckles and his mouth goes up higher in one corner.

"Why, Sophia? Are you uncomfortable with me here like this?"

Looking back at him, I shrug my shoulders, trying to play it cool.

"No, of course not."

Yeah, a little.

"Just thought, I don't know . . ." I gesture my hand up and down his mammoth body. "What if one of the guys comes busting through the door and sees you like this?"

Good one. He looks up at the ceiling and stretches, and I suddenly feel heat building in my core again.

He exhales and climbs to his feet. He has to crouch down a bit when standing in the bus.

"Yeah, I guess you're right."

He slips his jeans on with no boxers and walks past me, turning around and giving me one more full blown smile.

"Do you mind if I shower?"

I shake my head no at him and he turns and walks out. I'm so giddy right now I feel like shoving my face into my pillow and screaming in it. What the fuck, am I in high school again? Being with Tristan like this sure makes me feel that way, though. I decide to grab my iPad and go on Netflix. I come across Bill and Ted's Bogus Journey. Ooh, that's a good one. I click on it.

Tristan walks in five minutes later, jeans hung low, showing off his V. His hair is wet and brushed back off his face. He looks like he's some kind of model or something.

"What are we watching?" he asks me as he climbs in bed beside me, wrapping one arm across my shoulders, pulling me into him.

"Bill and Ted's Bogus Journey," I smile up at him.

He shakes his head a little and laughs again.

"Shit, I haven't seen that movie since I was in junior high."

"Oh, I love it. When I was younger I had the hugest crush on Ted."

He gives me this look like, *Really?* and I can't help but laugh back at him.

"Hey, I couldn't help it. Ted was the cooler one, if you ask me."

"Oh, fuck," he lets out, and rolls his eyes.

Everything I Want

We watch all of the movie, Tristan poking fun at some parts and myself defending it. When it's over, I hear some of the guys waking up and rustling around out front. I look up at Tristan, who's already staring down at me.

"Are you hungry?" I ask and his eyes darken again.

"Yes."

I feel like there's more behind his simple response. Easing myself out of his hold, I decide that now is a good time to ask him what he's doing here.

"Tristan?" I suddenly feel nervous, fidgeting in my spot. But he's still just lying there looking calm. "Wh— Why are you here?"

I'm having a hard time getting this out. I look down at my hands that are in my lap. I can feel his eyes on me, watching every move I make.

"I thought it was pretty obvious," he says matter-of-factly.

I look back up at him, and his gaze is intense.

"I— I know, but you were given a break. You should've taken it."

Breathe, Sophia! I don't know why, but I feel my stomach roll, in a good, excited way.

"I wanted to be with you. You didn't want to come with me, so ... And after last night you bet your ass that now I'm not leaving your side on this tour. No one touches you. Anyone were to ever lay a hand on you again, whether it be hurtful or sexual, I'll kill 'em."

Wow! His words send me for a loop. He has so much control right now I don't really know what to think of it. Part of me is flattered and turned on, but the other part is scared and unsure of it.

"What do you mean, 'sexual?'"

I quirk my eyebrow up at him, crossing my arms. His smile returns.

"You know exactly what I mean. You're mine, and no one lays a finger on you."

"How can I be yours? We've only fucked a few times."

When the words come out of my mouth, I instantly regret them. Tristan's face hardens and he gently pulls me to him, making sure not to hurt my already bruised stomach. I feel his mouth on the top of my head.

"The moment I first laid eyes on you, I knew you were mine."

Then he tilts my chin and kisses me. Hard.

We feverishly start making out, rubbing our hands up and down each other's bodies, when suddenly, I hear a knock at the door.

"You all right, Sophia?"

It's Roger! He must not know that Tristan is here. Well, Tristan had to see someone to get on the bus last night. Roger must've been passed out or something.

"Yep!" is all I can get out, my voice breaking a bit from our passionate kiss.

"All right. You coming out for breakfast? We're stopping in ten minutes."

"Yeah, be right out."

Tristan's hand is still feeling me up as I talk to Roger, and I hurry and slap it away.

"What are you doing?" I whisper-yell at him.

He smiles and shrugs his shoulders.

Everything I Want

"I was touching your perfect tits."

I push myself off of him and he laughs louder than before.

"Does anyone know you're here?"

"Yeah, Matt and Cory. Why?"

"I don't know, maybe I thought you just . . . I don't know . . . sneaked your way onto the bus."

Shaking his head, he stands to unzip his pants and my eyes fall right on his erection. Again?

"Calm down, Sophia. Just getting my boxers on. I don't think it would be a good idea to fuck right now. After all, your band is up now."

I throw a pillow at him. He's turned this around as if I started this. Well, maybe the morning one, yes, but he was the one that couldn't keep his hands off me just now. He laughs in my face again and gets dressed.

When I feel the bus stop, I open the door and look up at Tristan nervously. His eyes are kind and soft.

"What do I tell them?" I whisper.

"Tell them whatever you want," he says back to me.

I don't know, but right now I feel very small. I mean, I know they know we have a little something going on, but Tristan being here with me on the road for the next few days, without his band? That kind of says that we're more than fuck buddies. And I don't really know what yet.

I see Cory in the hallway and he glances at Tristan, then me.

"What up?" he says as he goes through the bathroom door, obviously not giving a shit. Jared is leaning against the sink, stirring his coffee. His smile is warm and playful. Aw, my. My sweet Jared. But then I hear Roger gasp.

"Holy fucking shit!"

Roger gets up and does that half-handshake, half-hug thing with Tristan.

"Thought you'd be in Seattle by now."

Tristan shrugs his shoulders and looks back at me, smiling.

"Change of plans, I guess." He faces Roger again. "You know how it is."

"No, he doesn't," Jared pipes in.

I giggle at his remark, and Roger flips him off.

"Fuck you, man. Why don't you go and spike your hair or some shit," Roger calls back.

Tristan takes hold of my hand in front of everyone, and I feel my cheeks warm up again. He doesn't care what any of them think. He walks us over to the sofa as we wait for the bus doors to open.

"You fucking nailed that guy last night, man. Shit!" Roger says.

I still at the thought as it crosses my mind again, and Tristan can tell that my body tenses. He rubs his thumb over my knuckles, trying to soothe me, and shrugs his shoulders, playing it off as nothing.

"Whatever, man. I've seen a couple of bar fights in Detroit and I've never seen anything like that before. That. Was. Awesome."

"Shut up, man!" Cory walks back out. "He would've never had to have done that if we didn't have our heads in our asses."

I instantly feel remorse, putting my head down. That this was all because of me makes me feel sick.

Roger tries to speak and looks down at me.

"Shit. I'm sorry, Sophia," he says, but I raise my hand to stop him from going on.

"Don't worry about it. Shit happens. It's no one's fault."

I just want to leave this spot right now. Tristan's grip on my hand tightens even more. Hearing the hydraulics from the brakes as the doors open, I feel relieved.

Chapter Twenty-Seven

It's already been two days, and we're almost to Seattle. Tristan and I have been low key pretty much this whole time, only really talking to the guys when we're stopping somewhere.

Other than that, we've just been back in my little area, fucking and watching movies. That's it. But it feels completely amazing. I love being with Tristan and that scares the shit out of me. This world we're living in is only temporary and I know it's going to end sooner than later. The tour is already half over.

Arriving in Seattle, Tristan's phone has been blowing up with calls and texts from Lux. He wants everyone in both bands to meet him at the hotel first before going to the arena.

Once we arrive at the hotel, I grab my belongings and stuff them into my bag. Tristan grabs his bag and reaches over to grab mine from me. Another simple gesture that I love.

Walking off the bus, Tristan grabs a hold of my elbow, stopping me. I turn around and look back up at him.

"What is it?" I ask.

He leans in and kisses me softly before releasing me.

"Stay with me tonight. In my suite."

I smile at him, then look back at the guys walking in, not even waiting for me. They probably know I'm in safe hands with Tristan. Turning back to face him I know I should start putting some distance between us. But I can't. Or I don't want to.

"Sure," is all I say and the corners of his mouth lift up. He drapes his arm over my shoulder as we walk in, carrying both of our bags in his other hand.

Lux is in the lobby and I still at the look on his face. Tristan doesn't notice or doesn't care. His arm is still draped over me.

Lux walks in front of us.

"The conference room. Now!" he says in a low voice.

Shit! I actually feel worried or something, like a teenager that got caught cheating on a test or got picked up by the cops. I sweat a little as we make our way to the conference room. The rest of the guys from both bands are sitting at the table.

"What, no food?" Roger jokes but Lux raises his hand to him.

"Not. Now," he says as he rounds the table.

Tristan and I take the only seats left; at the front, right in front of Lux, of course.

Tristan's legs are too long to fit underneath comfortably, so he pushes his chair back and sits lazily in it, folding his arms over his chest. He looks so calm and cool right now, like some bad boy. But I, on the other hand, am sitting straight up with my fingers laced and palms down on the table, trying to look proper and shit.

Lux pulls a few magazines out of his briefcase and slams them down in front of Tristan.

"What the fuck were you fucking thinking?"

Holy shit! I've never heard Lux say those words before, much less yell them, for that matter. I jump as he slams the magazines down, but Tristan doesn't budge, doesn't even bat an eyelash. Isn't he going to check them out? Lux's face is mad. I see Caleb's fingers dancing across the table to pull one to him, but Lux slaps his hand down on top of it, stopping him. Caleb starts laughing a little and Lux turns his glare to him.

"This is not a fucking joke. Do you guys have any idea what the media has been saying since Minneapolis? Do you?"

He looks around at all of us and notices me just sitting there. My tan skin must be pale because I feel like the shit has been literally scared out of me. Lux's face relaxes a bit.

"I'm sorry, Sophia. What happened to you that night was awful, and I'm so sorry for you," he says with sympathy before glancing back at Tristan. "But you can't just fuck someone up when they do something to piss you off. You're lucky that guy isn't going to take your ass to court. Believe me, he's already tried. I got my attorneys on it yesterday. Someone recorded him on their phone hitting Sophia."

He nods over to me.

"But now, some of those fucking magazines are making you look like you go nuts on your fans for no reason. You have an image to uphold, and you must think before you act out, in any circumstances."

Lux looks back over at me and I feel so embarrassed.

"I'm not going to let some motherfucker touch her and get away with it, Lux. You'd be out of your goddamn mind if you think I'm just going to fucking sit back."

Tristan's voice is starting to get that dangerous edge to it again. Lux looks down and shakes his head before looking back up.

"Tristan, you keep doing this shit, you might as well kiss your career goodbye. Like I said, good thing someone recorded this shit, because soon that footage will get out and shut those magazines up. But if it ever happens again, it will just look like you're one angry son of a bitch. Sophia, from here on out, you will have your own bodyguard with you now, so hopefully none of this shit happens again."

Everything I Want

Tristan sits up suddenly.

I shake my head at Lux. I don't want some guy following me around everywhere I go!

Maybe you should've thought of that before going into this career, I think to myself. Shit.

Saying nothing, I look back down at the table. I can't argue with him.

"Maybe you should've fucking done that before. You've seen how popular she was getting on the internet. Of course some fucking psycho was going to come out."

Tristan's voice is eerily calm.

The internet? Yes! I totally forgot to see what the reviews on the band are. Every time I would remember to do so, I would get . . . sidetracked.

"Well, I can't go back into the past; I can only try to make it better." Lux looks at the rest of my guys. "And you guys be careful out there, too. Just because you're men doesn't mean some idiot won't try something. After this tour is over, we will get you guys set up, too."

We finish our meeting and I slowly stand up, feeling light headed from all of what just happened. I could so go for a joint right about now to calm my nerves. Tristan grabs my hand and we start walking out when I hear Lux clear his throat. Both of us turn around. Lux stands there with his arms crossed.

"If you guys are . . ." He gestures to us. "Something . . . Well, be prepared for that backlash, too. You should really turn it down a notch if this isn't serious."

Lux's words come back to me later as I'm sitting on Tristan's bed. I can't stop myself from wondering what in the hell we are doing. I feel like I'm causing more harm than good to us, and to the rest of the guys. I didn't even think of the tabloid shit.

Quickly pulling out my phone, I skim through some articles. I don't have time for the ones that give positive reviews about my band, or the negative ones, either. After browsing for a few minutes, Tristan walks back into the bedroom, but I don't notice. My eyes are glued to the screen of my phone and my mouth pops open. There are pictures of Tristan carrying me, passed out, down a hallway with nothing but my bra on.

Shit! Must've been that night he was bringing me back to my room after the drunken 'Cherry Pie' incident. There's another picture of us at the pub in downtown Minneapolis with me sprawling across the pool table. I didn't mean for it to be sexual or anything. I just wanted to get a damn shot. But they sure made it look different. The captions with those pictures aren't great, either. First I'm some drunken groupie, then the next says, "Sophia Ariel of Dollar Settlement laying herself out for Tristan Scott, lead singer of Undead Society."

Tristan notices my reaction to my phone and grabs it from me. He looks down at it for only a moment then tosses it down on the bed.

"Don't read that shit," he says to me and walks over to place his phone on the iDock he has set up.

He presses a few buttons then turns around, facing me again. Stone Sour's 'Wicked Game' remake begins to play, but I can't shake the images of my photos on the internet. He saunters over to me and I can't help but gaze up at him. He takes my hands and brings me to my feet. Grabbing the hem of my shirt, he lifts it up and over my head. Now we're both just standing there, shirtless and staring at each other. The nerves I had from a moment ago are completely gone and new, excited ones take over.

Everything I Want

He places one hand on my waist and brings me close to him, and his other hand tucks a few strands of my fallen hair behind my ear. My hardening nipples rub against the strict confinement of my bra.

Tristan pulls me even closer to him and I rest my cheek on his chest. I close my eyes and hold on to the back of shoulders, as we slowly move to the song. I feel his warm breath on top of my head, ruffling my hair slightly. He starts to sing the song to me softly. I hold him tighter, feeling butterflies taking flight in my stomach. At least right now I can pretend that everything will be all right and none of that shit matters . . . that Tristan will always be there.

He tilts my chin up to meet his gaze. He looks so beautiful right now, but his eyes have this lost look in them. His breathing picks up, and then he leans down and kisses me. Opening my mouth up for him, his tongue enters, stroking mine sensually. His taste is so incredible. I feel like I could get drunk or high off of it. I wrap my arms around his neck and stand on my tip toes. He picks me up and carries me over to the bed, laying me down gently.

"You're so beautiful, Sophia," he whispers against my lips before kissing me again.

His hand caresses every inch of me as it works its way down my jeans. Too involved in our kiss, I don't realize that my pants come off. Tristan pulls himself off of me and kneels down at the foot of the bed. Taking hold of my thighs, he pulls them apart. Resting up on my elbows, I watch him. He starts kissing the apex of my thigh, working his way to my center, slowly torturing me with feather light kisses and nibbles. Then I feel his hot breath on my swollen clit and he carefully pulls it into his mouth, gently licking and sucking on it before he slowly starts to lick the entire length of me. I moan softly and my head falls back, closing my eyes tightly.

"Look at me," Tristan growls, and I lift my heavy head back up.

Even my eyelids are weighed down right now. I see my arousal on his lips and chin, and I want to look away again. But he doesn't let me. He holds my gaze with his as he takes me with his mouth again.

"Mmm . . . You taste so fucking sweet, my girl."

And with those words, and his breath speaking right onto my most sensitive part, I come for him. He laps up my orgasm with his tongue inside me. Without my realizing it, he has unhooked my bra. I feel his tongue licking around my nipples, taking each one into his mouth. When he is done with both, he starts kissing his way up. Moist, hot trails trace up my collarbone and then the nape of my neck.

Finally he reaches my mouth, and I gently suck on his tongue. Tasting the sweet, musky taste of my arousal on him only turns me on even more. And I know it does the same for Tristan. His moan is deep and low in the back of his throat.

"Sophia," is all that he says before he thrusts hard into me.

"Ahh . . ."

I grip the sheets tightly, twisting my head up and to the side with my eyes closed tightly again.

"Open those beautiful blue eyes for me. I want every part of you aware of me inside that sweet pussy."

Sweat starts to bead at his temples. Looking into his eyes as I feel him tunnel in and out of me only makes me wetter. My stomach tightens with my arousal.

"Tristan, I— I—"

"What, baby?" He cuts me off and begins to thrust even harder.

I can't remember what I was going to say. This is unbelievably hot. Staring up at him like this, seeing him watching me right now, is only pushing me over the brink even faster. I can feel his cock hardening even more inside of me, and I love it. He keeps up his rhythm when he asks me again.

"What is it, Sophia?"

Shit! The way he says my name right now sends me over the edge. I close my eyes and let it take me. My blood runs hot and my muscles tighten around him.

"I'm not done yet, my girl. I'm going to take my time on this sweet pussy of yours tonight. I don't ever want this to end. You hear me? Never."

Tristan slows down the pace once he finds his release, and I feel his chest pressing down hard on my breasts. I can feel another orgasm starting to build deep in me again as I try to catch my breath from my last one. Something about his words sends me instantly to a place of ecstasy.

Lying there in bed with his arms wrapped around me, holding me close to his chest, I inhale deeply. Taking his scent in, I'm filled with this strange feeling of hope. Hope that maybe Tristan and I could possibly be able to make this work. And I find that thought very comforting. I also find it very frightening.

Trying to push the negative thoughts to the back of my mind, I just try to enjoy this moment that I have with him right now. Tristan uses his fingertips to gently caress up and down my spine.

"What are you thinking?" he asks me.

Looking up at him, I smile. Should I really tell him what I was thinking? Or maybe I should keep certain parts out.

"I'm thinking about how nice this is. You know, being here, right now, with you . . ."

I decide to just get it off my chest. Hell, we've been getting a lot closer these past few days since Minneapolis, even if it's only all the fucking we've been doing. But now it seems more . . . more *meaningful*, I guess. Tristan smiles and bends over to kiss my forehead. He holds his lips there for a few moments before leaning back against the headboard.

"Good. I was thinking the same thing too," he says calmly.

I can't believe we're even here like this right now. Propping myself up on one elbow, I stare at him. My hair falls down all around me, covering my breasts.

"Tristan? What are we . . . or, um . . . What is going to happen?"

He looks at me in puzzlement, like I've grown a third eye or something. Great! Shouldn't have said a thing. Now he probably thinks I'm one of those clingers or something. Tristan interrupts my thoughts.

"Like with us?"

Nodding my head, I lay back down and pull the sheet over my body. But Tristan grabs my hand and stops me from covering myself. His eyes are soft and dark.

"What do you want, Sophia?" he asks me.

Leaning on my back and looking up at the ceiling, I say the first thing that comes in my head.

"I don't know, exactly."

There, the truth. I really don't know what else to say right now. Part of me was hoping he had a better answer.

"You don't know?" There's some amusement in his voice. "What is that supposed to mean?"

I roll over on my side and rest my elbow on the bed again.

"This tour is going to be over soon."

"So . . ." Tristan says, kind of wondering where I'm going with this.

"So . . . you're going over to Europe for another couple of months, and I'm going back to LA to start promoting my first album."

Tristan is staring at me intently now, his eyes not leaving mine. Not even blinking. So I continue.

"I just don't know if this—" I gesture with my free hand between our bodies. "—is going to work out to be anything serious. Maybe some kind of friendship could."

At my last words, Tristan's old mask comes back on, hardening up right in front of me. That mysterious dark side of him that I remember seeing when I first met him is back. Shit! I pissed him off.

"I mean . . ." I try a different approach, but I already think the damage is done. "What do you want?"

Tristan's staring at me, only his eyes showing me any kind of emotion.

"Please talk to me."

I'm now kneeling naked in front of him, but he still doesn't say anything.

I roll my eyes at him. I'm getting frustrated; then, right when I turn to look away, he breaks his silence.

"I want you, Sophia. Just you. I can't explain it and I don't want to. I just know that part of me needs you and I don't want to let you go."

His words pull at my insides, making my heart literally feel like it's burning. This gorgeous, mysterious man wants me, and I'm pretty much not letting him have me. What the fuck is wrong with me? A few years ago I would have jumped all over this opportunity, but now my career is just starting to take off. I don't know if I can.

Taking a hold of his hand, I gently squeeze it.

"Tristan, I think maybe it's best if we just keep having fun right now. I know I was asking what we were. But I think it's better this way, you know? You're busy with your own tour and life and I'm just getting started."

His eyes grow darker than before and he pulls his hand out of mine.

"What?" I ask, kind of annoyed. "I mean, look. We hang out a few times and the tabloids are already jumping on us—"

"I don't give a fuck about the tabloids!" he shouts. "I don't give a fuck about anything else but you!"

He's seriously trying to break me right now, isn't he?

"Tristan, come on. We've only known each other for a short time. How?"

He reaches out and pulls me close to him again.

"Sophia, I've been with many women before. And no one— I mean, no one! Has ever made me feel remotely the way you have these last few weeks. Shit. Since I first laid eyes on you."

With my head held to his chest, I let out a sigh.

"Tristan, I think we should just be friends right now. I'm sorry."

Everything I Want

His grip grows tighter around me, holding me. I can almost feel pain in the way he starts to breathe. I know after this that I shouldn't be staying the night with him, so I try to pull myself free. But he doesn't let me go.

"Tristan, please," I quietly beg him.

"Why are you doing this, Sophia?"

He gently pushes me off of him. I fall back on the bed. I'm shocked that he just did that to me. He stands and walks over to retrieve his jeans from the floor. I'm lying there naked and exposed. I know I should be covering myself right now, but I can't move. After Tristan zips up his jeans he bends down and grabs mine and throws them at me. Reaching out, I catch them before they whip my face. Okay, now I'm pissed.

Standing up abruptly, I haul my jeans on, not caring that I have no panties on. After I'm done with that, he throws my shirt at me, and when I grab it with one hand, I flip him off with the other. That sends him over the edge.

Tristan pounces at me, but I quickly dart out of his way.

"Fuck you!" I scream at him. "You act like a dick to me one minute, then try to come after me the next? You're so fucked up," I say more calmly to him as I put my shirt on. Tristan stands there, clenching his jaw.

"You want this, Sophia? You really fucking want this to end before it even had a chance to go somewhere?"

Looking at him, I say nothing. My face is as plain and emotionless as his once was.

I nod my head at him and his face drops. Hurt and pain steal over his broad features.

"Tristan . . . It's just not the time right now. I'm sorry."

He says nothing more to me; instead, he walks away and picks up his shirt and slams his bedroom door. Moments later I hear the main suite door slam. And he's gone.

Alone in his suite, I feel this incredible ache burrowing its way into my heart. My skin that once felt hot is now cold, and tears burn the back of my eyes. Shit! I gotta get out of here. Now.

Bending over to grab the rest of my things, I walk out into the living area and get my bag from the table. I didn't get my room key, so I guess I'll just text Frankie. I need somewhere to go, because I doubt that Tristan will want me to stay here now. I don't know why I said anything. I thought we should be open with each other, but I guess I was wrong. We were just starting to get somewhere, too. Fuck me!

Chapter Twenty-Eight

Walking out of his room, I head for the elevators, texting Frankie on my way.

Hey! Where you at?

A minute later, he replies.

In my room sweetie. What's up?

I step into the elevator and before pressing what floor I text him back again.

I need to crash with you tonight.

A second later, he replies.

Meet me in the hotel bar . . . NOW!

After a few drinks, I explain everything to Frankie. He sits there silently, listening to everything I have to say without judging. It feels so good to get this all off my chest.

Biting my lip, I wait for him to say something. He just twirls his drink straw around in his Roman coke, then picks it up and sips on it, holding the straw with his delicate pinky sticking out. Come on, Frankie! Say something, anything. Placing his drink back down, he looks me square in the eyes.

"Listen, girl. What I have to say, I mean with all the upmost respect to you, okay?"

"Okay," I say back nervously.

"I've been in LA and on this scene for quite a while now, and from Tristan's point of view, I can see where he's coming from. I can also see where you're coming from. But what I think is, it's not about the busy schedules or the fucking tabloids."

Everything I Want

He stops and takes another drink, and I lean in closer, resting my chin in my hand.

"Honestly, I think it's you being afraid, my dear."

What? Afraid of fucking what?

Frankie's face is stern looking, as if he was some professor that just threw a curveball on an exam at me or something.

"Frankie that's—"

"That's what? Think about it. You told me you've only been in three other relationships, right? Only three, but in each one you had your heart broken some way or another. I think you're trying to beat the punch on this one. Stopping it before it has a chance to grow."

I roll my eyes at him. Now it's time for me to take a drink. I grab my beer and finish it off.

Frankie reaches over and takes hold of my hands, stretching my arms across the table. His eyes are sincere right now, and as I think about what he just said, I guess he's right. I mean, I don't know how we're going to make this work if it *is* something, but I know I should at least try. I do care about him.

"You're right," I say quietly, casting my eyes down at the table.

Looking back up at him, Frankie looks shocked.

"I— I am?"

His response makes me smile. He's a very good friend, and in this case, he's dead-on. I just needed to let down the wall that I had built up for so long, I guess.

"Yeah, you're right. I should at least see if this could go somewhere."

Frankie lets go of my hands and reaches in his back pocket, pulling out his wallet. He lays a few bills on the table then pulls out his room key and hands it to me.

"Here, just in case you need this tonight. I'm on the seventh floor, room 709."

Taking the card from him, I check to make sure I still have Tristan's room key. And I do.

It's pretty late now. Frankie and I have been down here for a few hours, so I hope Tristan's not sleeping. I just hope he's even there.

Standing up, I walk around the table and give Frankie a quick hug.

"See you tomorrow," I say to him as I head out of the bar.

"Good luck!" he yells back.

Once the elevator opens up to the penthouse floor, I hear loud music coming from down the hall. It kind of sounds like Mudvayne's 'Happy.' I notice the guy that usually stands in front of Tristan's door sometimes isn't there. But that's definitely where the music is coming from.

My hands shake with nerves as I slide the card down. When the green light flicks, I press the door open slowly, peeking my head in. The music is so loud that I'm surprised the other guests aren't complaining. Actually, I think they reserved this whole floor for Tristan and his crew.

Still, I tiptoe my way through the room and it looks like a party has taken place. You would've thought that it would still be going on, though? I mean, these guys can party 'til the early morning hours. I see what looks like coke and pot on the tables and empty beer and mini shot bottles litter the floor. As I step up to Tristan's door, this shiny metallic paper catches my eye.

Everything I Want

Bending down, I pick it up. Rubbing the ends with my fingers, my gut drops. It's a condom wrapper! And not just any, but a magnum. Tristan's never used condoms with me, which is so bad on my part, but I do know that if he were to use one, then this probably would be it.

My blood starts to run hot through my veins and my stomach feels like I'm about to go on the biggest roller coaster of my life. I'm so scared to open this door right now, but now that I'm here, I kind of have to.

Squeezing the handle, I twist the knob slowly. The room is dark with only a flicker of the TV on. And that's when I see him and her . . .

My heart stops beating. Tristan and some Pamela-Anderson-from-the-nineties looking bitch are going at it. Tears sting my eyes as they burn down my cheeks. He has her bent over the side of the bed, and he's fucking her hard. I can't fucking believe this! He was just with me a few hours ago, and he's already with someone else!

Rage takes over me. Rage like I have never felt before, and I notice that bitch's heels lying on the floor. Seven-inch hooker heels. I bend down and pick it up, throwing it at him as hard as I can.

The heel hits Tristan dead on the side of his head and falls on top of the bitch.

"What the fuck?" she says slow and breathlessly.

Tristan jerks his head up and stops, staying still inside of her as he sees me standing in the doorway.

"Fuck you," I choke out, then I'm off as fast as I can go.

"Fuck!" Tristan yells. "Sophia!"

I slam the door shut and sprint down the hall to the elevators, more tears streaming down my face.

I press the call button fifty times in hopes that the more I hit it, the faster it will arrive.

I feel like bending over and throwing up all over the place. Did that really just happen? I can't believe this! This is just some fucked-up dream. It has to be!

The elevator door finally opens and I look over my shoulder to see Tristan running down the hall after me, wearing only a towel.

"Sophia!" he yells at me again, and I jump onto the elevator, hitting the seventh floor then fumbling with shaky fingers to hold down the close doors button.

The doors are only an inch from closing when I catch a glimpse of Tristan, out of breath, stopping in front of it. He notices my tears, but I raise my middle finger up at him, shaking my head.

I fall back onto the wall once I know that I'm safe from him right now. I cover my face with my hands and sob into them. I can't believe I'm fucking crying. I told him I just wanted to be friends; well, he definitely took that to heart. But the truth is, I want more.

I hope to God that he doesn't figure out that I'm in Frankie's room tonight. I only have a few more floors to go then I know I'm safe for the night for sure.

I hate him. I fucking hate him. I hate that I ever let the piece of shit lay his hands on me and make me feel safe.

I'm on the seventh floor now, and I look out of the elevator both ways to make sure Tristan didn't take the stairs or something. Good to go. I quickly scan the hall for Frankie's room.

709— there it is! I start pounding on the door as if some murderer were coming after me.

Frankie opens up the door with a toothbrush still in his mouth when his face drops.

Everything I Want

"What the fuck happened?"

He grabs me by the shoulders and pulls me into his room. And I can't help it. I let out a sob again. I hate that I'm acting like such a little bitch. What I really want to do right now is go back there and kick his ass and that whore's ass, too. I'm so angry and upset that I clench my fingers in my hands so tightly that my nails break my skin.

Frankie comes over and rubs my back.

"Shh . . ." he whispers in my ear. "Calm down, sweetie."

But I can't. I'm seeing red, and all I can do is freak out or cry. Being with Frankie right now, I decide on crying.

"I'm going to get something. Be right back. Here, take a seat."

He helps me over to his bed, and gently eases me down on it.

I grab hold of the pillow and start wringing my fingers through it. Pulling and stretching at it as if it were Tristan's face.

By the time Frankie returns to the room, I have managed to stop my tears.

"Sorry. It must have been the fucking beers that got me so emotional."

Frankie walks over and sits beside me on the bed.

"It's all right," he says softly, but I shake my head at him.

"No, it's not. I shouldn't be acting this way. I fucking barely know the guy. Who cares who he fucks?"

Frankie's eyes have pity in them. Pity that I don't want. He pulls out a joint and lights it up. Taking only one quick hit, he passes it to me. With still shaky hands, I take the joint from him and bring it up to my mouth, inhaling deeply as if somehow it will erase everything.

We sit there in silence smoking the joint until it is down to a roach. All I feel now is exhausted. My adrenaline has come down and the high is taking me over.

"What happened?" Frankie asks, finally breaking the silence.

I let out a scoff, not being able to grasp any words. I lick my lips; my mouth is so dry.

"I went up there. To talk to him. And—"

I hate this. All it's doing is bringing everything back into full view. Closing my eyes, I finish telling him.

"I went to his room to talk to him, and he was right in the middle of fucking some whore. She was bent over the bed, and he was pounding her."

Frankie brings both of his hands up to cover his now opened mouth.

"So I threw her hooker shoe at him and ran out. He tried to yell after me. As if I was going to fucking stop!"

"Oh, my God!"

Nodding my head, I pull back the duvet and climb into bed fully clothed. I'm done with this day and I just want to go to sleep now.

"What the fuck?" Frankie yells in his feminine voice. "Are you fucking kidding me?"

Laying down now, I reach over and turn the bedside light off. Not saying another word.

"That prick!"

I close my eyes, hoping that Frankie will just stop, but he doesn't.

Everything I Want

"If he comes here tonight . . ." Frankie stands now with one hand on his hip and the other using his finger pointing down. "I'm going to kick his whore ass!"

The thought of Frankie attacking Tristan makes me cackle. Yes, it would be nice seeing Tristan get hit right now, but I don't think Frankie stands a chance with him. Aw, my, though. At least he cares.

"Good night, Frankie," I whisper and roll over to my side.

I feel Frankie's lips by my ear.

"Night, girl. Remember I'm right over there if you need me."

With that he kisses my ear and walks over to the second bed in his room.

I awake in the night with a text. I jerk out of my dreamless sleep from the vibration of my phone going off in my back pocket. I pull the phone out and toss it to the ground, not caring because I know it's probably from Tristan. I roll back over trying to get comfortable again, but I can't, tossing and turning for the rest of the night with images of him and her in my head.

It feels like I just fell back asleep when Frankie starts nudging me.

"Wake up, girl. You have to get to the arena."

Moaning, I use my arm to cover my eyes. He must have opened the curtains, because light is filling the room.

"Come on, girl. It's already one o'clock. The boys are downstairs waiting for you. I'll be right over. I'm getting there early so I can be with you while you're setting up, okay?"

I'm still in the same clothes from last night, and I haven't showered. Great. Picking myself up, I glance around the room for my bag, which Frankie had set on top of the dresser.

"Tell them I'll be down in ten. I need to grab a quick shower first."

Frankie nods and gets up. Pulling his phone out of his back pocket, he calls one of the guys and leaves the room.

Feeling groggy from the restless sleep, I stumble my way to the bathroom. Closing the door behind me, I start the shower and strip out of my clothes. My skin burns everywhere that Tristan has touched me, and I need to scrub it off.

Climbing into the shower, I lather up my hair. Rinsing it under the hot water, I turn and grab the washcloth and pour some body wash onto it. I scrub myself so hard that my tan skin actually turns red. It could also be from the scalding water I'm standing in. My body doesn't feel it, though. I'm numb.

When I'm done with my shower, I dress quickly and brush my teeth. Jeans, t-shirt, and my hair pulled back into a sloppy bun. I don't care about putting on makeup. Just being clean is good enough for me.

Stepping back into the room, I notice all my boys are in there waiting for me. They all have pity in their eyes.

"What the fuck, Frankie?" I glare at him.

I can't believe he told them. Shit! Frankie shrugs his shoulders and looks down.

"I'm sorry, hun. But they thought something happened to you. Normally, you're never late."

Cory walks over and takes my bag from my hands and heads out of the room.

Matt steps in front of Frankie and says, "Don't worry about it, Sophia. We don't care . . . I mean, about him. You're better than that shit, anyways."

Everything I Want

He follows Cory out and all that's left is Jared and a very hung over-looking Roger. Jared says nothing, which I like right now, but walks over and squeezes me instead. Oh, my God, I want to die. It's really not a big deal, now that I think about it. I got screwed over. So what? I'll get over it. But come on. I don't need any pity.

When Jared leaves, Roger walks right up to me.

"You want me to kick his ass?"

I laugh at him. That's sweet and all, but Roger? He's so much like the protective big brother I never had. Thank God he's brought a genuine smile to my face. It actually feels good right now.

"No, Roger, I don't. I'm fine. Really."

"Well, if you want me to, I will. How can anybody hurt a sweet girl like you? If I didn't love you like a sis, you would be a great catch. Any guy can see that."

Roger's words touch me and I pat him on the shoulder.

"I'm okay. Now, let's go. Only eight more shows left and we got to kill 'em all."

"Fucking right! That's my girl."

Roger throws his arm around me and leads me out of the room.

"See you there, girl!" Frankie yells behind us.

I nod over my shoulder.

Sitting offstage, I watch the crew working. Thank God Undead is big and doesn't have to do this shit with us. I really don't know how I'm going to feel when I see Tristan later. I keep telling myself that this was just a few fucks' fling—what should I have expected?

Surprisingly, that seems to take the edge off. Yeah, fuck him! I will not yell or even exchange glares with him anymore. I will pretend that nothing ever happened between us. I know it's easier said than done, but hey, I have to try. It was my own stupid fault for getting such strong feelings right away.

"Sophia, you ready?" One of the crew members yells for me to sound check the mics and to see if I like the set up.

I do a quick scan of the set up, then I grab the mic and do some vocal warm ups to see how the mics sound with my voice. When I'm satisfied, I walk off the stage.

Frankie is waiting for me like he promised.

He wraps me up in a hug. I wish everyone would stop treating me like I just lost a relative or something, but I know the more I act like nothing is bothering me, the faster they will stop. Few long days, max.

"Girl, I have such a great costume for you tonight. I kind of got the inspiration when Holly Madison wore that peacock costume on that old show. Gawd that was a good show! They were all so funny," he giggles.

I quirk my eyebrow up at him.

"Wait a minute . . . You're going to make me wear feathers and shit?"

He shakes his head, laughing.

"No, silly. The colors. Oh, the colors! Deep blues and purples and green. The strapless corset with the sexy little short bottoms . . . You're gonna look smoking. And wait 'til you see what I have planned for your hair and makeup. We actually have to get started now, so come on."

He takes my hand and leads me to the back where they have a designated area blocked off for me. Frankie pulls up a chair and begins rolling curlers into my hair. "After all, it's almost Halloween.

Everything I Want

I figure we can dress you up tonight. I even got you a masquerade mask that looks so fucking hot!" he shrieks with excitement.

Frankie continues with my hair when I feel my phone go off again. Pulling it out, I see that I have four missed calls. All from my guys earlier and two missed texts. Both from Tristan.

The first one was sent at 2:45 a.m.

There are no words I can say.

Chapter Twenty-Nine

Rolling my eyes at such a shitty text, I scroll down to the next one he just sent me.

Please, Sophia. We need to talk!

Need to talk? Please! I set my phone down on the makeshift vanity Frankie has set up and lean back in my chair.

"Are any of the other guys partaking in this Halloween-style show?"

Frankie has this splitting grin going across his face.

"Maybe," is all he says.

What? He's up to something, I just know it.

"What do you mean, 'maybe?'"

I raise my left eyebrow at him, looking directly at him in the mirror.

"I just gave them a shout out this morning and told them that they had to wear masks, too. They were all for it. Well, not Roger, of course. But when I explained to him that their masquerade masks were more in a 'Slipknot' style, he was all for it. Yours my dear . . . yours is different. Edgy and completely sexy."

When Frankie is done with me, he spins me around in my chair to face the mirror. When I see myself, I go into shock. I look like I just stepped out of some mystical, sensual ball. My hair is full with these huge waves and my eyes are smoky with dark purple and blue and silver lining around. Teeny little gems are glued around the corners going down to my cheekbones. My lips are painted with this shiny deep plum lipstick.

Everything I Want

The outfit hugs every single curve of my body, with my breasts —like all the other costumes he's picked for me— bulging out. Really bulging, actually. I'm afraid that with one small move, nipples will be showing. My ass cheeks are peeking out of the thin black shorts he has me wearing. They're more like panties than anything else.

He hands me a pair of fingerless black elbow-length gloves to put on. Some parts of them have fabric missing which has been replaced with sheer black nylon. After I pull up the gloves, he turns around and opens an expensive-looking black box. Inside is the most beautiful mask that I have ever seen! Made up of velvet, it has the same deep, rich colors of my costume and makeup, with crystals lining the edges.

"One last touch," he says, then helps me get the mask on.

I feel incredibly sensual and powerful wearing this. For some reason, even with my entire body so exposed, when the mask is on, I feel protected. Shielded.

"Now, one more thing. To help loosen up your nerves."

Nerves? What nerves? As soon as he says that, Tristan comes to mind. Damn. I guess now I do feel some nerves. Tonight I will actually have to see him again. Shit! Thank God that we head straight for the bus after the show and hit the road to LA.

Frankie brings over two shot glasses filled with clear liquor.

"I don't want you ruining that beautiful lip job yet. So open your mouth and pour in."

"What?" I laugh.

"You heard me, girl. You need to look perfect. I mean you already are. But still, I just spent the last three hours on you, so . . . ."

Taking the glass from his hand, I cheers him without thinking of it and pour the liquid in my mouth. Wincing at the instant burn it has given me, I glare up at Frankie, who is laughing hard.

"What in the hell was that?" I stick out my tongue, trying to cool it off. "It tastes like rubbing alcohol."

Frankie is now laughing so hard that he's holding his gut.

"It's homemade moonshine! You love it?"

"How in the fuck did you come across this?"

"I have my ways. But give it time. You should be feeling pretty relaxed momentarily."

The sick thing is, he's right. When the burn finally subsides, my muscles feel much looser. Damn.

Exhaling, I turn and exit into the hall. Striding with a good pace, I hear my heels clicking against the tile. I finally notice my boys coming around the corner ahead of me and I smile in relief. They all stop and suddenly stare. I stop, too, and look behind me.

"What?" I say back to them when I see nothing behind me.

"Fucking eh, girl!" Roger exclaims and a slow smile creeps across my face.

Oh. I take it that I look damn fine. Good. This might sound petty, but if my own boys are reacting like this, then maybe someone else will, too. And right now nothing would give me more pleasure than to watch Tristan wriggle before me like a fucking worm on a hook. That also puts another devilish plan in my head. Okay, fucker, let's see how you can handle this extra little curve ball I'm going to throw at you tonight!

Walking up to them, I raise my hand.

"Hey, guys. Can we make a quick change to the ending tonight?"

Everything I Want

Approaching the stage, I still haven't run into Tristan yet. Which is kind of off because I always run into him before every performance. I hear the audience actually chanting our name.

"Dol-lar Set-tle-ment, Dol-lar Set-tle-ment!"

I can't believe this. We're actually starting to get recognized. I hope it's not from the video of me being gut punched. But it's still amazing hearing it come from thousands of people.

Right before I step onstage, I see Tristan standing off in the corner. His eyes drop and slowly rake up and down me. It's too dark where he's standing to get a good look at his face. Chills spread all over my skin.

I don't stand there long. I quickly pick up my pace and get up on stage. The lights are out, so no one in the audience can get a good look at me. Now that I'm up here, though, I feel an intense heat building up on my neck from Tristan's stare and I tremble.

Grabbing the mic, I get the whistle from Matt letting me know everything is all good. They play 'Everything Forgotten.' The lights beam softly onto the stage.

How ironically perfect of a song to start with.

The entire performance goes by in a complete blur. I would say a few things to the audience after every couple of songs, but nothing I really remembering doing. I don't think it's from the shot Frankie gave me, but that Tristan staring at me the entire time has me thrown off.

Finally I sing the last song of our set and the audience is clapping and whistling. I pick up the mic from the stand, raising my other arm up.

"You guys were awesome tonight. Thank you!" They start roaring even more. "I was wondering . . . would you guys mind if we do just one more for you?"

The audience grows louder, cheering and screaming. My stomach starts to flip with thousands of butterflies. I look over off the stage and Tristan takes a few steps closer. Oh my God! What is he doing? I hurry up and face the crowd again.

"Well, you see, it's not ours." I shrug my shoulders and smile. "But I fucking love this band so it would be an honor to play one of their songs."

With that being said I continue on.

"I've been called many things in my life, but never before was I called this. Well, until recently, on this tour. Hell, a couple of times this person dedicated one of their songs to me."

The arena goes still, and I finish up with what I need to say.

"I was called harlot!" My face breaks out into a splitting grin, and the audience starts cheering and whistling again. "Well, this last song I would like to dedicate to that motherfucker! We're going to do 'Whore' by In This Moment!"

Claps and cheers, screams and more whistles erupt from them.

I peek over my shoulder at Matt and nod to him, giving him his cue. The lights fall again and Matt starts to play with Cory.

Placing the mic back on the stand, I take hold of it with one hand while using the other to slowly caress the side of my upper body, swaying my hips slowly as I sing. The stand is right in between my legs positioned at a lazy angle.

Roger and Jared join in now, and we really jam. I place both hands on the mic now. I close my eyes tightly and grip the stand, pulling it down as I'm bending on top of it. I scream into the mic when the chorus comes.

The song is almost over, with only a minute or so left. I'm at the front of the stage, squatting down while singing one of the lyrics and slowly stand back up with my knees spread out to the sides. Kind of looks like some stripper move you'd see at a club, but hey. This song is called 'Whore' and that's pretty much how Tristan made me feel.

Fuck him. After the last couple of screams the song is done and I take a bow for the audience. The lights go and it's black everywhere again. All my guys walk up to me and we descend from the stage.

My nerves are back in full force again. I'm about to run into Tristan, and I have no clue what will happen. A couple of the Undead Society guys whistle, pulling me out of my thoughts. Looking over, I see Caleb and Ryan standing next to Tristan.

"Fucking badass woman!" Caleb says to me with his chin raised.

I give him a quick smile and turn to face Lux, making sure to not make any eye contact with Tristan. I feel safe because he won't just come up and try to explain his sorry self to me. I have all my guys around me, like I'm in my own little fortress.

Lux's face has this surprised look on it, as if he's seeing me for the first time or some shit. Maybe I should tell Frankie to tone it down on the sex appeal for the next show. Pulling the mask free from my face, I blink up at him.

"Wow," Lux says. "Great job tonight, guys."

I hear the guys chuckle behind me.

"Anyway, after Undead is done, you guys are getting right on the bus. We have a show in LA tomorrow night, then right after that in Denver. Sophia . . ." Lux smiles at me and nods in approval. "Excellent."

With that he turns and walks away to take a call. I start laughing. Lux's 'excellent' reminds me of Bill and Ted. But then my heart hurts remembering how only a week ago, Tristan and I were laughing at that movie.

Roger and Matt step away to grab a beer, so now I'm just standing there with Jared and Cory.

"Do you wanna drink?" asks Cory. "They got Coors Light."

Cory smiles, his tone a teasing one. He knows that I can't resist a nice cold Coors Light. My throat is so dry from singing.

"Yeah, please. That would be cool."

Cory walks over to where the drinks are set up and now it's just me and Jared. Jared is playing with his phone beside me when all of a sudden I feel intense heat and strength right behind me, pressing up on my back. Tristan!

Turning around I look up at him, exactly the way I told myself earlier I would act— as if nothing ever happened. He's nothing to me. His jaw is clenched, but his eyes look pained. I have nothing to say to Tristan anymore. Turning back around, I grab Jared's elbow.

"Come on, let's get a drink."

"Sure."

Jared tucks his phone away and as we turn away, Tristan reaches out and grabs my elbow, making me come to a sudden stop, which then makes Jared come to a stop, too. Letting go of him, I point to him to indicate I will be right over. He looks from me then to Tristan and back at me. He doesn't want to leave my side. My sweet Jared.

"Are you sure?" he whispers and I nod at him again.

"Well, okay, then."

He takes off. Whipping around to face Tristan now, I'm sure my expression says 'don't fuck with me.'

"What?" I firmly say to him. He just stares down at me with his lips slightly parted, breathing heavily.

"What?" I ask again.

Getting annoyed now, I take a couple steps back, crossing my arms.

"Tristan! Ready?" I hear his band call after him as they make their way on stage.

Tristan doesn't move. Instead he takes a step closer to me. I don't move back. His nearness sends a whirl of emotions through me, and I can't grasp just one to feel exactly at this moment. Breathing in his scent is starting to make my lungs feel full and my chest ache.

"Go, Tristan," I say to him softly, and I walk over to Jared and Cory for my drink. Tristan doesn't stop me this time, and instead, goes on stage.

Tristan is so calm right now that it's kind of eerie. He usually grabs me or yells. But this time, he just stood there. Well, he really doesn't have any right to be angry. He's the motherfucker who was fucking someone else when just a few hours before, he wanted something more with me. So yeah, he has no room to talk.

Grabbing my beer, I take a long drink. I hear the band starting up, and I certainly don't want to stand around this time.

"Wanna go down to the back and start our own little party?" I ask Cory and Jared.

Roger comes crashing into the middle of us.

"Fuck yeah!"

I laugh a little. Roger's so bold and blunt. I just love it.

We all grab a few beers each and make our way to the back room. I kick off my shoes when we walk in, so now I'm barefoot. Matt pulls out his phone and connects it to a dock. We can hear Undead Society faintly in the background, echoing down the hall.

Matt puts on some older Hollywood Undead and we sit around the table, laughing and drinking.

"To a great fucking show tonight!" Roger exclaims, toasting with his beer. "Remember that time Cory brought home those two Asian women? I asked him to share and he wouldn't."

"Fuck that, man! You'd get them dirty!" Cory laughs back.

"Oh, my God. You guys are so bad. I'm surprised your dicks haven't fallen off yet," I tease as I bring my drink up to my mouth. I'm feeling buzzed and it's so what I need right now.

"Hey, we use condoms! Shit," Cory retorts.

After a while of going back and forth with old stories, I realize that Undead is probably almost done with their set. Rising to my feet, I pick up my beer.

"Wanna head for the bus now?"

"Sure," they agree, standing as well.

We step out into the hallway and off to the left I see the guys from Undead heading our way from off stage. Then I notice Tristan. His eyes once again have this dangerous shimmer in them. He doesn't look around at anyone else, but makes his way toward me. I pick up my pace, sandwiching myself between Jared and Matt, with Cory and Roger a few feet ahead of us talking to Gunner and Caleb as they walk down the hall.

Everything I Want

I can feel Tristan coming up quickly and before I can sprint forward, he wraps his arm around my waist and pulls me back, crushing my backside into his hard chest.

"Don't," he whispers in my ear.

I claw at his arms to make him free me, but he takes his other hand and collects both of my wrists, holding them together out in front of me.

"Just fucking listen to me, please!" he says a little louder.

Jared and Matt have now stopped, watching us. Matt starts to come in closer.

"Let me fucking go, Tristan! I don't want to hear anything you have to fucking say!" I yell at him.

Now Roger, Cory, and all of Undead stop, looking back now.

"Hey, man. Let her go," Matt says to him as he walks up trying to grab my arm to pull me away.

I hate this. I hate that I hate him, I hate that everyone is watching this and I also hate how good it feels being close to him again. Feeling myself fit perfectly in his arms.

"Fuck off. This is between her and me," Tristan growls at Matt and at that, Matt steps in firmly, grabbing my arm to pull me away.

I feel like a doll that's being played tug-of-war with by two kids.

Tristan easily pulls me back though, with Matt releasing my arm. Tristan spins me around so I'm facing him. I can hear voices in the background but I can't make them out. I'm locked in Tristan's gaze. His face looks pained.

"Please listen, Sophia. I fucked up. I was high and drunk. I didn't know what I was doing. Please . . . I never meant to hurt you. I would kill anyone who would try to hurt you. Please!"

"Hey, man. You better back the fuck off!" Roger comes stomping in and Caleb and Gunner place themselves on either side of him

"Just leave it, bro!" Gunner yells.

Tristan shakes his head. I can feel his hold on me getting tighter. It's actually hurting my skin. Fucking tears burn the back of my eyes again when I see Tristan's lost look of denial.

"Let me go!" I scream at him.

When I open my mouth, I feel tears loosen from my eyes and spill down my cheeks.

"No!" he roars.

Caleb and Gunner rush in and push him back by his shoulders as Matt and Roger rip me out of his grasp. Tristan starts swinging his weight around, shaking Caleb and Gunner off of him. I'm trembling right now. Literally shaking. Cory wraps his arms around my shoulders and quickly turns me around to get me out of there. Jared is walking close by me on my other side. I hear shuffling and yelling behind me.

"Sophia!" I hear Tristan shout, and I turn to look over my shoulder.

Gunner and Caleb are holding him back as Roger gets into his face.

"Don't ever fucking touch her again! You hear me? She's not yours!"

Roger definitely has balls. He's the biggest guy in our band and the second biggest of the tour, but he still looks smaller than Tristan. Roger doesn't care, though. He's right in Tristan's face.

Everything I Want

The tendons in Tristan's neck are flexing, and his mouth is set in a hard line as he stares darkly at me. Suddenly, I feel a cool breeze hitting my hot skin. We're outside and the buses are parked fifty feet away.

"It's all right," Cory whispers in my ear.

I try to calm my body's shaking. Jared runs ahead to open the door and Cory leads me inside the bus. Once I'm inside, I see the heavy metal door from the building bust open. Tristan barrels out with his shirt ripped and the rest of the guys race after him. Roger runs out in front of him, pushing on his chest to keep him away from the bus. They're all yelling at each other, or at least, at him.

Tristan says nothing but stops in front of the window, looking up at me. Staring down at him, I feel completely bad. This is all my fault. I should've pushed him off me back in Detroit. I should've kicked him off the bus when we were heading out west. I knew my feelings were going to get hurt, but at the time, being with him was more important. I didn't care. Now the guys are fighting, tabloid shit is out, and my heart is heavy with pain.

Tristan raises both his hands up like, "come on."

Then he takes a few steps back, still staring at me but not fighting any of the guys anymore trying to get to me. Instead, he slowly turns around and starts walking over to his bus, with his guys breaking apart to give him space. I don't even notice when Roger and Matt step onto our bus. Roger comes stomping over.

"Fucking eh! You all right, Sophia?"

Still looking out the window with my hands pressed against it, I nod, but I can't speak right now.

Jared comes up to me and rubs my shoulder.

"Shit. I don't know what to say."

"Nothing," I say, turning to stare at him and seeing the concern on his face. "There's nothing to say."

This night is done with now. I'm humiliated and I just want to crash. After I wash my makeup off and slip on shorts and my very large Pantera shirt, I'm ready for bed. Crawling into bed in my little cove, I grab my earbuds and place them in. I need to go numb for a while right now and listen to music. I might as well feel sorry for myself too, because I choose Slipknot's 'Snuff' to listen to.

When the music starts to fill my ears, I close my eyes, roll on my side, and squeeze my pillow. Corey Taylor's voice runs through me and sets me off gently crying into my pillow. Before the song is over I fall into another dark, dreamless sleep.

Chapter Thirty

When I wake up, we're somewhere in Northern California. I try to comb my fingers through my hair and they instantly get tangled up. With all that product Frankie put in it and me not taming it last night before going to bed, my hair is now the worst nest that I've ever had. Shit!

My eyes feel swollen from the crying that I did once again last night, and my mouth is dry.

I pull the earbuds out. I must have slept with them in last night; now my ears hurt a little. Looking down, I notice my phone must've died. I reach over and grab the charger that's plugged into the outlet and connect the phone to it. A few moments later, it turns back on. I slide my finger across it and a message alert pops up. My eyes grow wide when I notice a long text from Tristan.

I can't even begin to tell you how fucking sorry I am. For everything. Sophia, these past weeks with you were some of the most frustrating and happiest times of my life. No one has ever set fire to me the way you have. I miss you. I miss the way your skin tastes and how soft you are. I miss your laugh and how you mumble in your sleep. I miss your blue eyes piercing into mine when I'm taking you. The way you feel when I'm inside you. I know you probably won't ever forgive me. But I have to let you know that I'm so sorry. She meant nothing to me and I wasn't in my right mind that night. I was angry at you for throwing us away before giving us a chance. I was pissed at myself for falling so quickly. And I hate myself for hurting you. I will leave you alone now. But just remember, Sophia; you will always be mine. Even when you're not with me. You'll be what I will always have on my mind.

Oh my God! My heart constricts inside my chest again. Dropping my phone on the bed, I try to shake off Tristan's last text.

What do I do? Do I text back or leave it alone now? I do miss him, but I don't want him thinking he can just fuck around and I will be one of those weak bitches I used to pity for going back.

No! This is the best thing. The tour is winding down now. Only seven more shows to go and then we go back to LA and Undead will go overseas. Maybe in time I might be able to have a polite conversation with him, but it will never go back to where we were going. I know that day was my fault, wanting to be "just friends."

I was just scared. I was going to tell him, forget everything I said earlier and let's try, but I guess I was too late. He probably would've done the exact same shit to me even if we were together, so maybe this is a blessing in disguise.

After I'm done showering and brushing my hair for like an hour, I am ready to join the guys. They're acting like nothing happened last night, and I'm truly grateful.

"So after LA's show, we're going to fly out to Denver. So that means that we'll have a night in LA," Cory says, smiling. It's like he has some plan going on. "Sophia, you never went out with us when we were there for that month before the tour. We should go out after the show so you can check some shit out."

I don't really feel like partying, but I guess I should at least go with my boys.

"Sure. Why not?"

"Sweet," Cory says.

Jared walks over with a pop tart in his hand, nibbling around the edges. After taking a couple bites he speaks up.

"Lux called while you were passed out. He just wanted to let us know that everything will be ready in LA. Pretty much all we have to do is get on stage. Our show tonight is late, like nine or something."

"Really?"

Wow, that is a little later than we've played before. But I don't care. All I want to know is, where exactly are we?

"Hey, where we at?" I ask looking around at all the guys.

Matt walks over and sets his coffee down.

"I don't know," he says. "Probably like eight hours away, still. The bus only stopped once last night to refuel. I'm guessing we're going to stop again soon, though, which is good. I want some jerky."

"Oh," I say, getting up to head to my room. "Let me know when we stop."

"You going back to bed?" Cory asks me, and I stop, feeling bad that I was trying to go and hide.

Turning back around, I walk over to the table and take a seat.

"Nah. Who's got a joint? I bet I could kick some ass in Euchre."

"You're so fucking on!" Roger shouts, coming over with a deck he pulled out.

I quirk my eyebrow at him.

"How about we make a wager on that, then?"

"All right, but you have Jared on your team. Cory, wanna be on mine?"

"No. I wanna be on Sophia's."

Jared strides over to the window, next to Roger.

"Looks like it's us, buddy," Jared smiles at him.

Everything I Want

"Oh, Christ," Roger groans.

This is exactly what I need right now. My friends, a little weed, and a good ole game from back home. Roger starts dealing the cards, but I still can't shake Tristan's sad eyes out of my head. Shit! I have to get over him. And soon.

Frankie has me dressed more casually tonight than usual in black, low-riding leather pants with a tight white belly shirt. My make-up and hair are styled as always. Walking up to the stage, I don't see any of the Undead Society guys. I think Lux has them waiting in the back or something; maybe he heard what happened last night.

The crowd is huge and I methodically go through my routine. It's so hard to get into it with Tristan on my mind. This is the first show that he hasn't watched me do. Maybe I should go and talk to him later? Just to clear the air a bit. I hate this tension. It's so thick you need a chainsaw to cut through it.

Cory was on top of his game tonight, showing off more than he has in a while. He loves LA. The look on his face is like a kid on Christmas morning. When we're done, we leave the stage. Tristan is not waiting there, only Lux.

"I have a limo out back for you guys, but remember, the flight leaves early tomorrow morning, so no getting in trouble."

He winks at us then walks off.

Biting my lip, I'm about to text Tristan when all of a sudden I run forcefully into something hard, almost sending me back. Long, strong arms reach out and pull me back in. I look up to see Tristan, studying me with his eyes.

"S— Sorry," I say so low that you can barely hear it.

He doesn't say anything, but gently moves me to the side and continues to make his way on stage.

Wow! What the hell just happened? I kind of wanted him to say something. Anything, for that matter. I guess last night's scene got it through his head to leave me alone. I slide my phone back in my pocket and follow the rest of the guys out the door.

I look back to see if Tristan is watching me. He isn't.

Later that night, the guys end up dragging me to some stupid strip club. We're all wasted and Roger looks happier than a pig in mud. Cory keeps going off somewhere and I'm scared to think of what he's doing. At the last bar, I tried asking him where he was going, but he shrugged it off, not answering me.

Meanwhile, Jared is getting a lap dance from some woman they call "Jasmine." Funny, she even looks like the chick from the Disney cartoon. Leaning over to Matt, I yell in his ear because it's too damn loud in here.

"I'm heading. I'll send the limo back for you guys, though."

He smiles at me.

"Why? You don't like it here?"

I flip him off and he starts laughing.

As I'm walking out of the bar I notice Cory standing down the dark hallway to my right, by the restrooms. I stop and call out to him.

"Hey! Hey Cory!"

He doesn't turn to me, so I walk over to him. What the fuck is he doing? When I approach him, he jumps back, startled. Looking down at his arm, I notice blood pouring out of his vein. I yank him by the wrist.

"What the fuck are you doing?" I scream at him.

He laughs coldly at me and shrugs.

"It's cool. It's cool."

"Really? Now you're doing fucking heroin? Out in the open, no less!"

Cory smiles at me and his eyes look lost.

"Sorry, Sophia. I guess I just had too much to drink. I never did this before. But don't worry . . .

brand new needle."

"Cory, you're so dumb! Fuck! Once you start dancing with this shit, it's going to be really fucking hard to get off. Do you even realize that?"

I feel like I'm talking to myself. Cory is standing there smiling at me, but his eyes are like a shark's. Dark and empty. I feel myself getting emotional and a tear slips down my cheek. What is happening to my friend?

"Shh . . . It's okay, Sophia, I promise. I got this under control. Hey, I didn't do coke tonight."

He sounds like he's proud of himself. But I know that's a lie, too. Why else has he been running off all night? Just using the bathroom? Right!

"Please, come back to the room with me?"

Cory leans in and gives me a tight hug.

"I'll be back soon. Just going to hang with the guys for a little bit. I promise you, tomorrow you can have me on the tightest leash you want. I'm just happy about the show tonight and being here. I promise you I'm done now, okay?"

He steps back and wipes away the one tear that was resting on my cheek.

"I swear, Sophia."

"Please don't do it anymore. Please!"

"I promise. Now go to bed. I'll take you out to breakfast in the morning. My treat."

He shows all his teeth in that one smile he gives me, and I can't help but smile back.

"Let me see your pockets first," I demand.

Cory does as I ask and cleans out his pockets, pulling out the syringe he just used with the cap back on, a lighter, some kind of device he used to heat the heroin up, and a pack of cigarettes. I open the pack to make sure nothing is in it. Only cigarettes.

"Where's your ID?"

I don't know why I ask, but I don't want him losing it. He flips it up, showing me.

"Right here. I don't have any more cash, so Roger will just have to buy my drinks now."

I shake my head at him and point to his arm.

"You doing that shit, you don't need any more to drink, all right?" I say as sternly as I can. "And if I find out one more fucking time that you're doing this, I'm letting Lux know and your ass will be off to rehab. Got it?"

Cory nods and gives me a hug.

"Got it. See you tomorrow for breakfast."

Everything I Want

He turns and goes back into the bar. I still feel nervous at leaving him, but I'm tired and drunk. So, I text Matt. I don't care if Cory gets mad at me, either. I love him too much to look the other way.

Hey, just caught Cory doing heroin . . . He's going back with you. Please keep a good eye on him tonight, okay?

I press send and make my way out back to where the limo is parked. I get a text back from Matt when I'm outside.

WTF?! Yeah, he's here right now. I will and good night.

I feel a little relieved that Matt knows, too. He's the second most responsible one of the group, and he doesn't usually get too drunk. Roger and Jared are wasted right now, so I know they wouldn't be that good at keeping an eye out.

I'm back at the hotel and I feel my phone go off again. This time Tristan's left me a text.

Just wanted to let you know that you looked beautiful tonight.

My insides turn to goo. I would give anything to not care what he does and to be with him right now, but I just can't push things aside that easy. I brush my teeth, barely, plop down on my bed, and pass out.

My room phone is ringing off the hook. I slowly blink my eyes open. Shit! Head-fucking-ache.

I still feel a little buzzed. The ringing noise is just slamming my ear drums right now. I open my eyes and it's still dark in my room. I try to feel around for my cell to check the time, but I can't find it. The phone is still ringing so now I'm wondering what is going on?

I pick up the phone.

"Hello?" I answer in a raspy voice.

It's Matt and he's crying. Hysterically. I can barely make out a word. I shoot straight up in the bed. My stomach drops and my body tenses.

"What? What is it?" I yell.

"It's . . . it's Cory! He— he fucking OD'd!"

Everything goes numb. I go deaf and blind. I can't make out what Matt is saying to me. It just sounds like static. Images of Cory from earlier start racing through my mind. His smile, his eyes. On stage tonight just so happy and then catching him with that fucking needle. This is all my fault! I shouldn't have left him. Oh, my God! Matt screams into the phone bringing me back to reality.

"Sophia! Sophia, please. Get to the hospital."

I don't say anything, I just run out the door in my clothes from earlier, leaving the phone off the hook in my haste.

I can't take this shit right now! I start bawling as I race down the hallway. My shoes are barely on my feet. I have no cash or phone on me. I just know that I have to get there as soon as possible. When I approach the elevators, the doors open. It's Tristan and Caleb. They're laughing but when they turn and see me choking on my own tears, Tristan's face drops and he quickly pulls me into his arms.

"What the fuck's happened?" I hear Caleb ask, but I can't talk.

The only thing I can get out are hard sobs. I use my hands to cover my face, trying to calm myself.

"I-I need to get to the h-hospital," I choke out, stuttering.

"What's going on?" Tristan asks softly in my ear, but I freak out at the thought that Cory is lying in a bed at the hospital, possibly dying.

Everything I Want

"I need to get to the fucking hospital! C-Cory!" I scream in Tristan's face.

Tristan doesn't flinch, but presses the button down to the first floor. Caleb gets on his phone and dials a ride.

"Shit! Shit! Shit!" I hear him say.

I'm crying so hard now that my vision is blurred when we reach the ground floor. I can't even walk right. Tristan picks me up and cradles me in his arms and carries me through the lobby. Cory, my poor sweet friend. Please, God, let him be all right. Please . . .

We fly through the neon streets of LA and pull up out front of the hospital. I don't wait for the car to stop. I quickly jump out and tear off into the building.

"Sophia! Sophia, wait!" I hear Tristan yell after me, but I don't stop. Sprinting through the glass doors, I head for the reception desk.

"Cory. Cory Thompson?" I ask, out of breath with tears all over my face and my mascara running down my cheeks.

The nurse types on her computer and directs me to the correct floor. Tristan and Caleb are by my side now, but only for a moment. Once I find out where my friend is, I go running off again, not waiting for anyone or anything. I start pressing the button to the elevator. When it doesn't arrive fast enough, I hit it. Tristan reaches down and grabs my hand and pulls me into his chest.

"Shh . . . Don't cause a scene. You don't want to get arrested or some stupid shit. They'll report on you out here. Just wait, my girl."

I'm breathing hard, as if I've just run ten miles. The doors open and I push myself out of Tristan's hold. I can't focus on him right now. The only thing on my mind is Cory.

Chapter Thirty-One

We arrive on Cory's floor, the intensive care unit. Oh, my God, my heart is breaking. I round the corner and see my guys and Lux waiting out in the hall. I run up to Matt who is crying and his usually perfect hair and clothes are a mess. I fall on him and let go again.

"Where is he?" I look up into Matt's bloodshot eyes.

"He's in room 310," Roger chokes out behind me. "We can't go in there right now. The doctors are evaluating him."

Lux walks over to me and places his hand on my shoulder. He doesn't say anything, but lets me cry while I hold on to Matt.

Twenty long minutes later, the doctor comes out. He's an older man who's balding on the top of his head. The look on his face makes my knees weaken. He looks over all of us and back to Lux. He looks down at the white tile floors and starts shaking his head.

No! No! Please, God, help!

I begin to shake uncontrollably. The doctor clears his throat and speaks gently.

"We tried everything that we possibly could. His organs are shutting down, and he is on a ventilator to keep him breathing, for now. Just long enough to say your final goodbyes."

He looks over at Lux and continues.

"We have notified his parents back in Michigan. It will be their decision to shut the machines off. They should be here in about six hours. They want to be here with him when we do."

I hear Jared and Roger crying even harder, with Roger taking his fists and shoving them into his face with his eyes closed tightly. I can't sob any more, but tears continually stream down my face. I'm in total shock. I feel like this isn't happening. That the guys are still out and I'm still in my room passed out. Not in some cold, sterile hospital.

The doctor looks back at me.

"Would you like to go and see him now?"

Nodding to him, I follow slowly behind. I feel like I'm floating down the hallway, as if my legs aren't even moving. The doctor steps in front of the room and moves aside.

"I will send the gentlemen in one by one. But you can stay in here with him until his family arrives."

I just stare up at the doctor's face. His eyes are filled with sorrow. Pushing open the door, I see my sweet friend laying there motionless on the bed. So many machines and ventilators are hooked up to him. It's so loud in here with all the beeping.

I creep toward him and he has this tube shoved down his throat. His eyes are closed and the only sign of life left is the way his chest is rising and falling from the machines. He looks so pale, his beautiful color completely washed from his skin. I reach over and take his cold hand into mine, for some reason trying to warm him up. I gently sweep my fingers over the inside of his palms and up his long, callused fingers. These hands of his had such amazing talent. So much life he had left in him, and now?

New tears sting my eyes and I bend over him, holding him the best way I can with all these machines hooked up to him. I kiss the side of his face. It's cold and clammy. I start crying even more.

"Oh, Cory! Why?" I whisper to him.

All I hear in return is the beeping of the machines. I will never hear his voice again. I will never get to see his teasing smile or the way he holds me when I'm upset. I will never again get another guitar lesson from my friend after having a few drinks, and him telling me that I'm good when I know that I'm really not. I will never get to hear his laughter or get to see the excited look on his face before performances. It didn't matter how big or small they were. He loved doing each of them.

Sitting next to him now, I keep his hand in mine and softly sing 'Freebird' to him. It's the only one that came into my head. My Cory.

As I hum the rest, the door opens and it's Jared. His face looks broken and tears are also streaming down his face. He doesn't say anything, but walks up to the other side of the bed. I continue to hum softly to my friend, hoping he can actually hear it and find comfort in it.

Jared takes hold of Cory's other hand and puts it to his cheek, kneeling beside him. Jared just stares at him and cries softly to himself. He sits there like that for five minutes before gently resting Cory's hand back down on the bed.

"See you later, man," he whispers, and walks out of the room.

Still holding tightly to his other hand, I rub circles over his knuckles when Roger comes in. He only takes a few steps inside, then stops. His eyes are bloodshot. He falls to his knees and starts sobbing into his hands.

I carefully let go of Cory and kneel down beside Roger, rubbing his back. I have nothing to say but I cry with him. After a few minutes, Roger gets up and uses the back of his hand to roughly wipe away his tears. Blinking rapidly, he continues his way over to the bed and hold Cory's lifeless body.

"Fuck, man! Why? We need you so fucking much," he weeps, his voice cracking.

Everything I Want

The sound makes me cover my mouth with my hand to try to stop myself from bawling again. Roger cries over Cory. I have never, in all the years that I've known him, seen him cry. This tears at my insides even more.

When Roger's done, he starts to leave, but stops and turns back to Cory. Putting his head down, he walks out the room. I don't think I can take any more of this, but I don't want to leave my friend alone. I sit down beside his bed again and take his hand in mine.

Matt comes in next. Taking his place at the other side of the bed, he shakes his head. Matt looks at me and starts crying even harder.

"He told me he would be right back. He told me."

I know what Matt is getting at and I don't want to hear it. I look away at the clock on the wall and try to focus on the hands. But Matt fucking goes on.

"He left my sight only once, and I didn't think anything of it. It was getting late and we were getting ready to leave. Just fucking once."

I lose it and start bawling, not even covering my eyes this time. I let it all out.

"Please, Matt. Just stop, please," I beg.

"I love you, man," I hear Matt say to Cory. "I'm so sorry I fucked up."

Turning back to them, I see Matt rest his forehead against Cory's. This is all like some fucked up nightmare I can't escape.

Matt says nothing more but kisses his friend on the forehead and walks out.

To kill the sound of the machines and waiting for the next person to come in, I start singing again. I sing the first song I ever sang. I was six years old and it was at some church festival, but the memory makes me smile on the inside a little bit, because it was then that I realized that I wanted to be a singer. A classic. 'The Rose.'

As I start off singing this one to him, Lux walks in but doesn't come as close to him as the rest of us. Instead he just stares and gently wipes away his tears.

"How are you holding up?" he asks me after a few minutes.

I let out a scoff and look right at him. What fucking kind of question is that?

Lux's eyes are soft and he nods his head slowly and walks out.

I continue my song for Cory while using my other hand to gently stroke his face. So fucking cold, yet he's still breathing. But my friend is already gone.

I don't hear the door when it opens again. This time, it's Tristan. He creeps up to my side and stands over me, gently placing his hand on my shoulder. I don't jump, but still singing, I look up at Tristan's face. He looks like some dark angel right now. His broad features are soft, almost weak, and his eyes are filled with remorse and sadness. He cups my face in his hand and wipes away my tears with his thumb.

Tristan stays silent and just stands next to me. He takes hold of my right hand and laces our fingers together, resting them against my collarbone. Eventually he lets go and bends down to face me. I turn to him and his eyes are cast down at the floor.

"If you need me, I'll be out in the waiting room."

Nodding silently, I let go of his hand and watch him walk to the door. His back muscles tense through his t-shirt. He turns back to look at me once more. I'm just sitting there, frozen.

"I'll be right out here," he says again, quietly.

Everything I Want

And with that, he walks out.

Hours pass, but I can't really tell. My eyes burn from the tears that they've shed, and from lack of sleep. I'm afraid if I close them, Cory will be all the way gone.

Sunlight starts to slip into the room, shimmering on top of Cory's blond head. I hate seeing all these tubes and IVs hooked up to him. I admire Cory's beautiful features one last time. The door opens and it's Cory's parents; his mom, a short, petite woman with the same piercing blue eyes as his, and his dad, tall and lean with gray-blond hair. I see Cory in both of them and my heart breaks all over again when I see their faces at the sight of their only son.

Cory's mom holds on tightly to Mr. Thompson and starts crying. He wraps his arm around his wife, just staring at the bed. His mom lets go and runs over to the bed, throwing herself on her son.

"My baby. My sweet, handsome little boy."

She sobs into Cory's chest. Cory's dad walks around to my side and I quickly stand, giving him better access to his son. He looks down and hugs me hard.

"Thank you for being with our boy tonight. He would've been so lonely if you weren't here."

His words break me again. I hold on to him tightly. After letting my tears out again, I leave the room so his parents can be with him.

It's ghostly quiet in the hallway. Some of the guys have fallen asleep against the wall, and Tristan is standing off the right with a coffee in his hand, looking out the large glass window. I walk over to my boys and lean against the wall by Jared.

Tristan turns around and notices I'm out of the room. He gives me my space and just watches me. I take a seat against the cool wall and pray. I pray that maybe some kind of miracle will wake my friend back up.

An hour later, the doctor from earlier and a nurse go into the room. Oh, my God. What's going on? A few minutes pass and Cory's parents walk out with Cory's mom burrowing her head into her husband's chest, sobbing uncontrollably.

They say nothing, but walk down the hall. And in that moment, I know. He's gone . . .

Chapter Thirty-Two

Lying on the bed in the hotel room, I stare up at the ceiling. I tried going to sleep, but I'm afraid to. I'm afraid that I will see Cory's face again, full of life. Right now I don't think I would be able to handle that; believing for just one minute he's still here and everything is fine, and then the next getting it all taken away from me again. I just can't bear the thought.

It's already almost five o'clock in the evening and our Denver show got canceled.

Lux texted me about half an hour ago wanting everyone to meet up at his office if we could. What in the hell is that supposed to mean? I don't want to leave my room, but I know we have to go. We're in the middle of our tour. I have no idea what's going to happen next. And as of right now, I don't really care.

Pulling myself up, I drag myself into the shower, standing there for I don't know how long. The water starts to run cold and I'm shivering, but I welcome the cold right now for it makes me feel something other than emptiness.

I slide on my jean shorts and my hoodie. My hair is a mess and there are big dark circles underneath my blue eyes. My eyelids look and feel heavier, as if I haven't slept in days, and my lips are chapped and dry.

Sitting back down on my bed, I call Roger up to see if they're going to Lux's. The phone rings a while before he answers. His usually loud voice is quiet.

Everything I Want

"Hi, Sophia," he says into the line. Already I feel like choking back tears.

"Are any of you guys going over to see Lux?"

The line is quiet for a moment, then he exhales loudly.

"Yeah, hey, I guess we should."

His voice breaks and one tear glides down my cheek.

Wiping it away I go on.

"I just don't know, Roger. I just don't know what to do right now."

"Yeah, I know. I know," he sniffles into the phone.

"I guess I'll meet you downstairs, then? Like in five?"

I'm trying not to let my voice break, but I give away at the end, my lip quivering.

"Yeah."

Roger quickly hangs up. I sit on my bed and cry softly to myself for a few minutes before gathering the strength to pick myself up. I dig around in my bag and find my sunglasses, which I slide on quickly before leaving.

Once I'm downstairs, I notice Roger, Jared, and Matt walking down the hall. All of them are wearing sunglasses, too. Cory died only five hours ago. Died, meaning the cord was officially pulled. We all sit in the taxi cab in silence, just staring out at the busy streets of LA. When we pull up to the studio, I climb out first. Matt climbs out next and hugs me hard. The last time we were here was when we were just finishing up the album and getting ready to go on tour, only a couple short months ago.

We arrive on the floor where Lux's office is. It's quiet. As we approach his door, I hear him talking. It sounds like the guys from

Undead Society are in there, too. My stomach feels like it's filled with lead. I'm already suffering inside. The last thing I need is to be around Tristan. Yes, he was a gentleman with me last night. Or was it today? But that still doesn't change the fact that I don't want to be around him right now. Actually, I don't want to be around anyone.

When we open the door, Lux stops talking and looks over at us with sorrow in his eyes. The other guys in the room follow suit.

"Hey, guys. Come in," Lux says in the gentlest tone I have ever heard him speak in before.

We all enter the dark room with our heads hung down. I walk over to the table and sit. Tristan is on the couch behind me. I know he's staring, but I face away from him.

When we're all seated, Lux walks over to his desk and leans on it. He's rubbing his hands up and down on his face, taking deep breaths.

"What happened today . . . I mean, it is, without a doubt, the darkest day you guys have probably ever had. Cory was an exceptional guitarist and musician. He was also a very good friend to everyone. I know that no amount of time will heal our hearts at his loss. That being said, Dollar Settlement, you guys will be flying back to Michigan tomorrow on my jet to be with your families and Cory's. I will find out the arrangements and make sure to be there myself. He was very special to us, and we will truly and utterly miss him. I'm sorry. I'm not good at talking about these kinds of things. And I really hate that I have to be having this kind of talk with all of you."

Lux stops and looks around. He grabs some tissues off his desk and brings them over to the table, where I'm sitting. I take one from him and lift my sunglasses a bit and wipe the corner of my eye.

"But, the show does have to go on. Dollar Settlement did sign with the label. The company is very understanding right now, but they would like it if you guys showed up at the final show in New York before Undead Society goes over to Europe. I was thinking that maybe we could look for a sub to fill in for Cory at that show—"

"Fuck that!" Roger yells. "No one can replace Cory. No one!"

Lux just stands there quietly and lets Roger finish. I hate that we're having this conversation, but I know we have to.

"I know how you feel, Roger. Believe me, if it were up to me, I wouldn't even have you guys come back, at least for a couple months, but there are other members on the board. I'm so terribly sorry."

The room goes quiet as Lux finishes up. Shit, he has a point.

All of a sudden, Caleb clears his throat.

"I can do it. I mean, I know I'm nothing like Cory was, but I will definitely do it if you guys want me to."

"I think that's probably how Cory would've wanted it." My voice comes through soft, low.

Staring at the floor, it feels like I'm having an out-of-body experience right now. Everyone stops talking and I can tell they're all looking at me, but my head is still hung low, with my hair falling around my face.

"Really?" Lux asks me and I look up and see Jared nod, then Matt. Finally I look over at Roger, who speaks.

"Yeah. I mean if we have to finish, then I think Caleb would be good. But what about their show?"

Caleb would have to play two whole sets that night. I turn around in my chair and face him and Tristan. Caleb shrugs his shoulders, like it's no problem.

"I have no problem learning the material. It will take extra work on my part, but I would be glad to help you guys out."

The tears that I've been fighting back since I came in here stream down my face. I stand up and walk over to Caleb. He gives me a gentle smile and stands, too. I wrap my arms around him tightly.

"Thank you," I whisper.

"You're welcome," he whispers back.

After releasing him, I see Tristan looking up at us. But he doesn't do or say anything but pat his friend on his shoulders when Caleb sits back down.

I take my seat again Lux goes on.

"Okay, then. Caleb, if you wouldn't mind, you can start learning the new material soon so you don't burn yourself out too much before New York."

"Yeah, okay," Caleb says.

"Well, now that we have taken care of that, I will send a car for you guys tomorrow morning to catch my . . . Well, the company's jet."

I stand up again, getting ready to leave. Lux walks over and hugs me one more time. I can barely hold on to him. I just want to leave now. Memories are flooding back of the last time I was in this room. When all of us were in this room.

Not saying anything, I give a nod of my head and follow the rest of my guys out. I don't even look behind me when I shut the door.

It's the day of Cory's funeral. It's November, so it's very chilly out, but the sun is shining. We're in Cory's hometown, a beautiful suburb outside Detroit where his parents still live. Putting on my dark coat, I pull my phone out of the pocket and call Roger. He answers on the first ring.

"Hi," Roger says, infusing that one little word with so much more meaning than what was said.

"Hey."

I bite my lip, lost for words. Tears start slipping down my cheeks.

"Are we going to do that today?" I choke out, though I'd tried to keep my voice calm.

Being calm is not going to happen today, I realize.

"Of course. Cory would've dug it."

Roger voice breaks up now. Holding my mouth with one hand, I use my other to run my fingers through my hair, resting my phone between my cheek and shoulder. Even though Roger can't see, I nod into the phone.

"Okay, well I guess I'll meet you guys there then."

"See you there, Sophia."

"Roger . . ." I pause.

"Yeah?"

He's trying to clear his throat.

"I love you, all of yous. I— I just wanted to let you know that."

"Love you too, Sophie."

He hangs up.

The funeral is very beautiful. His mother, God bless her, has done an amazing job pulling this together. I couldn't even imagine having to plan my child's funeral. It's being held at his childhood church, with fall flower arrangements bringing in colors of orange and yellow and red. Chrysanthemums are everywhere.

As we stand outside, the wind begins to pick up, but the sun is shining. The guys and I have planned something special for Cory before they lower him. All of his family and childhood friends are here. Even Lux and the guys from Undead Society are here to pay their respects. Tristan stands in the far back wearing all black, with his hair pushed back and sunglasses on. He's standing off by himself, probably trying to give me space as well.

I don't look at him during the funeral even once, though. I don't want to bring up those memories of him at all while I'm here with my friend for the last time. What can I say? Life sucks sometimes, but I can't let trivial things, like Tristan being a man, slow me down. That was my own mistake for even getting involved with someone in this line of work.

"Are you ready, girl?" Jared whispers in my ear, holding on to my shoulder.

"Yes," I say back to him.

Before the pastor continues, he stops to announce us.

"Today, Cory's friends and bandmates would like to do something very special for him. I will let them proceed up here now."

Matt and Jared pull their acoustic guitars out of their cases, and Roger pulls his harmonica out of his pocket. Walking up, I kneel down beside my friend and place my lips on the cool casket and whisper to him.

"This is for you, my friend. You will always be in our hearts, forever and ever."

I face the crowd. Clearing my throat, I begin to speak as the guys set up a few folding chairs for us.

"Cory was our very dear friend. He has touched so many lives and helped so many people. His smile would light up any room and

Everything I Want

his enthusiasm could bring cheer and hope to anyone. He was not only our bandmate, but our friend and our brother."

My throat begins to tighten and I'm praying that I can get through this. One tear slides down my face and I don't bother wiping it away. Cory's parents look so lost right now without their boy, that it breaks me.

Tristan moves closer, and for some reason that helps me. I feel comforted by his presence right now instead of angry at what he's done. Taking a deep breath, I continue.

"Today we would like to do something special for our dear friend. We will be singing one of his favorite songs."

The pain in my chest is lifting and light begins to fill the ache that's in my heart at the memory of Cory and this song.

"You see, Cory wasn't all about rock and rap. He really loved older folk music, too. He always would tell us that growing up, his parents would listen to Terry Reid and sing to him."

Cory's mom looks up at me, wiping her tear-soaked face. Cory's dad smiles, with tears still escaping his eyes.

"Cory actually tried to teach me this song on the guitar once, but it didn't really work out."

I hear quiet laughter from the crowd.

"I can hold on to a guitar, but that's pretty much it. But what we did do is this— he would play and I would—" shrugging my shoulders, looking down at my feet, "sing."

Tristan is now standing off to the far left in the front row now. I look over at him, giving him a gentle smile. He gives me a small one back and looks down at the ground. Facing Cory's parents again, I finish.

"Cory loved 'To Be Treated Rite,' and I would love to get a chance to sing it to him. I won't say 'for the last time,' either. I will be singing to him every day that I'm on this earth. And one day, we will be able to jam together again."

Turning around, I nod at my boys and place my right hand on the casket.

"See you later, Cory," I say.

Matt and Jared start strumming the soft, mellow chords, and I take a seat beside them, staring at Roger.

He's watching me, holding on to his harmonica. I close my eyes and begin to sing softly; Roger's hand reaches over and holds on to mine, comforting me. Opening my eyes, I gaze at him with my eyes full of unshed tears. He lets go and brings the harmonica up to his mouth, and begins to play. Cory's parents sit listening with gentle smiles on their faces.

When we finish the song, applause fills the church. Cory's mom comes over to me and the guys with her arms out, trying to take us all in. Holding on to her side, I rest my cheek on her narrow shoulder.

"Thank you," she whispers. "Thank you."

When the funeral is over, I take my time leaving. Everyone else is going back to Cory's parents' house, but I just don't feel like going. Sitting here staring at the dirt mound that's covering my friend, I have to keep reminding myself that he's not there anymore, but everywhere now. Still, I hurt, and I really don't know if any of us will ever be the same again.

"Are you all right?"

I hear Tristan and I slowly look over my shoulder and nod before turning back to face Cory.

Everything I Want

I can hear him stepping closer, but he doesn't say anything more. He stands behind me the entire time, never leaving, but not pushing, either, and that endearment I will always hold on to.

Chapter Thirty-Three

Madison Square Garden. We're all sitting around the table, silently. It has been a few weeks since Cory's funeral. I've neither seen nor talked to Lux since then. Tristan stood with me that day 'til I was finally ready to leave. He drove me back to my apartment in Ann Arbor. The only thing that came out of his mouth was a request for directions to where I lived. I can still remember though, what he said to me when we pulled up to my apartment.

"This is where you live?"

"Yes."

We sit there for a moment in silence again. I find silence right now very peaceful. Once upon a time, I hated the silence; but right now, I find it soothing. I just don't want to think about anything. I like this numb feeling I have going on. It's almost like I'm walking through a dream. Looking out my window, I know I should be getting inside, but I can't.

"Do you want me to come up? You know, for some company," Tristan says to me softly.

Still looking out the window, I shake my head no.

"Well, would you mind if maybe I call you sometime?"

I look over at him; his face is gentle and caring. His once-dark eyes are now soft and filled with remorse.

"I don't think that would be a very good idea, Tristan."

My voice is low and flat. I don't have the strength to show any emotion right now. I feel as if it has all bled out of me. Tristan's eyes pinch together as he closes them tight, as if he were in pain. I turn to look out the window again, reaching for the door handle. Tristan gently reaches over and stops my hands from grabbing it.

Everything I Want

"Wait."

Looking back at him, his eyes are still pinched together, trying to find words.

"I'm sorry."

"What for? For Cory?" *I ask, looking down at his hand holding mine.*

Opening his eyes, he looks completely lost. He shakes his head. I know what he's sorry for, and I really don't want to hear it. I take my other hand and place it on top of his. His grip on my other hand loosens. Biting my lip, I pull his hand off mine and he lets me. Opening the door, I exit the car, but before I shut the door, I lean in. Tristan is holding his breath, his eyes pleading.

"Thank you, Tristan. Thank you for everything."

With that, I shut his door and wave him off. He's still parked out front when I enter my apartment complex. Turning back around to look out the window, I see his tail lights pulling away.

I want to so badly to forget everything that has happened, but I know right now, it's not the right time.

We hear a knock at the door and then Lux peeks his head in. Still dressed as sharply as ever, he approaches us tentatively.

"Hello," he says.

He brings over a chair and sits beside Roger and Jared, across from me. Looking at each of us in the eyes, Lux goes on.

"I just want to thank you guys for making it tonight. Also, I just wanted to let you guys know that Caleb has been working very hard on the material. I know he's not Cory, but I believe that his heart is in the right place and he's just as good."

I know Caleb can play just as well as Cory. He's been in a rock band for almost ten years. But Cory had his own flair, one that I know we'll never hear or see again.

"Anyway, after tonight's show, you guys will have a couple months off before we start promoting and marketing. I need everyone to try and be in the best mindset that they can be at that time. Cory would've wanted that. He worked very hard with you guys to get Dollar Settlement somewhere. I know it hurts, but you can't just throw that away."

Lux's words strike a chord in me. He is absolutely right. Giving up now would mean everything we've worked so hard for would be wasted.

Smiling, I reach over and pat Lux's hand.

"You're right, sir."

Lux smiles back and looks over at the other guys.

"Yeah you are. He would've wanted that," Jared says to him.

"Yeah, he would be so pissed if we pussied out like Jared's hair over here."

Roger points at the new 'do Jared's been trying out. And that little comment, well, insult, makes us all start laughing. Who would've thought that something so small would finally bring laughter back into our lungs? Jared is smiling, shaking his head.

"Whatever, man. You're just jealous."

"Jealous of what? Flat ironing?"

Watching these two go at it really helps right now, and before I know it, it's time to go on. Lux stands, straightening out his suit.

"Are you guys ready now?"

"Yeah," I say, and we file out of the room.

Everything I Want

Caleb meets us by the stage, actually looking nervous. I've never, in all my time with him, seen him nervous. He turns around and looks at us.

"Hey," he says and I walk over to him.

"How you doing there, Caleb?"

"Oh, you know. Good, I guess. How are you guys doing?"

"Good. We're doing good."

Looking around, I notice that Tristan isn't standing nearby. For some reason, I was kind of wanting him to.

"All right guys; it's showtime."

Lux walks up and points to the stage. Thousands of people are here. It's Undead's last show before they start the European leg of their tour.

Looking back over at my guys, I open my arms so I can take them in before going on stage. Roger, Matt, and Jared all come around and we form one big circle, holding each other for a moment with our heads touching.

"God, please give us the strength to do this. Cory . . . this is for you."

Pulling away, we turn and walk out on stage. The lights are off while the boys rush to their spots. I walk up to the mic and pull it off the stand.

When I look over my shoulder to see how Caleb is doing, Tristan catches my eye. He's standing in the exact same spot off stage where he would always stand when we performed, only now I don't feel a cold stare or intimidation. I feel comfort and peace. Even though we're not together, and a lot of fucked up shit happened between us, I still find that seeing him always there is a great comfort. Looking straight ahead again, I speak into the mic.

"Hey, New York!"

Applause and cheers come from the audience.

That sensation that I thought I would never be able to feel again is back. The one you only get when you're onstage— the excitement you feel coming off the audience and the thrill of performing. This is why we started this band. This is why we're here. Caleb begins to play and the boys follow suit.

After our set is over, I turn around and jog over to Caleb. Before he can even set the guitar down, I wrap my arms around his neck, pulling him in.

"Whoa!" he says, laughing.

"Thank you so much."

I kiss him on the cheek, then release him.

"You're welcome."

He winks at me then walks off the stage, talking with Roger and Jared. I slowly trail behind them when Tristan steps in front of me, stopping me.

"Sophia, I need to talk to you."

Oh, boy. I have a good feeling what he wants to discuss. But now isn't the time nor place for this. Stepping aside, trying to get out of his way, he moves swiftly back in front of me.

"Please . . . I haven't texted or called you. I left you completely alone just like you wanted. Can you just give me one damn minute, please?"

This isn't the Tristan I know. He used to intimidate me almost threateningly when not getting his way, but now he seems panicked and uneasy. Nothing like his usual collected self. Glancing over my shoulder at the roadies setting up the stage, I turn back and face him.

Everything I Want

"You literally have *one* minute."

His eyes light up and he gently pushes me off to the side so we're in the corridor.

"Listen. I know I fucked up," he says softly, searching my eyes.

I roll mine. I've already heard this shit a hundred times before.

"Damn it, Sophia! Just stop it. Stop it!"

My eyes widen. He has my attention. Old Tristan is making his comeback. Blowing out a breath, he relaxes his shoulders and cups my face in his palms, so that I'm staring right into his eyes.

"I mean it. I can't tell you enough. That night, I was angry. At first I thought I was angry at you for turning me down, but that wasn't it. I was fucking angry at myself for falling for you. And that threw me off, so I handled it stupidly. I got wasted and did the first thing I thought would help. I never really did the girlfriend thing before, and I wanted to with you. That scared and pissed me off so fucking much. I really can't explain it, but when I saw you in the door way like that, what I really wanted all came back to me. Shit! Sophia, I love you . . ."

My eyes sting. Oh, my God. Don't cry. Don't cry over him. He's a rock star. He's done it once when we weren't even together— just think if we had been.

I try to shake my head free but he holds on tighter, pulling me in closer to him.

"I love you, Sophia. Hurting you was the biggest fucking mistake I have ever made. I was protecting you from everyone else, but then I ended up hurting you the most. I'm so fucking sorry. But please . . . Please give me a chance. I will never hurt you again baby, please."

"You guys are on!" I hear one of the roadies yell over Tristan's shoulder.

He doesn't budge.

Reaching up, I gently pry his hands off my face. My eyes are glassy, but I still manage to hold my tears in.

"No!"

"Wh— What?" he asks in disbelief, his face falling.

"Thank you for apologizing, but it's too late. I forgive you, really, I do. But right now, you have your tour, and we have to deal with a loss and our album. This is just not the right time."

Tristan takes a step back.

"You're afraid, Sophia. You're a fucking coward!" he shouts back at me.

What?

"Excuse me?"

"You fucking heard me! You're afraid to fall in love. Shit, I can't tell you enough how fucking stupid I was, but you'll just have to believe that I will never hurt you again."

"I'm not afraid of falling in love, but in the short time we were together, you fucked someone else! Like I said, I've forgiven you for that, but I will never forget. Right now, I want my band to go somewhere. We've come too damn far to turn back now, and I'm not going to throw it away."

"Tristan! Come on, man!" I hear Gunner yelling at him from the stage.

Tristan doesn't care. He's just standing there, glaring at me.

"Go on, Tristan . . ." I tilt my chin toward the stage. "Thousands of people want you right now. Don't worry about me."

Everything I Want

"I don't fucking care what they want! I want you!" he yells, and everyone around us stops and stares.

Shit! Why is he making a scene? Crossing my arms, I roll my eyes at him.

"Bye, Tristan. Have a good tour."

I turn on my heel and take off down the hallway so he doesn't try to leave the stage.

"This isn't over yet, Sophia. This isn't over!" he shouts after me.

Waving my hand up in the air toward him, I duck into the nearest room, falling down hard on the chair.

A minute later, Frankie comes in.

"Tsk tsk . . ."

Looking up at him, I run my hands through my hair.

"Girl . . . What are you going to do?"

Confused at what just happened between me and Tristan, I stare up at him blankly.

"Mm-hmm. That's what I thought."